Kim ten Tusscher

HYDRHAGA

Alter Ego Press

Welcome to the city of dreams and nightmares...

HYDRHAGA

ALTER EGO PRESS

First published in The Netherlands in 2008 by Ardor House
Published in The Netherlands in 2013 by Zilverspoor
English edition published in 2013 by Alter Ego press

Cover design by Studio Zilverspoor
Portraits cover: Jacob Gregory, Dmitrijs Bindemanis/shutterstock.com
Other cover images: Lukiyanova Natalia, sdecoret/shutterstock.com
Designed and typeset by Studio Zilverspoor
Translation by Judit Coppens
Copy Editing by J. Kevin Thomas

kimtentusscher.com
Facebook: kimttee
Twitter: @kim_t_tee

www.alteregopress.com
info@alteregopress.com
Facebook: alteregopress
Twitter: @AlterEgoPress

ISBN 978 94 9076 737 2

Alter Ego Press is an imprint of Zilverspoor, www.zilverspoor.com.

PROLOGUE

Centuries ago, the city was still called Arminath. No sign of the war between elves and men yet marred the city. It was a peaceful time, in which the elves had the chance to develop their talents.

Elvish architecture closely resembled the natural environment and it served to camouflage the city from the eyes of strangers. To the outside world, Arminath looked like a hill overgrown with trees. On closer inspection, however, the buildings of the elves could be discerned, spiraling from the boughs on high, down to the ground below. The center of the city was hidden from view by a circle of high birch. White and green marble had been skilfully carved into the likenesses of trees, each bent to form the graceful arch of our city gates.

Inside a ring of tall, living birch, structures towered above the surrounding treetops. While the elves were unable to fully disguise these buildings as natural formations, their great artistic flair and love of nature was still evident upon them. Finely-wrought latticeworks served as the walls, ushering the outside world into the interior of the buildings. Such was the skill of the craftsmen that these lattices seemed less like handmade artifice and more akin to flowering tendrils and vines that draped the buildings. The roofs of the houses were shaped like flower buds and were made from a yellow material that shone in the sun. Because of the organic nature of the architecture, not one building in Arminath was exactly alike. Flowering shrubs and bushes sweetened the air with scented perfumes, and at the intersection of every street there were bubbling fountains. The city was split in half by the river, which flowed through its heart and irrigated its soil.

This was my town. My whole life has been dedicated to the elves, with my wealth allowing the realization of my vision for Arminath, much to the satisfaction of its inhabitants. During this time they accumulated ever more wealth and knowledge. Due to my own reforms, science was lifted to a higher level. I introduced the guilds and each masterpiece they manufactured was proof of our artisans' masterful talents. During that peaceful time we mostly made luxury goods, such as silver brooches or gold bracelets and glittering tiaras. Weavers produced supple fabrics with complicated patterns, which the tailors then fashioned into glorious attire. Even though they severely limited movement, these clothes provided an unparalleled silhouette, and they were designed primarily for the many feasts that made life in Arminath even more pleasant. In everyday life we wore simpler clothing, though no less ornate in detail.

That is how my future should have been, living without a care in the luxuries Arminath offered. Together, with my beloved, I wanted to enjoy all that I had achieved, while the elves were held in high esteem near and far.

Unfortunately, I had not foreseen that the many riches I gave to my people had a downside. Arminath was theoretically accessible to everyone, and yet no other race than the elves lived there. Humans only rarely showed themselves in the center, much to the increasing satisfaction of the elves. Our preference for beautifully-crafted items slowly changed into vanity, which made us feel even more superior. We saw the humans as lesser beings, and instead of feeling compassion for them we emphasized our superiority by arrogantly looking down upon them.

This attitude was not wholly unfounded. The humans that lived in small villages close to our city shamelessly lived like fleas off of our society They greedily collected the items we carelessly threw away, resulting in a blooming trade of castaway elven goods with distant tribes, bringing great wealth for the humans living in the shadow of Arminath.

I did not see much harm in it, at first. It was a simple form of charity, allowing the humans to create a better existence for themselves, but many of the elves disagreed and despite repeated pleas for more compassion with the humans my words fell upon the ears of the deaf. Of course the humans did not have the means of survival without our people, but more and more elves could not bear their profiteering from an aspect of our society that we would have rather forgotten. Before long, contempt changed to disgust, and nobody bothered to hide it. Whenever a man or a woman dared enter the city, they were avoided on the streets like lepers. We turned our backs on them, and the negative tone was clear when the elves spoke of humans.

Naturally, the humans reacted in kind. They did not feel inferior to us at all; to them it was a sign that we lacked wisdom while we indulged upon and wasted such riches. In return for our derision, they treated us as we had them. Very soon, villages near Arminath adopted the same sneering tone that marked our speech when dealing with humans. We discredited and slandered each other; every offense met in kind by the opposite faction and were soon embroiled in a downward spiral of prejudice.

Unfortunately, I seemed to be the only one who noticed the situation as it steadily deteriorated, and as tensions rose, distrust heated to outright hatred. By then, it was too late for anyone to stop it. The elves closed Arminath to the humans and nobody dared venture outside of the city's birch walls without protection.

The final spark that ignited the fury within the hearts of the elves was the burning of the richly-embroidered banners that flew outside of the elven council house. While there were no witnesses to the crime, the humans were blamed for this most recent display of hostility.

Nobody discarded their unwanted goods any more, and the human economy quickly collapsed. It was obvious now that we had been right, that the humans could not survive on their own when they could no longer lean on the crutch of elven society. Their riches quickly evaporated as hunger and poverty spread through the villages. Instead of showing remorse about their condescending attitudes towards the elves, the emptiness in the humans' stomachs only increased their hatred of our fair race.

I can only guess at what happened that one night, but it lead us all beyond the point of no return. A few humans had been drinking in one of their many taverns, while in their cups the conversation must have turned more and more often to the elves and their pompous attitudes. I can picture it now: someone taking the floor and stirring up the others with a rousing speech while everyone listened to an ever-increasing list of crimes that were laid at the feet of my people. Perhaps only a few people react to the words at first, when the man was silent long enough to take a swig of ale from his tankard, but by the end of the evening, when the beer had flowed in abundance, the men and women would cry out in agreement, punctuating each sentence spoken by the drunken demagogue with a cheer of their own. As they egged each other on, the accusations grew worse. The atmosphere in the tavern must have bristled with unfounded anger and evil plans.

Unfortunately, an elvish woman was forced to leave the city that night. To her misfortune, she chanced upon the mob of drunken men. Incited by the talk in the tavern, steeped in alcohol as they were, they ravaged the woman. We found her maimed body the next morning, hanged from one of the new banners decorating the council house.

What the humans had done to her was horrifying. It gave witness to the barbarity of their race, and our smugness felt justified. A group of elves, incensed and in haste, went to the human villages seeking justice and a slake to their thirst for vengeance. They were unkind in their search. Their anger seethed, and in their quest for information they mishandled the humans. For all of their inquisitions, the elves found only grim silence. The culprits were never caught.

I do not believe the humans approved of what their own men had done to the poor woman, but our own rash acts only made the situation more untenable. The villagers ended up protecting the culprits and part of the blame for the whole mess was put on our doorstep. After all, we had taunted them with our contempt and now we raged violently through their villages. Under the cover of darkness, the humans struck back and Arminath's isolation increased. Repeated retaliations from both parties fanned the flames of revenge and both races suffered.

And so things went for a time, until one day the humans decided that the situation could no longer continue. They sent a group of men and women to Arminath to negotiate; these messengers were unarmed and carried with them a white flag. Suspicion and paranoia, however, had taken possession of the elves to such an extent that nobody could or would believe that these men really wanted peace.

I knew we were about to make a capital mistake, but I was powerless to prevent it. For hours I pleaded to the Senate, but my words came too late and in the end my attempt at reason was in vain. From the tower of the council house the humans were shot down by arrows, before they could even make their motives for the visit known.

Of course, this further stirred up the anger that the humans felt towards us and they formed an army. Humans from outlying regions came to aid their brethren who dwelt in the villages. Full of disbelief and indignation, we witnessed the proceedings and hurriedly readied an army of our own. After years of veiled tensions, the siege of Arminath was a fact.

The bloody war dragged on for more than a year, in which the elves were forced to acknowledge the humans as their superiors. It appeared that I had made another mistake, one which cost our race dearly. Our armors were beautiful, artfully crafted and fluted with designs that declared our superiority to all who chanced to gaze at them, but on my orders the masters of the blacksmith's guild had spent less and less time refining the key function of any article of war; to protect the bearer and defeat the enemy. Our armor was too thin to effectively protect the wearer, and as we had not waged war in a long time, we had thus neglected to forge new swords. In our arrogance, we presumed that none would dare attack us, the greatest of races. Our old blades proved serviceable, but there were not enough to equip a whole army.

As time went on, the fighting became more grim. Men were hanged at the gates as a warning to the humans not to enter our city. Elvish women found the heads of their husbands on their doorstep. Even the children of both peoples were not safe from the warring adults. We were less versed in the art of war when compared to the humans, and I am ashamed to admit that we resorted to the use of underhanded and dishonorable techniques. Our victims were mostly humans who were either too sick or too old to properly defend themselves, but their race had left us with little choice.

More and more people from the surrounding areas started interfering with the war, so that the elves slowly reached the conclusion that we were far outnumbered. It was a lost cause. The only thing we could do was run, leaving the humans behind as victors. They celebrated their victory by destroying our buildings, tearing down our graceful city. From afar, I watched as fire consumed my city. Everything I had lived for was destroyed, reduced to ash and broken husks of its former grandeur. Their own structures seemed to spring forth from the very ground, such was the speed at which their city replaced our own. Only an errant fountain or paved street section remained to indicate that elves had once dwelt in that place.

Still, the destruction of our race was not complete. The new kings arose, and as is the way of victors in any war, history was rewritten to fit their purpose. Their history depicted my race as diabolical monsters who arrogantly hoarded their wealth and fortunes over a repressed human race. The overturning of such a corrupt society was justice for the many human lives which the elves had destroyed. Conscience and the humans' own mistakes were conveniently forgotten as the true account of things was buried.

Our flight left us as nomads, with nowhere to go. When we had left behind the turmoil of battle and the quiet had returned, the shame for our own actions quickly followed. The history written by the humans was spread across the land, and soon, everybody looked down on us. Generations passed, but nobody in our region had forgotten what the elves had done. We stayed hidden, and, contrary to most guilt-stricken elves, I never could forget what had really happened.

Since then, I have been searching for a way to undo the damage of the past. I did everything I could to secure the future of my people. The road was longer than I had foreseen and I even walked among the people I despise so much. But every sacrifice I made was meant to restore the honor of the elves, because they deserve better than the way they have been treated since the end of the war. For all of those centuries I brooded on my revenge, but—soon now—the fate of the humans will be sealed...

1

The gondola rocked as the airship banked right and Lumea saw Omnesia laid out below her. She could clearly see the rectangles that formed the city, with their narrow and dark streets running between them. Even though the lanterns were lit, she couldn't see anyone moving in the streets.

The sun had all but disappeared behind the horizon when the bird-like airship hovered over the city. She heard the wooden wings creaking as the captain steered the ship from the helm. A long sigh followed, signaling the air releasing from the balloon, and their altitude decreased. Lumea looked out over the countryside. Somewhere nearby, hidden in the gloomy twilight, there was another city. Omnesia, the gondola's current destination, was only a brief stopover on Lumea's journey.

The gondola's interior lights came on, and Lumea's face was suddenly reflected in the window. For a moment she studied her features, pulling back her hair to reveal the tattoo etched on her temple and cheek, with its elegant lines connecting the different symbols. Her clothes covered the golden-hued drawings from her neck down. The airship's light was weak, but still the tattoo shone as if it were reflecting sunlight. Lumea was proud of the ceremonial decorations. They proclaimed her heritage even though, at times, her faith and culture felt as confining as a straight-jacket. That was her main reason for responding to the letter she had received some months ago.

The letter had explained that she had been chosen to live in Hydrhaga, which was described as a peaceful land where everyone could live without worry. Lumea felt honored to be chosen and the letter had made her feel special. She had begged her parents to let her go on this journey, and though at first they had not wanted her to go, after a lot of begging and fighting her father had relented. Now, after a long gondola flight, she was finally getting close. Though she knew Hydrhaga was out there, she couldn't see it anywhere in the twilight that encroached upon the city of Omnesia.

Hundreds of lights lit up beneath her. A colored platform emerged underneath the 'Phoenix' and the ship descended rapidly, accompanied by the tell-tale whistle of released air. A soft *thud* announced that the airship had landed. Almost immediately, the door opened and two men rolled a staircase from the side of the ship. After that, they helped Lumea descend the stairs. As she stepped onto the ground, whorls of sand clouded her feet and were summarily carried away by an errant gust of wind.

As she scanned her surroundings, Lumea felt disoriented. The distance to Omnesia had seemed insignificant in the airship, but the reality was that the city still lay an hour distant by foot. She was nervous, for she knew neither the way nor the people in this faraway place. Until now, she had never set foot beyond the countryside that surrounded her village, and most of her life had been spent within the walls of her family's house.

The men pointed to a high building and as she hurried towards it, her cape flapped in the wind, which had free reign over the near-empty airport. A small, elderly man in formal dress approached her.

"Welcome to Omnesia, my lady. My name is Gabe, and I am a coach driver. Is there anywhere I can take you at this late hour?"

"Thank you, lord Gabe, but I was hoping you could tell me where I might find an inn? I'd rather walk there. I could use some fresh air."

"Of course. I know where to find an inn, and if you would like, I'll tell you how to get there, but I would still advise you to use my coach. The nights here are clear, it gets cold fast, and the city is farther away than you think. A ride isn't expensive, so if money is a concern, you shouldn't let that stop you."

Lumea hesitated. She would much rather walk, but the man's words sounded like an honest warning.

"If you want to walk, it'll take you about an hour, but I can have you at an inn within ten minutes. Of course, if you still need fresh air by then, you can always take a walk through Omnesia. Most inhabitants don't step out of their houses at this hour, and the quiet gives the place a special atmosphere."

Lumea's doubts were dispelled, and Gabe opened the coach door for her. He climbed onto the box seat and pulled a lever, which made a cloth roof close silently overhead. Then the man shook the reins. The trip started slowly, but the pace increased quickly as Gabe spurred on his horses and the sand whirled up behind them. Every now and then, the coach shook violently, and Lumea had to hold on tight to the handle on the inside of the door to prevent a tumble through the carriage.

From the driver's seat, Gabe yelled his apologies to her, but his words were lost in the rush of wind caused by the speed with which the horses raced. As they arrived into Omnesia's city limits, they slowed their pace. The houses here were still low, although the farther they went into the city, the buildings grew taller.

Finally, the driver stopped in front of an inn. Murmured sound hinted at the occupants on the other side of the door and light shone through small, bare windows. The old man laboriously climbed down from his seat, opened the coach door and helped Lumea out. She paid Gabe and stroked the horses, silently thanking them their speed. Their sides steamed and the cold night air changed their heaving breath into fine, white fog that escaped in irregular puffs. Lumea was glad the man had convinced her to change her mind about walking. She gave him a friendly wave and opened the inn door. When she stepped over the threshold, she turned around, but Gabe had already pulled his coach back into the dark city streets.

"I should have asked him to bring me to Hydrhaga tomorrow," Lumea realized, too late, as the light of the coach's lamp shook around a corner.

The inn was crowded, and some men looked up at the new stranger. They were all dressed in the same fashion: their breeches reached to their knees while the shirts had a smooth cut to them. Their half-length vests hung over their chairs, the materials dyed in dark, sombre colors. Women carried platters deftly between the patrons, tables and chairs. Their clothing were of the same colors as those worn by the men, and their dresses were cut in like fashion. At the far wall, a fire crackled.

Lumea went over to the bar and waited for someone to notice her. She looked around uncertainly. In the end, the bartender had to summon the innkeeper, the latter having sat himself down with some patrons. The bartender informed him that Lumea was waiting for him. The innkeeper stood but didn't walk away from his table immediately. Instead, laughter filled the air and bounced back off the bare walls. Only then did he approach, giving her the opportunity to study him. He was dressed entirely in black, his collar high and clasped with a silver pin. Around his waist he wore an immaculate apron. Everything about him was dark, including his hair and eyes, but his appearance was friendly, nevertheless.

"Welcome, my lady. I apologize for keeping you waiting."

Lumea smiled at him and asked for a room. He nodded and handed her a book, and while she filled it out in her elegant hand, she felt him scrutinizing her. She returned his pen and he skimmed over the page.

"Lunadeiron? That's quite a journey."

She nodded.

"It is an honor to receive such a high guest in my inn," he said, judging her by her clothes.

Lumea had pulled back her cape, which allowed the man a glimpse of her red skirt made of silk, with large embroidered birds, and while she didn't know it, in this town bird heraldry was reserved for royalty. Lumea shook her head. "I am but the daughter of a musician."

The innkeeper did not press the issue and opened a drawer. Lumea was obviously not the only guest, for she noticed that most of the key shelves were empty. The innkeeper gave her a key and pointed to the stairs, as Lumea's room was situated on the fourth floor.

Her ascent through the inn gave her a view of each floor as she passed. All were solid oak and uniform in their clean corridors. Lumea arrived before her own door. She opened it but did not step inside, instead she halted on the threshold and looked into the small space. Next to the window there was a simple table with a chair, but most of the room was taken up by the bed. Its frame was also made of oak, with long corner-posts that gave support to beams from which light curtains were hung. The curtains were the only decoration in the otherwise bare room. Heavy curtains hung to either side of the room's only window, which seemed heavy enough to shut out all light. In a corner stood a simple screen with a toilet behind it, as well as a small wash basin with a towel and a sliver of soap. The wooden floor creaked as she entered the room.

Lumea walked over to the bed and sat down on it with a tired sigh. She collapsed backwards onto the immovable and too-firm mattress. She stared at the white ceiling and the single lamp hanging from one of the wooden beams. The lamp suffused the small room with a wavering light. Almost immediately someone knocked, startling her. The door opened and a woman silently brought her something to eat. Lumea asked if she knew where Hydrhaga lay, but the woman disappeared without speaking a word. Pensive, Lumea stared at the closed door of her room.

"Perhaps she didn't hear me?" she wondered aloud.

She stood up and moved to the table, where she sat down again. She shifted her drab food with the fork, before taking a tentative bite. It tasted as nearly as bland as the Omnesians looked, and while it offered nutrition, that was all. She had to force herself to swallow the stew, but took a second bite nonetheless. When she was halfway through dinner, she put down the fork. The food was so alien when compared to the meals her mother used to cook. Those were colorful, beautifully presented, and almost a shame to eat. When you finally bit into them, the exquisite flavors and aromas were intoxicating.

It was a skill that her mother had undertaken countless attempts to teach her. In the hours they spent together in the kitchen, the woman bored her to tears with the exact proportions of different ingredients while Lumea had stared out of the window. Her mother had organized many parties designed primarily to emphasize what a wonderful housewife she was, but Lumea had not learned fast enough and it had not been long before she was banned from the kitchen when the house had guests.

Her relief was short-lived, because her mother relentlessly continued the lessons, determined to try and force her daughter into a 'proper' lifestyle. It had become a battle between the two women, but Lumea had stubbornly held on to her resistance. The way her brothers were allowed to live their lives appealed to her more than what her mother wanted her to swallow, but in her culture that type of lifestyle was out of the question for a woman.

Lumea took up her fork and sniffed at the stew again. It smelled just like it tasted, but she reluctantly decided to finish it anyway. Afterward, she went to bed, for she wanted to be up and about early the next morning. She could hardly wait to continue her journey and finally get to Hydrhaga. She was convinced that, like everything else, the food there would be better.

2

The following morning, Lumea awoke to a single beam of sunlight piercing through the curtains, which she had failed to close properly the night before. Judging by the light, the morning was still fresh, which was just what she had been hoping for. She got out of bed and opened the window. The rising sun painted the sky in bright hues, and a cool wind caressed her face, carrying with it the scent of herbs. From the window, she could see over most of the city. The sun painted the yellow stone buildings an orange hue, and cast long shadows on the ground. Omnesia was still slumbering, the only people on the streets were a couple of men who had spent the night carousing and were only now staggering their way home.

Lumea could see the grassy plains stretching out behind the city, and beyond them the salt plains. She could discern some scattered clusters of trees, but otherwise the landscape consisted solely of plains. Contrary to her homeland, Omnesia's surroundings were savannah-like. The waving, yellow landscape piqued Lumea's curiosity, so she quickly dressed and threw on her cape. She decided to go and see if the cook had some breakfast for her, the better to be on her way without wasting any more time.

When she stepped out of the door half an hour later, workmen were already busy in the streets. Their job was burdensome, and the men looked tough. Their clothing looked very different from that of the other townsmen, and was threadbare from their heavy labors. The men wielded their foreign tools skilfully and did not stop working even when they looked up as she passed. Inexplicably, Lumea found that was afraid of these men. She pulled her cape tightly around her, as if the azure fabric could ward off anyone with evil intentions, and she hurried on.

On a street corner, she paused and surveyed her surroundings. Far away, she could see the fields that she had seen and smelled that morning, so she turned right down the fork in the road which lead to the distant fields. She had always felt more comfortable in nature than among people and buildings. She was curious about what she would find, and expected to see Hydrhaga nearby.

She soon found herself outside of the city. A soft breeze caused the verdant plains of grass to dance and weave underfoot, rustling and disguising the sounds of a slowly-awakening Omnesia. Setting her feet on a drover's trail, Lumea headed west, chasing her slowly shrinking shadow. For some time, she saw nothing interesting. The grassy plains stretched on with no sign of Hydrhaga, the green vista was broken only by a single hill a short distance away. She left the path and angled toward the hill in the hope that higher ground would provide her with a view to her elusive destination.

The sun was reaching its zenith when Lumea finally came to the foot of the hill. Brimming with anticipation, expecting to catch her first glimpse of the promised Hydrhaga, she crested the hill. To her dismay, the grassy plains extended as far as the eye could see. The verdant green fields swayed in the breeze, defying her perception that Hydrhaga would be within sight. Deeply disappointed, she decided to return to the city.

Back at the inn, she found a place near the hearth from where she could observe the patrons. The innkeeper brought her a pot of tea and a cup.

"Is there a farrier nearby who I can borrow a horse from?" she asked when he had filled the cup.

He put the pot down in front of her and plucked a small feather from his apron. The Omnesian inhabitants usually went around on foot, he explained, in the narrow streets it was the best and safest way to get from one place to another, especially during the day when everyone was heading for work. There was, however, a woman who lived on the outskirts of the city who owned many horses. He provided Lumea with directions, and she noted that the horse woman's stables were only a few streets away

"Omnesia doesn't seem to be your final destination. It is rare for anyone to venture out of the city limits, foreigners especially take care not to go outside. Do you mind my asking why you came here?"

"Of course not, actually, you might be able to help me. I'm looking for Hydrhaga. Omnesia is only a brief stop on my journey.

"You'd do better not to continue your travels."

"Why is that?"

The innkeeper did not answer, and quickly continued with his work instead. Lumea was perplexed and wondered why the man had reacted like that. Lifting her tea and enjoying its warmth, she took a sip and let her gaze drift over the common room. The place was filling up, but nobody spoke to her. She noticed some men at the other side of the room who were obvious foreigners. They wore long, light-colored robes and talked together loudly in a language Lumea did not understand. She refilled her cup and settled back into her chair, deep in thought.

The following day, Lumea went to find a horse at the residence recommended to her by the innkeeper. The woman's stables were at the very edge of the city. A brass knocker in the shape of a horse's head was mounted on the door, and Lumea knocked upon it once. Immediately, she heard noises coming from behind the closed door, but it soon opened. Before her stood an elderly woman, dressed noticeably different from the rest of the Omnesians that Lumea had previously witnessed. Her overcoat was long, reaching down to her ankles, and it was dyed a warm orange color. Her hair was tied up in three different braids. The old woman seemed to have been expecting Lumea's visit and she led her towards the stables.

As they walked past the stalls, curious horses poked their heads out. At times, the old woman's hand would disappear into a deep pocket and bring forth a bit of apple. She would feed it to the horse with one hand and stroke its nose with the other. The row of stables seemed endless, though the woman eventually selected a small gray for Lumea. They saddled the animal and, taking the reigns, the pair walked the horse to one of the farrier's gates. In silence, the old woman handed the reins to Lumea before retreating into the stables and out of sight.

Lumea climbed into the saddle with a practiced movement and shook the reigns. As soon as she was outside the city, she increased their speed, and soon they they were at the hill she had visited the day before. They rode on, but the landscape hardly changed, and all she saw was the yellowish-green grass rolling ahead of her for miles. Guiding her horse, Lumea circled the city, hoping that she had merely been seeking her destination in the wrong direction. Eventually, dark and imposing shadows marred the horizon, and Lumea's heart leaped with the hope that they were distant buildings. Sensing her change in mood, the horse increased its pace, and the shadows grew in size, until she realized that what she saw were enormous trees. Her initial disappointment, however, quickly changed into wonder.

She had never seen trees like these, and if someone had told her about them, she would not have believed they existed. The trees towered above her, defying her senses that anything could grow so large; their bases were so thick that Lumea guessed it would take ten men to encircle just one. It seemed to her that the gods themselves must have planted these trees. The multitude of branches overhead were crowned with tiny leaves, which seemed incongruent when compared to their enormous trunks.

Lumea discovered one tree that was not as tall as the others and decided to climb it. She pulled herself up, using the rough bark as leverage for her feet. When she reached the top a small flock of brightly-colored birds flew from out of the boughs, surprising her as they screeched their indignation. Curiosity compelled her to look down for the first time. Where the branches met the trunk a depression formed natural bowls which caught rain and dew. She quenched her thirst with water from one of the depressions, and as the birds returned to their perches she surveyed the vista afforded to her. Everywhere she looked there were trees. Most of them were standing alone, but farther on they became a dense forest. However, the only thing she saw was nature. Nowhere could she discern a sign of the city she was looking for.

For days on end she and the gray scoured the countryside surrounding Omnesia. In the south, she discovered a forest. She dismounted and left the horse near a small pond, tying the reins loosely around a branch. She enjoyed walking among the shadows of the trees. Springy moss softened her footfalls while insects buzzed about her head. Then she saw it: a pile of rocks which could not possibly have been formed naturally. Her pace quickened. She discovered more and more stones, shaped by hands, and finally she arrived at a gateway. Vines reached up over the arch, dotted with flowers that hung down in white clusters. They gave off a sweet scent and attracted busily-flying bees.

Hesitantly, Lumea walked under the arch and into the square beyond. Everywhere there were ancient buildings, all of them with plants and roots growing over their long walls, grasping at the ancient carvings. They must have been wonderful buildings once, but all that remained now were ruins. Time went on inexorably as Lumea wandered between the buildings, struck by the atmosphere of this place. The air was oppressive and stale and, at times, she thought she saw parts of the buildings' past. For the briefest of moments she would glimpse stately creatures walking about, dressed in extraordinary robes, but when she tried to focus her eyes on them, the visions would disappear, leaving Lumea to wonder if she had really seen them.

Suddenly the young woman realized she was shivering. The sun had gone down behind the walls and from far away she heard her gray neighing. She hurried towards the animal, climbed on, and galloped in the direction of the Omnesia. It was not far, and on the horizon she could soon see the glow made by the city's lamps. She rode into the city just before the true darkness of nightfall. It was not long after she had returned the horse to its stable that she herself retired to her rented room in the inn.

That night she decided to change her tactics. No matter how far she rode, she could not find what she was looking for in the country around the city. Starting the following morning, she would stay in Omnesia and ask its inhabitants if they could help her. She just hoped that one of them would know where Hydrhaga was.

3

Lumea slept halfway through the next morning, but she was in no hurry to go anywhere. By the time she left the inn, it was noon. Once again, she found herself alone out on the streets except for the groups of workmen. The morning was quiet and peaceful, and as she cast her thoughts back to the view afforded to her on the approach via airship, Lumea recalled how the city had been planned, with every street forming neat blocks. From the ground, the layout was just as obvious. Every street corner was marked by a lantern, and the watery light they provided emphasized the straight lines and corners of the surrounding buildings and lanes.

To Lumea, the streets seemed like an endless repetition of the same building, interspersed at regular intervals with street-lights. The buildings all had multiple floors and were huddled close together as though to waste as little space as possible. The houses loomed over the narrow streets, reducing the sky to a thin strip of blue which was dotted by the occasional airship that passed overhead. The walls of the houses had small windows, as if the people living there wanted to separate their own little world from the public community. The only discordant notes of design within the city were the wells, and those had been placed around the town seemingly at random. Like the men working on them, they did not seem to aesthetically belong.

Lumea did not understand how the Omnesians could feel comfortable here. In her own country, the villages were a lot more spacious. The buildings there had slender frames and subtle construction, allowing for trees to grow amongst the streets and lanes. Each building held effigies of the gods, with a strong predominance towards the Goddess Isil, the goddess of the moon and mother to her race. Her own people knew that their race needed to coexist with the natural world, and every effort was made to cohabitate with the land.

Here in Omnesia, that order seemed to be turned upside-down. Nothing whatsoever indicated the Omnesian's faith, and they had even changed the course of the river for the convenience of the city folk. Their redirection of the river, however, was poorly-done and now a dry bed lay where the river once flowed. The arid riverbed was the reason the city was dusty, and the wind was constantly blew yellow sand through the streets. In some corners the sand and dust piled up higher and higher. The people did not seem to care, however, for once the sand settled in its corners and alcoves, it remained there for years, as no one cleaned it away, nor did they seem to care that the piles steadily grew larger.

Walking through an archway that spanned the street, Lumea paused. The adjacent wall held a small plaque: *South, 42nd, Quarter of Knowledge*. Her curiosity was piqued and she decided to see where it led. A lack of pedestrians meant she could not ask for directions, and she was resigned to rely solely on her gut feelings. From time to time she stopped and looked back, but she had no way of judging how far she had walked. The buildings she passed now had broad, double doors, but still she could see no sign of life either inside the buildings or out.

The still street was suddenly thrust into organized chaos, as bells began to toll in long sonorous peals. Doors lining the streets disgorged their hidden tenants as the inhabitants of Omnesia took to the streets in their dull gray, uniform dress. The masses formed orderly lines and headed towards the city proper, back in the direction from which Lumea had just come, and they walked with a lack of spirit that blurred the crowds from individuals into a monotone vista. With her back against a wall she watched the mob pass, and she was intrigued by their behavior and apathy. Lumea decided to follow.

The crowd moved under the gateway and began to split up. More and more people disappeared into their homes, and the streets slowly emptied again. Lumea stopped in the middle of the road, wondering about the Omnesians' behavior. For a brief moment the city had come to life, but now everything around her was quiet once again.

Twilight fell, and the young woman saw a light go on in the distance, and then another. More and more lights turned on, a little bit closer each time. Then she heard a curious ticking sound, as of metal striking the cobblestone streets. There were a few seconds of time between each tick, but they grew louder, seemingly moving closer.

Lumea was curious enough to stand her ground and peer into the growing darkness. From it, a man on high stilts emerged. He walked through the dark streets and lit the gas lanterns flanking either side of the street. His work seemed superfluous in light of the fact that the streets were abandoned of people after nightfall, but on he went. The man passed her without a word and disappeared into the darkness again. The sound of his stilts disappeared with him, but his passage was marked by the luminous glow of lanterns being lit at regular intervals.

An evening chill settled over the city, and the wind blew unhindered through the long, straight streets. Lumea walked after the lantern man, hoping to reach the inn soon. Far away, she could see yet another lamp being lit, and she increased her pace. The walk back to the inn was likely going to take some time.

In the days that followed, Lumea discovered just how hard it was to make contact with anyone, as the city's inhabitants kept very much to themselves. In the meantime, her searches led her deeper into the city, where she discovered more about the way it was constructed. There were three distinct districts laid out in concentric rings. The inn where she stayed was situated in the outer ring. The next ring was the industrial hub of the city, where a great many offices and manufacturing buildings were located. The people working there all lived in the outer district as well, but the owners of the companies lived in the center circle, together with other prosperous men and women.

Each district was separated from the others by a high wall. The walls had intermittent gates that allowed passage between the various districts. On her first day, Lumea had followed a street that ran parallel to the center instead of leading towards it. Now that she had spent some time wandering the city, she knew that the inn was not that far from the center if you knew the way.

There were more people on the streets in the middle district. At times there were small groups of Omnesians talking to each other, although the conversations never lasted for very long. Everyone here was always busy.

Lumea had addressed several inhabitants, but she could have been talking to walls for all the reaction she received. The people walked away from her, often without waiting for her to finish asking her question. Once or twice, someone took the trouble of listening, but as soon as the name Hydrhaga came up in conversation, they said they did not know and that they had to go.

The longer she stayed in the city, the more it seemed as though the inhabitants were avoiding her. She grew furious, because nobody was polite enough to answer her decently.

Several days later, Lumea had a strange encounter with one of the citizens of this very alien city. He approached her as she was sitting on a bench, resting and observing her surroundings. He was one of the workmen, and he had muscular limbs and was covered in a patina of dirt from his daily labors, but she pushed aside her initial fear and made room for him on the bench. She gave him a friendly nod, for she was afraid of insulting him if she ignored him. The man was dark from his work outdoors, and he smelled strongly of sweat. Lumea was surprised to find that the smell was not wholly unpleasant. His scent triggered distant murmurings in the depths of her mind, and she had the feeling that this was a smell she should know. The workman was dressed in a green tunic, but it was threadbare with traces of rich embroidery. Wrapped around his head he wore a kerchief, which Lumea assumed was part of the worker's outfit, for the workers all wore similar kerchiefs. The man sat down next to her silently, but his face was open and friendly.

After a while, he said, "I am Elion."

Lumea was taken aback for a moment, for she had almost forgotten about him and she had been deep in thought. She looked at him, confused, and he repeated, "I am Elion. That is my name."

Lumea smiled at him and introduced herself. Elion nodded and they sat in silence once again. In the end, Lumea got up and bid the man farewell. She looked around before crossing the street, and then disappeared around a corner.

That same day Lumea came upon an imposing building which was surrounded by a cast-iron fence. Behind it, soldiers marched down lanes that ran between fields of freshly-mowed grass. At the gate, four men were standing guard. Lumea straightened up and walked towards them. The four soldiers seemed to confer with each other as she came closer. One of them looked at her over his shoulder, and when she neared, they turned toward her. Lumea bowed and waited for a reaction, but none was forthcoming. Hesitantly, she righted herself while she devised a new plan.

"Good afternoon, gentlemen."

Still, they gave no reaction.

"Might I inquire as to who lives behind this fence?"

The men seemed relieved that she asked that question. One of them answered, "That is the palace of the King of Omnesia and his royal family."

"Oh, of course. I should have known. You should be proud to guard the royal family. It must be honorable work?"

"You're right, it's not easy to become a guard. First you have to go through years of intense combat training. Only those with the best fighting skills have a chance to be promoted to this duty."

Lumea was glad that her plan was working and the men were talking. She forced herself to stay calm and pushed on, flattering their pride.

"But fighting skills are surely not the only criterion on which you were selected? You must have a great knowledge of this land and its history?"

The men nodded proudly. They explained that they had been trained to fight from childhood. This was normal in Omnesia, as all boys were obligated to master the martial arts. The talent shown by their physical prowess determined the status of their families. The four men had hardly been able to walk when their fathers had brought them to a fighting school. It had not been long before their talent distinguished them from other boys their age, and they had been transferred to the school within the royal compound. There, the boys were also trained in history and heraldry.

Lumea knew that now was the time to strike. Maybe they would let something slip that they normally would not.

"Then you must know where Hydrhaga lies?"

One of the men made as if to answer, but the eldest of the four was quicker. "I believe this conversation has lasted long enough."

None of them spoke another word. Lumea bowed again and walked away. She was disappointed that again she had found out nothing at all about Hydrhaga, and wondered why nobody wanted to help her. No matter how long she walked around and no matter how many people she asked, she was no closer to her destination than when she first arrived.

4

It was the end of Lumea's second week in Omnesia. Her confidence had grown as she learned how to navigate the thoroughfares and streets of this foreign city. It was on one of her excursions into the center district that she encountered a sound that had previously been absent from the other sounds of the city: music. A simple tune played on a flute reached her ears, and, intrigued, she quickened her pace toward the direction of the sound. She encountered a group of fighters. They marched in orderly lines to the beat of the music, and wore magnificent orange robes with embroidered, black symbols. Their faces were hidden behind beautifully-painted wooden masks. Their appearance struck a chord within Lumea, as she desired to be like them with their stately posture, their supple movements, and outfitted with a variety of weapons. They seemed to be the very definition of precision.

The citizens of the city emerged from their homes, forming a procession behind the fighters. Some women had tied orange ribbons in their hair, lending the entire scene a sense of exuberance and vitality that was normally lacking in the austere streets. The atmosphere was alien to what Lumea had decided was the norm for Omnesia as the people laughed and called out to one another. The strange behavior made Lumea curious, and so she joined the throng of people now striding purposefully behind the fighters.

They approached the center district, and more people joined the crowd. When Lumea looked down a side street, she saw another group of fighters marching towards the city center, with each group dressed in a different color.

Finally, the throng of people arrived at the arena. The whole city seemed to have congregated here. Their normally sombre clothing was adorned with the fighters' own colors. Although people were betting on the outcome and challenging each other, the atmosphere was filled with excitement.

The arena doors swung open and Lumea had no choice but to

go into the arena, swept along by the flow of the crowd. The people around her were apparently supporting the blue team, and that helped to calm Lumea's nerves because her blue dress did not stand out overmuch. Everyone quickly spread out and took a seat while Lumea found a place somewhere in the middle. The amphitheater was built in the shape of a star, although the outer ring of seats was round. The star's points were painted in the different colors of the fighters. The populace of Omnesia continued to flow into the arena, filling every seat with excited spectators, all of whom were obviously eager to observe the upcoming spectacle.

An announcer's voice could be heard naming the different fighting teams. Each time, a different section stood and cheered for their favorite group, while all the other sections taunted, hooted and booed. The blue supporters stood and cheered as loudly as they could to drown out the jeers of the opposing fans. Lumea joined in, gripped by the excitement in the packed arena. She was very much enjoying herself, and though she had no idea what was about to happen, the charged air was pleasingly infectious.

A hush spread through the crowd as the announcer cried that the king had arrived, and everyone rose to their feet. On the opposite side of the arena from where Lumea sat there was a box, where doors were now opened. The royal family entered the amphitheater, with their royal garments displaying all the colors of the rainbow. The fabric dragged on the floor and glittered in the sunlight. The queen and her daughter took their seats within the box, seeming deep in conversation. The princess's cheeks were bright red from all the excitement, and the anticipation was clear on her features. The king remained standing, and while a flag was being raised in the center of the arena, he seemed to be looking straight at Lumea. Uncomfortable from such a scrutinizing gaze, she turned away in discomfort.

The flag stood atop an artificial hill which dominated the center of the field, and the dry wind caused it to stir briefly. The creak of wood drew everyone's attention to fortified double doors that stood directly beneath the royal enclosure, and four men emerged into the light of the stadium. They surveyed the crowd briefly before starting toward the hill, striding with purpose and holding aloft a golden spear. Upon reaching the top of the hill, one of the men thrust the spear into the ground before they turned and walked back through the doors from whence they came. The entire spectacle served only to pique Lumea's curiosity further as there was no overt reason given for such a display.

Then the gates of the outer points of the star opened and the groups of fighters wearing masks entered. The King was given a bow, and he notched a blunt-tipped arrow. He took aim and drew back the string as far as it would go, and then let go. The arrow buzzed through the air and hit a gong at the opposite side of the arena. The sound was the signal for the fight to start, and the different teams started to move.

The difference in tactics among the groups was clear from the start. Some of them stormed forward and were immediately engaged in hand-to-hand combat. Others held back and let the other teams do the fighting, waiting for the opportune moment to join the fray. The fevered pitch of the crowd grew as the melee soon engulfed all of the contending teams. The cheering tapered off from the orange section of the stands, as it was obvious that their team was the weakest on the field. Lumea was glad that luck had allowed her to enter the arena with the blue supporters, for the blue team seemed to be the stronger contestants on the field, and the electric atmosphere had her shouting her support at the top of her lungs.

Her cries did not go unnoticed. One of her fellow blue support-ers was wearing a very amused expression at her enthusiasm. She flashed a smile in his direction. Her enthusiasm was unrestrained, and he nodded at her in return. Not long after, he was standing next to her.

"You're obviously enjoying the fight. Do you know the rules, though?"

Lumea shook her head.

"The goal is to get the spear. The team that captures it, wins. While it is in every team's interest to balance offense and defense, the com-petition usually boils down to hand-to-hand combat. There's a per-fect example right now..."

The man pointed to the left, and Lumea's eyes followed his out-stretched finger. A blue warrior was fighting with a player from the red team. It looked as though the blue player was losing; he was already fighting without weapons. Then a great cheer of triumph erupted from the blue supporters. The exchange was over so quickly that Lumea had almost missed it. The red warrior had made a bold thrust at his blue opponent in an effort to the end skirmish quickly, but the blue warrior pivoted and snatched off his opponent's mask.

"The blue fighter has won. This fight is not about victims. Nobody has ever even been killed. As soon as you have your opponent's mask, he is defeated and leaves the field. This elimination leaves fewer fighters on the field."

The red fighter who had lost bowed to his opponent, picked up his weapon and made his way over to a special stand that was guarded by two soldiers, where he took a seat between orange-clad figures.

Just that moment, a yellow fighter defeated his blue opponent. He quickly exchanged masks and walked over to the blue team. There was some confusion, during which he easily unmasked two of the blue fighters before being unmasked himself. Laughter sounded from the stands as spectators applauded the crafty move. It had brought a comical turn to the fight that even the blue supporters could appreciate.

The event lasted the entire afternoon, and Lumea's companion provided a running commentary of what was happening and where Lumea should look to appreciate the most interesting moments of the game. At the end of the day, the green team won by virtue of having the majority of players still on field. One of their players ascended the hill with little opposition from the remaining members of the opposing teams. He picked up the spear and the game was over. The green seats shook with the force of the spectator's enthusiasm. Cheers and stamping feet drowned out all other sound. Lumea was disappointed for a moment that her own team had not won, but everyone around her was in high spirits, so she celebrated along with them. It was an extraordinary experience, and while there was obvious rivalry between the groups, nobody let the defeat of their own team ruin the celebratory atmosphere.

She was exhausted by the time she returned to her room that evening. Before she fell asleep, though, she thought about everything that had happened since she came to Omnesia. She had spent the last two weeks walking through the city, looking for the place mentioned in her letter, the place that had taken her so far away from home but which she could not find. When she asked passers-by if they knew of Hydrhaga, they gave her a typical blank stare. Some of them even seemed to be afraid, though that could have been just her imagination.

That night, Lumea decided to look for Elion. He was one of the very few people in the whole of the city who had talked to her in a friendly manner. And who knew? He might even be able to help her. Lumea had a feeling she could trust him, and for some vague reason she expected him to know about Hydrhaga. She hoped to find him soon.

5

It still took Lumea several days to locate Elion in the city's streets. He was at work restoring one of the wells that were dotted around the city. The elves had made the wells a long time ago, the Horse Lady had told her, but the negligence of the human kings had allowed them to fall into disrepair. When the waters of the river dried up, the humans had to reconsider that negligence. The elvish wells proved deep enough to supply the populace with clean water, and so men were hired to repair them. The work was laborious under the unrelenting sun, and though many seemed to be having difficulty completing their tasks, Lumea could see that Elion was experienced and suffered little discomfort.

He was stationed beside an odd-looking machine that fed a constant stream of air into a furnace. The cherry glow emanating from within tinted the workmen red and distorted the air with ripples of heat. Atop the squat furnace was a solid-looking crucible, into which other members of Elion's work group tossed chunks of metallic ore. The fiery temperature was allowed to do its work on the metal above, and some minutes later Elion pulled a lever that toppled the crucible, spilling its molten cargo into a mold which was positioned over the ancient elven well. While the workmen operating the furnace and smelter wiped the sweat from their brows, a second workman bathed the mold with a jet of liquid nitrogen from a canister, solidifying the metal. The men carefully removed the mold and proudly surveyed the result.

They had enough experience that it almost always went well, but sometimes the metal cooled down so quickly that it cracked. Apparently there was no problem this time, because an older man installed the piston and another workman welded the on lid. After a moment, clear water clattered from the pump and into the basin. The workmen drank greedily from the fruits of their labor.

All this time Lumea had been standing hidden in the shadow of the buildings, watching the man she had wanted to find. She had not counted on the gang of workmen around Elion, though. They still scared Lumea, and the fire and cinders from their work fed into her fears, and now she was too afraid to go and talk to him. She was on the verge of returning to the inn when Elion turned around and looked straight at her. He said something to his neighbor, and then made his way over to her.

"My Lady Lumea, what an honor..."

Lumea was surprised by the formality of his greeting, but Elion started to laugh.

"I'm sorry. I didn't mean to startle you."

Lumea did not react to this statement, but he was obviously happy to see her.

"I was hoping that you might be able to help me," she said, coming to the point immediately. "Nobody seems to know the place, but I received a letter that I should come to Hydrhaga."

Lumea studied Elion's sooty face. Maybe she would finally learn something—anything—about the place she was looking for. But Elion's face remained open and friendly, without any trace of fear or even recognition.

"Hydrhaga? You received a letter?"

He continued to look at her, his face showing no hint of recognition.

"Never mind," Lumea said, disappointed. "Apparently nobody here in Omnesia knows of the place. Perhaps it would be best if I just return home."

When she turned to go, Elion grabbed her arm.

"Meet me tonight at Achnon's Ruin," he whispered. He let her go, then returned to his fellow workmen. He put his all into that afternoon's work, for he knew that it would be his last day toiling on the wells.

Lumea stood in the shadows for a moment longer, too surprised to move. It took her some time to shake off the unstated implications of Elion's fleeting remark. Upon returning to her room at the inn, she rifled through her belongings and drew out the letter. There didn't seem to be anything unusual or out of the ordinary about it. It was a simple letter, addressed to her, with an invitation to come to Hydrhaga. She had gratefully accepted the opportunity, for it was her chance to escape the stifling walls of her parents' home and to see the world she had longed to see. Even the journey seemed full of exciting prospects, as she was going to sail and fly. She would meet new people, but more importantly, see new countries. The journey had turned out to be harder than she had expected, and in her heart she most looked forward to the time when she would actually arrive in Hydrhaga. Yet, the letter had given her a different feeling as well. That was the reason she took it up yet again.

It still said the same things, but she could not shake the feeling that there was some kind of secret hidden within the words, some secret subtext that tantalized her and remained elusively beyond her grasp. The reactions she had received in Omnesia did nothing to comfort her. Lumea did not enjoy this vague feeling; she was not used to threats. Up until now, everything had gone smoothly in her life, her only true sense of discord coming from her parents and her own imagination. Her gut feeling told her that this was something else entirely, and Elion's behavior intensified the feeling of unease. Why did he act so mysteriously? Still, she was glad that he wanted to help her. Something deep inside her wanted to believe that she was worried for nothing, and that Hydrhaga was a good place to be.

When twilight fell, Lumea packed her things. The innkeeper shook his head when she paid him for the time she had spent there. He muttered something nearly unintelligible about making the wrong decision. Lumea ignored his warning and flung her cloak around her shoulders as she stepped into the rapidly-approaching chill night. She took a fleeting glance at the lantern lighter, who was striding down the street atop his stilts, before turning down the street that would lead her out of the city. Achnon's Ruin was close by. She had been there before.

By the time she reached the ruin, the sun had disappeared below the horizon, and the moon stood high in the night sky, arcing through its last quarter. When she had asked about it, the Horse Lady had told her that the ruin had been built by the elves a long time ago. The pale light did little to diminish the loveliness that the ruins held during the day, but now that beauty was displayed in contrast to the radiance of deep night. The shadows of the ruins lent an eerie sense of foreboding to the alcoves and arches. Positioning herself on one of the boulders that dotted the area, she thrust her imagined fears from her mind and settled in to wait for Elion.

After sitting there for some time, Lumea started to fear that Elion would not come after all. Then she heard muffled footfalls, and there he was, emerging from the shadows that blanketed the ruins. The wind tore at his cloak, revealing for a moment the richly-embroidered tunic that he wore underneath. The patterns were old, definitely not from the current fashion that the Omnesians wore, but the tunic itself looked almost new. The contrast to the clothing he had worn during the day was startling, and again Lumea found herself taken aback by this man. His face was grave when he finally got close enough to speak with her.

"You said you have a letter inviting you to Hydrhaga, and asked me if I knew where it lay. My heart has always longed to go there. I will show you the way, but only if you will take me inside the city with you, as your guide."

For a moment Lumea recognized the formality in his voice, just as he had used earlier in greeting her. She could not quite put her finger on it, but it did not fit at all with the image of a workman she had in her mind. Her mind flashed to the brief glimpse of rich clothing hidden under the folds of his cloak and she decided then and there to bury her prejudices.

Elion's words comforted her. He wanted to go there too, so it must be the beautiful place that she imagined it to be. He would show her the way, and he even wanted to go inside the city with her. That was comforting, too. She wouldn't be alone.

"I would like for you to come with me," she answered truthfully.

They shouldered their belongings and set off on their journey. El-ion seemed to know the way, for his feet found the path even though it was hidden in the dark. Their first night's travel was a short one, with Elion leading Lumea to a small building a short distance from the ruins. Though it appeared of the same architecture, and would be of a similar age, it had weathered the ravages of time better, and provided shelter for travelers.

They swiftly made camp, with Elion disappearing to gather firewood. Lumea dug through her pack for some of the food she had the foresight to bring. It had been several hours since she had last eaten and hunger was beginning to gnaw at her stomach. Upon his return, Elion piled up the wood and in short order had a small fire burning. It was clear he had done this before. Handing some of the food over, Lumea noticed that Elion ate slowly, as though he needed to control himself from devouring the meager meal. As they sat there, the light from the flames glistened off a lighter patch of skin that ran from Elion's wrist to his hand, a large scar.

"What happened to your hand?"

Elion immediately pulled his sleeve over the hand and folded his arms in front of his chest.

"You saw the job I did," he answered, averting his eyes.

"You were burned? That must have hurt terribly!"

He answered her comment with silence, and a non-committal shrug. Understanding that this was not a topic he wanted to discuss, she let the matter drop.

It was some time later, when the fire had died down to a cherry-colored bed of coals that Lumea finally drifted off to sleep. Her dreams were full of rolling landscapes bathed in warm light, with folk enjoying simple, but fulfilling lives. The light from the rising sun woke her from the dream. Elion was already busy cleaning up the site where they had camped, extinguishing the last embers of the fire with sand. They ate a small breakfast, and afterward broke camp before the sun was fully above the horizon.

It was during these early hours of the morning that Lumea had the chance to glimpse the animals that she had previously only seen the tracks of: gemsbuck, hare, and all manner of other creature emerged from their dens to lap at the cool dew that blanketed the grass and foliage during the chill night. The animals were shy, and the hares fled very quickly, warning others by the rapid cadence of their retreating hind feet. The antelopes, grazing in herds, turned their heads as the man and the woman neared, but decided that they posed no threat and continued to graze unperturbed. At times, their path took them through plains where the grasses reached above the waist. Their passage occasionally caused hidden flocks of birds to burst from concealment, which startled them both. It was an overwhelming experience to stand in the middle of their flapping wings, while they screeched in an attempt to chase them off. They soon gave up the fight, though, and the quiet returned. The sun soon crested the horizon, and the day warmed the last vestiges of dew, drying it up. With no other reason to remain in the open, the animals disappeared from sight again, and Lumea wondered where they went to be hidden so quickly and completely.

As the day wore on, their journey was marked by a notable silence. Although Elion had seemed glad at first to have been invited on this excursion he now wore an expression as though he were passing judgment, but it was hard to determine whether it was positive or not. Aside from that, he automatically took charge of everything, which annoyed Lumea.

The uncomfortable silence lasted until he asked her why she wanted to go to Hydrhaga so badly. Lumea explained that it seemed to be the place where she could lead her own life. "That is something I can't do in my home country. The law prescribes how a woman should act, but that is not the way I wish to live. Hydrhaga seems to be a peaceful country, and I hope to find a carefree life there."

Elion had seemed honestly interested in her reasons for wanting to build a new existence far from home. Now, however, she could read the disapproval in his eyes. She was disconcerted by the contempt, but she asked, "Why do you want to go there, then?"

His reply was a barely audible murmur about a man he was supposed to meet there. He resumed their trek, and it was the way he just assumed she would follow that made her stay put as her anger rose. He soon returned and looked at her impatiently, but she stared back defiantly.

"Come on, we have to move on," he said.

"And who made you leader?"

"I'm guiding you to your land of milk and honey. That would seem like enough of a reason to me."

His sarcastic words rankled her, and Lumea brusquely confronted him. She wondered what made men around the world decide that they could boss women around, so she snapped, "You could at least consult with me."

Elion shrugged and remained silent, but afterward he did adjust his behavior, but only just a little.

6

They traveled for six days, and Lumea enjoyed the unknown surroundings, with its fresh sights. The journey was easy, even if the uncomfortable silences between the two of them continued. At first, they walked over the grassy plains, then under gigantic trees, but they also passed the salt plains that Lumea had espied in the distance during her stay in the city. The sun glittered on the wide, whitish landscape, blinding them both. These plains formed when the salt water that collected in the region evaporated, leaving its crystallized load behind.

At times they saw vultures circling the plains, looking for a gemsbuck or some other hapless animal that had taken its chances on the plains and lost. Elion always led her around these places, traversing paths that were considerably safer and more hospitable.

The vegetation gradually changed. The grassy fields gave way to clumps of cacti, which grew in all shapes and sizes out of the arid earth. Elion cut off two bulbous stems from one of the cacti with his knife. Then he easily rid them of their spines and made a hole in each, after which he gave one to Lumea.

"Ever had cactus-milk?"

Even as he asked it, he raised the second plant to his lips and drank. Lumea followed his example, and was surprised at how bitter it tasted.

The lands changed and continued to surprise Lumea with the variety of different plants which grew in this corner of the world. They passed beyond the salt plains and once again entered verdant valleys, dotted with with thickets of trees. Their stunted trunks supported branches bedecked with broad, waxy leaves. The valley floor was covered in shrubs and flowering vines of varied hue, and Lumea found pleasure in the different colors and smells that wafted from them. This was similar to the vistas of her homeland, but of a softer cast, less rugged.

Finally, they reached the edge of a lake. Figures of strange creatures carved from thick, wooden poles stood in the water, supporting a bridge that led to Hydrhaga's main gate. The bridge had no railing, and seemed to be suspended dangerously high above the water. Elion was the first to step onto the wooden boards, but Lumea hesitated for a moment before following him. She kept meticulously to the middle and tried not to look down between the boards.

At the other side of the lake they saw a tower. As they got closer, they realized it was part of a greater structure. To the left of the tower there was the gatehouse, which guarded the interior from the outside world. The wall surrounding the gate was the only straight one in the whole of the structure.

All of the other walls were built more to the front or to the back, and they rose higher or rolled lower almost like a wave. It altered the perspective, so that it was impossible to say if the wall was high or low, near or far. The building was mirrored in the water, and the glint of the sun on the lake was reflected in the smooth marble walls. The overall effect only added to the confusion. It was impossible to say where the wall ended and the water began. Everything came together in one grand design, which as a whole, conspired to make her feel insignificant.

On the wall above the gate, bronze spikes were mounted. Behind them, Lumea could discern the silhouettes of guards with their weapons at the ready. At first, because the light was shining in her eyes, she thought they were statues, but just as the two of them approached there was a change of the guards. All the other walls sloped forward at the top. Even if you could climb the slippery walls, that slope would prove insurmountable. Where the walls drew back, they were decorated with bronze statues that seemed to tumble and dive into the lake. Over time, they had turned green.

The most noticeable feature of the whole structure, though, was the enormous tower they had first seen. Halfway up, there was a door with stairs going down on the outside. When the two travelers finally arrived at the tower, a man came down to meet them. The robe he was wearing clung tightly to his upper body, though it fanned out from his waist down. The underside of his skirt trailed behind him on the stairs. He lifted the front of the skirt just a bit so that he would not stumble over it. This action allowed Lumea to see that he was wearing boots with high soles, which added to his height. They waited for him to descend the stairs. When he was standing in front of them, it was clear that even Elion was smaller than the man welcoming them, even considering his platform boots. Lumea handed him the letter.

"I bid you welcome, Lumea Ouinwred," he said after reading it. "We expected you sooner, and alone." He regarded Elion with a suspicious glance.

"This is Elion. My father sent him along with me because he thought it would be irresponsible for me to travel alone."

The man seemed to believe her as he nodded and asked them both to follow him. With a triumphant smile, Lumea looked over her shoulder at Elion. They were both glad to finally enter Hydrhaga, but for Lumea there was also the pleasure of knowing that Elion would not have succeeded in entering the city without her.

The massive metal gate opened. Behind it was a broad corridor leading to the next gate, and the next. All of them opened to allow the new guests inside, seemingly of their own accord. As Lumea and Elion walked, they were watched by stone gargoyles glaring down at the gates from both sides. The stone gulleys through which water had once run were now dry, and had apparently been so for a long time, as mosses now covered the bottom of the trenches.

Beyond the fourth and final gate a man waited for them. Before Lumea and Elion stepped through the gateway, the man spit into his hand and with a quick movement brushed his hair backwards out of his face. Then he clasped his hands behind his back again. It was an unconscious gesture, almost as if he did not realize that he was doing it. The locks of hair immediately fell back into his face. The man bowed and introduced himself as Ward. He had a careful look about him, and because of his stooped shoulders, his deep-set eyes seemed to be searching everything around him with suspicion, peering from under small, thin eyebrows that served to give his face a pained look. He took a quick step back when another man passed them. Again he spit into his hand and brushed his hair back. His voice was soft and on occasion it broke into a higher register.

"I will be your guide through Hydrhaga today and show you

where you will be staying. Should you have any questions, do not hesitate to ask."

He turned around with a jerky, halting movement to walk in front of the newcomers. Elion looked back for a moment. The last gate was already closed, and above it soldiers marched, guarding the exit. He took one last, lingering look at the gate, and then quickly caught up with Lumea and Ward as they headed deeper into the city.

Hydrhaga proved to be a country with an abundance of water. Lumea lost count of the number of lakes that dotted the green pastures and fields that surrounded the city: ten… twenty? She did not know. Ward proudly explained that some of them were thousands of feet deep, and the the darkness of the water seemed to confirm his claims. The murky depths consumed all light, and nowhere in sight was there a sign of a bottom. In the middle of the lakes, dozens of small boats sailed the waterways. The shores were busy, too, with people basking in the radiance of the sun and others enjoying a cool swim. Lumea looked forward to taking a dive later in the day. Both she and Elion could not help but notice the seemingly carefree way of life in Hydrhaga.

Dotted around the landscape were several buildings. They were oval in shape and were partly covered by earth, making them resemble natural hillocks. Each building had its own flag and the walls that were visible had windows that allowed sunlight to pierce the near-subterranean abode. The dwelling Ward led them to, however, had the curtains drawn, blocking the light, and as they walked along the corridor their guide explained the layout of the houses.

"Each house is built much like a tree. You could say that we are walking along the trunk now. Further on it is divided, as if into branches. At the end of the branches are seven leaves, which are the living spaces. Both of you have been given a room in this building."

Ward stopped talking just as they arrived at the intersection where the hallway branched off and shortly thereafter he opened the door to Lumea's room. Elion's room was the one next door. Ward left them there, saying that they could always find him if they needed him.

Lumea closed the door of her room behind her. It was somewhat of a relief to be alone again after the journey with Elion. There was a chair standing against the wall, and when Lumea lowered herself into it, she sank into its soft cushions. Looking around at the pentagonal room, she noted that every effort had been made to make the guests feel at home, to feel comfortable. Long, velvet curtains hung down from the ceiling, swathing every inch of the walls in the luxurious fabric. Next to the chair, there was an oaken table, polished and varnished so that the wood held a deep shine, setting off the natural texture of the grain. Against the opposing wall was a large bed with what appeared to be a fine down mattress, the sort Lumea had only dreamed of. The last piece of furniture was a marble wash basin, a sculpted branch decorated with ivory leaves hung suspended from the wall, upon which cascaded a constant stream of cool, fresh water.

Lumea got up and walked over to one of the curtains, which she drew to the side in single sweeping motion, revealing ornately-carved window frames. From her room, Lumea could see the woods of Hydrhaga before her, like a personal piece of woodland paradise. She drew open the other curtains, determined not to closet away a single avenue of her breathtaking view. The wonder over the beautiful landscape lasted only until she noticed something strange. Nothing moved. Not a leaf stirred in the wind, not a bird flew through the air. The clouds retained their shape and stayed in the same place.

She reached out with her hand, and under her fingers she could feel the texture of the paint. Remembering that this building was buried in sand and earth, she suddenly felt a need for fresh air. She walked out of her room and knocked on Elion's door. Together they left the building and went to discover more about Hydrhaga.

The lakes were busy, because the temperature outside was so pleasant. Elion and Lumea found a place under the shadow of a solitary tree.

"Going for a swim?" Lumea asked Elion.

He shook his head in answer.

Lumea shrugged, took off her dress and walked into the lake. The ground immediately disappeared from under her feet, and she sank under the water. She tried to scream, but instead she swallowed a gulp of water. She had been caught unawares, because she had assumed that the bottom of the lake would fall away gradually. Instead, it was a steep drop. Her feet couldn't find purchase, bringing on a panic she would not normally have felt. For a moment that seemed to stretch on to eternity, the water seemed to be dragging her down and into its crushing embrace.

In her mind, she returned to the time when she was just a little girl. Lunadeiron had seen its first signs of winter. The land was covered in a white blanket and the brooks and lakes had frozen over during the night. Her brothers had challenged her to step out onto the fragile ice. She wanted to impress them and she had done what they said. However, the ice was still too thin to support her weight and it broke, sinking her beneath its glass-like surface. She was gripped by the cold; all she could see was a blurred light. She tried to find the hole she had made, but time and again she bumped into the ice instead, and she was too weak to break through. It had seemed like lifetime before someone had finally pulled her out of the icy water.

Now Lumea panicked again, beating at the water with her arms as if looking for something to latch onto, even though there was nothing there. The panic made her forget how to swim, and she felt like that helpless four year-old again. She desperately tried to reach the surface, but instead she seemed to sink farther.

Suddenly, somebody grabbed her and pulled her ashore. She was lying on the ground, breathing heavily. The sun quickly warmed her, but the incident had upset her.

"Are you okay?" Elion asked when he helped her to sit up.

Lumea nodded. "I'm a bit dizzy, is all. Must be because of the shock and all the water I swallowed." Then she stood up. "I'm going to my room."

Lumea noticed that Elion was concerned, and she felt touched that he cared about her, as well as surprised to see this new side of him.

From that time on, the dark water looked much less inviting, and Lumea preferred to remain ashore. Nobody had witnessed what had happened; the other people seemed to be enjoying themselves too much to pay attention to the newcomers. In Hydrhaga, everybody was happy.

In the dark of night Lumea had a sudden bout of anxiety, when her heart leaped into her throat. She seemed paralyzed as she watched formless ghosts approaching her from all sides. They reached out for her, threatening to deprive her of air, the way the water of the lake so surely had. She gasped for breath, but none came. It was morning by the time she fell into a dreamless sleep. When she woke up, the pains from the previous day's experience had nearly passed.

On the second day, Ward had sought Lumea and Elion out, intent on continuing their tour. He sounded businesslike as he pointed out the different sights and provided brief explanations about them. Then they reached a fenced-in terrain that seemed to have been dug out some time ago. Ward explained that inside Hydrhaga's walls the remains of a strange creature had been found, which the discoverers had named the Thuranc. The pit that lay before them was the archaeological dig-site. The guide told Lumea about the great importance of the find, and how, through further research, they hoped to uncover the secrets of the past.

Elion was only partially paying attention, as his time was mostly spent simply examining the surroundings. Lumea, on the other hand, was engrossed. She immediately recognized that their quiet and nervous host had a passion for the Thuranc. His voice became louder and less guarded. Lumea asked him many questions, enjoying the fact that her interest brought on such a change in their guide. Ward became more animated, he talked faster and his voice seemed to break less than it had on the previous day.

They had been standing there for some time, examining the excavation site while Ward indicated the specific locations where various segments of the Thuranc had been found, all carefully marked with small stakes and signs. It was unexpected when Ward suddenly asked them to wait for a moment. He disappeared into a nearby building, leaving Elion and Lumea behind.

When he returned, his eyes were twinkling with anticipation, and he gestured for the two of them to follow. They entered a long hallway with closed doors on either side. At the end of the hallway there was another door which was securely locked. Ward held his hand against a palm scanner and the locks opened with a loud click. The door opened and they entered behind their host. When the light was turned on, they could see the Thuranc behind a glass wall.

Lumea had never heard of anything like it, not even in the many myths that her own country knew. The creature on the other side of the glass was slim and towered high above her. As far as its build was concerned, it looked almost human. It was naked, and its muscles stood out prominently. The muscles in its arms were especially large, like cables coiled beneath its smooth, nearly-translucent skin. Its long fingers sported sharp claws. Its hair was braided and fell down his back, and Lumea couldn't help but notice that it was the only hair anywhere on its body. Its head was oriented downward, giving it the appearance that it was looking down upon any visitors. Its dark eyes seemed to look right through her as she stared at this relic of a distant past.

The creature looked as if it had never known life, but at the same time Lumea imagined it would have no trouble breaking through the window and killing them all in one fierce, terrifying display. It confused and even frightened her, and she found that she was afraid of the Thuranc. She was not sure why, but as Ward became more enthusiastic, her fears grew, but she kept them to herself. Lumea did notice, however, that for the first time since arriving here, Elion actually seemed interested in something.

7

After that, Lumea and Elion only saw Ward from a distance. New guests had arrived and it was his duty to showcase Hydrhaga to them as well. Lumea wondered if they had been permitted a look at the strange creature by some higher authority, or if Ward had broken some rule that now prevented him from speaking to them further. She worried that they had gotten him into trouble. Aside from that sole fear, their carefree stay continued. There was always enough food and the temperature stayed pleasantly consistent. The days were quiet, the nights passed without any more nightmares of clutching hands or crushing watery depths. As her fears abated, it became logical for life to be centered around the lakes, with their cool, calming waters. Lumea's existence, as with all of the other guests, continued in ignorance of the secret research being conducted in Hydrhaga.

Lumea did not speak much with Elion, even though he was always close by. She was surprised by his constant presence. There was barely the need for his protection in this safe environment, and over time his overprotective nature began to grate on her. She did not confront him about his behavior, hoping that it would subside in time. It was the carefree attitude displayed by others that eventually served to relax him a little, and it was not long before Lumea started getting used to having people around her. She even started to recognize the more common faces, learning their names and developing acquaintances. Curiously, at times people seemed to simply disappear. She assumed they had gone back home, but nobody ever talked about it. The reason why she and the others had actually come to Hydrhaga remained likewise unclear, but it all appeared unimportant, with life continuing on at its calm pace.

Even with the communal atmosphere and pleasant days, boredom struck Lumea in the evenings. As soon as it turned dark, everyone retreated to their rooms. The window-paintings were lit differently during that time, but the knowledge that none of it was real detracted from their beauty. They would look exactly the same tomorrow, and the day after that, and the one after that.

Lumea spent most of those lonely hours reading, but one night she put aside her book. It was impossible to concentrate on the words for some reason. She had read the last page three times already, and still she had no idea what it said. She thought of her parents, and wondered if she had made the right choice in coming here. What would she have been doing now, if she had stayed? Quite likely, she would have been surrounded by guests who would end up spending the night.

Those evenings were always full of company. The guests would tell stories and sing songs. When she was little, she always tried to find a small corner somewhere so that she would not have to go to bed. There, she would sit quietly and fight against sleep, a battle she would always lose. Her father would then take her into his strong arms and place her gently into her bed. She would wake up for a moment just as he tucked her in and wished her the sweetest dreams.

As she grew older, her father would often ask her to sing for their guests, who listened breathlessly. She loved those moments, because they made her feel as though she actually belonged. It was a feeling she did not have very often, for most of the time she felt more like an outsider.

Lumea stood up and walked out of her room. She knocked on the door next to hers. A woman opened it.

"Hi, good evening. I was thinking in my room just now – well, actually I was being bored in my room, and I thought maybe it would be nice to get together with the people in this corridor, you know, as a way of getting to know each other? What do you think?"

The woman's reaction was enthusiastic, and they agreed that she would come to Lumea's room in a moment. Others agreed as well, and before long they had all gathered. Most of them had brought a pillow with them so that they had a place to sit, and some brought food and drink to share. Elion chose the window sill to sit on, from there he could survey the group. Lumea sat on the floor in the center of the gathering.

The impromptu party started out somewhat stiff and tense, because they did not know each other, but soon enough, conversations started up among the gathering. Except for Lumea, all of them came from Omnesia, and they started comparing memories of home. The atmosphere grew more animated and even though she could not join in many of the conversations, Lumea was visibly enjoying it.

Suddenly, everything turned dark; the lights in Hydrhaga went out at a certain time. The only light that remained came from the emergency lamps within the corridor. Some people got up to go back to their room, but Elion had brought a lamp which he lit and handed to Lumea. She put it in the middle of the group.

The atmosphere turned mysterious as the lantern's light was not quite strong enough to reach the corners of the room. Elion sat in the dark and watched how the light shone on Lumea's face and made her tattoo glitter. Almost as if she was conscious of this fact, she started singing. It was a song about Lunadeiron, in her own language. Nobody understood the words, but even so her voice took them to the mountains and vales of her home. At times her voice was warm, like a summer's day, and at others clear and clattering like a waterfall. Everyone listened without even a murmur.

At the end of the song, they remained quiet for a moment longer, then a woman asked her to sing another song. Lumea remembered the beautiful duet she used to sing with her father. She was sure it would sound less magnificent if she sang it alone, but as she searched for a different song the melody of the duet kept intruding, making it impossible to think of anything else. She started singing, but her voice was unsure during the verses that her father normally sang.

Suddenly, Elion's voice joined in with hers, and she was surprised as he took her father's part of the song. The language he used was different—she did not know it—but it complimented the song very nicely. She looked up at the man sitting on the window sill. He smiled at her and nodded encouragingly. She felt her cheeks flush, but nobody knew that he was not singing the song the way it was written. The fact that he seemed to know the words only convinced them that he must come from Lunadeiron as well.

When the song ended, a man got up and left the room for a moment. When he returned, he had a small harp tucked under his arm. At first he played and sang alone, but the songs became rowdier and soon people were singing along and laughing. Even Elion laughed exuberantly at some of the lyrics. Everyone was in high spirits and by the time they got up to leave it was late. Lumea stopped Elion as he was leaving and looked at him enquiringly.

"Your song reminded me of one my parents used to sing. I only used their words in your song, that's all," he told her. He quickly walked through the door before she could ask anything else. She accepted his answer.

Similar nights followed, and Lumea and Elion relieved the boredom of the lonely nights in Hydrhaga through their parties.

Weeks passed this way, with nothing of importance to mark the passage of time, until one day, months later, Lumea discovered something new. For once, Elion was nowhere to be seen, and as she walked towards one of the lakes movement in the air caught her attention. When she turned towards it, she realized she was looking at kites. Some of them hung motionless in the air, except for their tails, colored ribbons that fluttered in the wind. Other kites swooped and dived in front of the passing clouds. They were made of thin paper and the sun shone through them, intensifying their colors, which stood out against the lavender sky.

The play in the air made Lumea feel cheerful, and she walked in the direction of the flying kites, her pace quickening, until finally she was running. When she crested the top of a small hill she stopped. Beneath her she could see a man operating all the kites. Most of them were attached to poles in the ground, but the man was holding two lines.

Two butterflies were dancing in synch through the air. The paper of the kites made a clapping sound in the wind, which sometimes changed to a low hum. Once or twice, the kites looked as if they would crash into the ground, but just before it happened the wind would pick them up again and they were flying high once more.

Lumea slowly approached the old man. When she was close to him, he nodded at her, though his attention quickly returned to his kites. The young woman did not say anything, but lay down in the grass and watched the kites play.

After a few minutes the man attached the lines of his kites to some poles and sat down beside her. Lumea sat up but waited for him to speak.

"In all my twenty years here, you're the first one to actually come and watch my kites. I'm glad you came. My name is Aeron."

He held out his hand and Lumea took it, although she was not used to this type of greeting. The man shook her hand heartily.

"My name is Lumea. Your kites are magnificent, did you make them all yourself?"

The man nodded. By way of proof he showed his hands. His nails were spotted with paint, his fingers full of small cuts made by the lines of his kites.

Aeron and Lumea lay in the grass for hours that day, companionable but not speaking. Eventually she said her goodbyes and went to look for Elion.

After this initial meeting, she went to Aeron more often and helped him keep his kites up in the air, or would hold parts of the kites so that he could repair them. It was magnificent seeing these silent creatures riding the wind and Lumea could watch them for hours on end.

One day Aeron was waving merrily as she descended the hillock. By the time she was near him he had reeled in his kite and walked towards her.

"Hi Lumea! I'm glad you're here. I have something for you."

They walked back together and he picked up a brown bag.

"It's a kite!"

Lumea happily took the package and carefully unrolled the paper that came out of the bag. Her friend was excited and had to keep himself from tearing it out of her hands and revealing the gift himself. As she unrolled it, the image of an eagle appeared. Its body, made out of balsa wood, was carved with incredibly lifelike feathers. Every little barb was visible. It must have taken Aeron hours—maybe even days—to make, and all this time he had kept it hidden from her! The beak was sharp and the eyes looked alive. The wings were made of paper painted in brown, ocher and gold colors.

Lumea turned the eagle in her hands, watching it from all sides.

Then she gratefully looked at the kite runner, who was smiling proud-ly.

"I saw that your tattoo has the wing of an eagle in it. I hope you like it."

"Like it? I love it! It's beautiful!"

She carefully put the kite down on the ground, then hugged Aeron and gave him a kiss on his cheek. He blushed, but his eyes were glow-ing with pride.

"Do you want to release it?" he asked.

Lumea shook her head. She was afraid that she would do some-thing wrong, and she didn't want to rip the paper. So she watched as Aeron launched the bird into the air. Just like all his other kites, this one came to life under the subtle movement of his hands. He let it swoop down like a real bird of prey hunting a small animal. Then he gestured for her to get up and handed the line to her.

At first she was cautious, but the eagle seemed to have a will of its own. Within moments it was soaring through the air. After a while, the man took the line back and attached it to one of the anchor poles so that it hovered in the sky, as if searching for prey. Lumea had brought food for the both of them, so they picnicked on the grass. It was late in the afternoon by the time she said goodbye to Aeron, thanking him again for the wonderful gift.

8

Hydrhaga did not seem to know seasons. The sun shone every day, the summer seemed without end, and everybody lost their grip on time. That was about to change.

The day started out much like any other. Lumea and Elion were sitting in the grass near one of the smaller lakes. The lake had a bottom that sloped down gradually and in the middle it was only a few dozen feet deep. Ward had tried to convince Lumea to swim again, but the woman had ignored his arguments. After her close brush with drowning, she did not trust the water any more.

When they arrived in Hydrhaga, Lumea had taught Elion a game that she had brought with her from Lunadeiron, but he had defeated her every single time they played, and he was well on his way to best her again. With a sudden burst of anger, she swept the pieces from the board.

"I give up, I will never beat you."

"Let's try again. Maybe this time you'll get lucky."

"Oh, never mind," Lumea replied testily.

Elion was amused by her mood, but just as he wanted to remark about it, one of the Hosts approached and told them to hurry back to their rooms. His eyes were hidden behind dark glasses. No emotion registered on his face.

"When summer ends, winter comes," he muttered. The remark did not seem to be meant for either of them.

Lumea gathered her things quickly, and Elion helped her up. Everywhere, the inhabitants of Hydrhaga rose obediently to comply with their Hosts' orders. They walked towards their rooms in long lines. Elion held Lumea by her arm as they joined the line, gripping it tightly. She wanted to tell him that he was hurting her, but something stopped her. His eyes flitted from left to right, as if searching for a means of escape.

As they neared the buildings, the number of Hosts increased. They formed a silent hedge next to the path that the guests were following.

Like the Host who had told Elion and Lumea to go to their room, all of them wore dark glasses, but Lumea felt that they were keeping a sharp eye on everyone. She also noticed that their clothing was too warm for the temperature, with thick, long mantles. All of them kept one hand hidden from sight under the folds of their cloaks. It scared Lumea. What were these surly men hiding? And why did the guests have to go to their room so suddenly? When Elion looked at her, he saw the fear in her eyes. He tried to give her a reassuring nod, but his eyes suggested that she not say a word.

A woman somewhere in front of them began to cry hysterically. Elion gripped Lumea's arm even harder, and the pain caused her to let out a soft, involuntary moan. Elion didn't seem to notice. The Hosts hurried to the woman and pulled her out of the line. The mood turned ugly and threatening. The other guests walked past, though, as if they were oblivious to the woman's plight.

It was the moment Elion had been waiting for. There was a door to their right and he quickly opened it, dragging Lumea inside. Another man followed them. Lumea looked over her shoulder and saw how one Host had drawn some kind of weapon from under his mantle. Instinct told her that the woman was about to die. She wanted to scream, but Elion put his hand over her mouth.

"Shhh, don't say anything, or we will know the same fate," he whispered into her ear.

The last thing she saw before the door closed behind them was the lifeless form of the woman lying on the ground. Nobody had noticed how the three of them—Elion, Lumea and the stranger—had left the line. She looked at the two men, confused.

"What's happening? What is going on?" she asked, the panic obvious in her voice.

"Later," Elion answered shortly as he walked through the room and to a dark staircase that spiraled down into unknown depths. After descending the stairs for a while they reached a heavy door, behind which could be heard the thudding sounds of industrial machines.

The thudding sped up and became louder. The door opened. Lumea barely had time to think, but she pulled the two men into the shadows. As it opened wider, the light crept closer and closer over the wall. The three runaways crouched against the wall and held their breath as the light approached without mercy. Lumea's heart kept skipping beats, convinced as she was that within moments they would be discovered. She wondered what would happen to them if they were caught. To her great relief, the worker who had opened the door let go of it again. The light disappeared as the door closed. The worker walked past them and into a corridor without spotting them.

They were safe again, so Elion continued to lead them down. As they descended, the metal staircase ended and a stone one began, cut out from the living rock. The steps were worn and wet, and the footing was precarious in the dark. Finally, they reached some caves, and after a while they found one that seemed as if it had not been used for a long time, since there were no signs of human activity. The corridor leading into it twisted and turned, so any light they made would not be seen from the other caves.

"Lumea, this is Siard," Elion said, introducing the other man.

When Lumea looked at him the young man nodded at her in a friendly manner. He wore clothing cut in the Omnesian style, and his hair was blond and reached just below his ears. From one buttonhole of his cotton overcoat ran a twisted silver chain down to his pocket. She could see the thin metal arm of a pair of glasses poking out of the pocket. He sat proudly upright, his long legs folded beneath him.

Lumea was surprised that Elion knew this man. She had never seen them together. Nevertheless, Siard seemed to know about her, since Elion did not take the trouble of introducing her. She looked at Elion.

"I think you have some explaining to do."

"I know as much, or as little, about this place as you do, Lumea. But I never trusted it here. Siard came a lot earlier than we did. I wanted to come earlier, but they would not let me in."

"So the two of you have known each other for a long time?"

"We both came here from Omnesia. When we heard the stories about Hydrhaga, we had our doubts about the things that happened here. Unfortunately, I was unable to enter on my own. You saw just how tightly secured this place is," Elion said. He paused, frowning slightly. "Or, maybe you didn't."

Elion's voice was irritated, and Lumea thought she heard something like contempt there. She was angry that he had not told her earlier how dangerous he thought it was here.

"You just used me to get inside the city!" she hissed angrily.

"Look, I just saved your butt out there, so stop whining!"

"Oh really? You saved it? From what?"

Elion looked the other way with an annoyed grunt.

"If you want me to help you, you'll have to tell me everything," Lumea said decisively, even though she knew that her words made very little impression on him. There was something in his eyes, something that she suspected was disapproval. She felt that he thought of her as nothing more than a burden, and she was determined to prove him wrong.

"If you didn't want me here, you shouldn't have dragged me through that door."

Siard tried to mediate. "Thank you for pulling us into the shadow back there," he said.

Lumea did not react to his words, but kept her eyes on Elion, who in turn avoided her gaze. Then she stood up and went to lie down in a corner, and though the floor was hard she tried to get some sleep. She heard the two men talking quietly, and although she had taken to the solitude of her own free will, she felt left out. It was obvious that they did not want to tell her everything. It took some time, but eventually she fell asleep.

"So, did you find your brother?"

Siard shook his head. "It's almost like he has never been here. I didn't want to ask too many questions, but it seems that most of the guests haven't been here for very long."

Elion pondered for a moment. "But we know that elves and humans came here ages ago already."

"I haven't met anyone inside the walls who could confirm those stories," Siard said.

The whispered conversation turned to the Thuranc and the strange, eerie glow that Elion had often seen in the lakes' depths. It was the reason he did not trust the water. Siard had seen it too, but he had no idea what could be the cause.

"I came here looking for answers and all I found were more questions," Siard said.

Elion nodded and started talking about something else. "Did you see what was going on in that hall upstairs?"

Siard shook his head again. From his position he had not seen very much.

"There were all kinds of machines. I was hoping you might have seen them, maybe you would know their function. There were workers there, and they operated the machines with a strange kind of automatism. Almost like they..." Elion tried to find the right words, "... like they were programmed for the work. On the ceiling there were rails, and from those hung metal parts of some sort."

"But what are they making?"

Elion shrugged. "I saw one man enter the hall with a handcart. But the door closed before I could get a better look at it."

"Can you remember what it looked like?"

"No, I can't. Sorry."

Elion seemed to hesitate for a moment, but he did not say anything else. If he had not seen that the thing was made from metal, he would have sworn that what he had seen was a living creature, but as that seemed too unlikely to be true, he did not say it.

"We will find out what they're making here," Siard said before lying down to sleep.

Elion stayed awake. As usual, he could not sleep, and besides, someone needed to stand guard. When he looked at Lumea, asleep in her corner, he stood up and grabbed his cape from the floor. He knelt beside her, and carefully draped the cloak over her.

The following morning Lumea awoke to the sound of Elion and Siard's voices. It took a moment for her to remember where she was and what had happened on the previous day. As soon as they realized that she was awake, they stopped talking. Lumea immediately felt last night's anger returning in full force. She stood up and went to sit with the other two, but she left Elion's cloak lying in the corner.

They did not have any food with them, so Elion took charge once more and the three of them started out. They halted for a moment near the stairs they had descended yesterday, but then they turned into the caves, which had been empty for quite some time, though the thudding of the machines could be heard everywhere, louder in some places, quieter in others. They reached a small, narrow passage, which they entered single file: Elion at the front, then Lumea, and Siard at the rear of their line. The thudding became quieter as they pressed on until, finally, they could not hear it at all.

The passage sloped gradually upward. They felt a cold draft and occasionally heard the splatter of drops of water dripping to the floor. After a long time they reached another cave. Six stalactites hung down from the ceiling in a perfect circle, around an air vent leading up into darkness. Underneath the circle was a small pond, fed by the water from a rivulet which entered the cave on the right and exited it again on the left side. Six different corridors led out from the cave.

They stopped and rested near the pond, though Elion forbade them to drink the water. He looked around thoughtfully before resting his eyes on Lumea, who looked away with a frown on her face. She could see his thoughts as clearly as if he had said them. If it was not for her, he would not have had to explain anything. Siard would follow him without question.

"We have to find something to eat and drink," he said in an attempt to break the silence. "Quite likely it really is winter out there, so it might be better to get warmer clothes for the two of you. I will go see what I can find. Lumea, stay here with Siard."

He walked toward one of the corridors, but at the same time Lumea stood up. "If you go that way, it will take too long to find what you're looking for. I'll go get the food and the clothes. If it takes too long for your tastes, then you can go on without me."

Before Elion could answer, she stepped into the corridor from which the water flowed, in order to follow it upstream. She had noted with satisfaction that Elion did not know his way down here. On their second day in Hydrhaga, however, Ward had told her about this place, and she had taken the opportunity to ask many questions. This was her chance to show the men that she was valuable to the group. She knew that the archive was located upstream. Ward had wanted to show it to her, but he had not been granted permission. Still, he had proudly told her about everything that was stored there. Lumea was sure that she would find the clothes there, as well as something to eat. Ward had told her that the archive was used quite often.

After following the rivulet for a while, she could see a light at the end of the corridor. She stood still for a moment to let her eyes adjust. When she heard nothing, she turned left.

Farther on, there was a room where people were working. She slipped past it, laughing to herself. She had done this quite often while at home. Her father was a light sleeper, so she had trained herself to walk silently whenever she had sneaked out of the house at night.

To her right, there was a double door leading into the archive, and she quickly slipped through them. The space that she had entered was partly darkened with heavy curtains hanging in front of the windows. The other windows allowed shafts of light to enter the dusty hall. Along two walls there were high cabinets where the larger artifacts were kept. The cabinets themselves were beautiful works of art, ornately decorated as they were. In the middle of the hall, there were low showcases exhibiting the more-important artifacts.

Lumea's fingers felt the carvings and she read the labels hanging on the items. It was an amazing collection. There was a half-burned banner, and its label revealed that it had once been part of a council house. Farther on, there was a piece of green marble identified as being 'from the east gate', and it was next to a simple bottle which apparently contained water from the Fountain of Life. The showcase in the very middle was the biggest, and it contained a magnificent dress. It was obviously the most cherished piece of the collection, but its label was blank, as though the curators had never found the words to describe it.

It was obvious that these items were elvish in origin, which amazed Lumea. Why had the people of Hydrhaga so carefully collected and stored them? The whole place had a kind of nostalgic feel about it that Lumea did not understand. The atmosphere in this room was so different from the sterile rooms she had passed earlier. She opened the big cabinets and felt the rich fabric of the clothes.

A sudden sound startled her and she silently closed the cabinet doors. After a quick look around she chose one of the back showcases and hurried towards it. Hiding underneath it, she tried to make herself as small as she could and waited for what would happen next. She heard footsteps approaching, just before the doors opened with a soft squeak. Lumea saw a long skirt, and when it whirled up for a moment she could see the high-soled boots. She trembled when she realized that it was a Host who had entered the archive. Her heart jumped up in her throat when the skirt came straight for her hiding place.

The Host stood still for a moment, then turned around and made as if to leave. Lumea could not stop the relieved sigh that escaped her. Immediately the feet stopped. Convinced that she was caught, Lumea squeezed her eyes shut and held her breath. Moments later, the doors clicked shut.

Seconds passed, and Lumea concentrated on every little sound she could hear. Maybe the man was still in the room, approaching from the other side. She was afraid to move, and the high showcase with the dress hid the other side of the room from sight. But everything was silent, so Lumea crawled carefully out from under her hiding place. To her relief, the rest of the archive room was empty.

She was physically shaking as she gathered warmer clothes. She also found a large bag and a waterskin, which she filled at a faucet. She would have liked to take it with her while it was still empty and fill it at the little pond, but she trusted Elion's judgment not to drink the water. She looked for other things that might come in handy wherever it was that they were going, and quickly left as soon as she had everything. She had been in the archive far too long.

Amazed by Lumea's decisive actions, Elion sat down on the ground next to Siard. They looked at each other, and Siard started laughing.

"The lady sounded like she knew what she was talking about. Who knows what she'll come back with."

"It's not safe for her out there. She could be caught."

"That could have happened to you as well. Anyway, there's nothing to do but wait. I assume you still don't want to leave her behind."

Elion shook his head. "I'm annoyed with her naivety, but I couldn't leave her in the hands of those Hosts."

"You can't blame her for being young, Elion. She hasn't experienced even half of what you've been through."

"You're right, Siard, but you're only a little bit older than she is, and you notice things that she does not."

"Perhaps, but I came here knowing that something might be wrong, which always makes people notice more than when they think they're safe."

After that they remained silent until they heard someone approaching. They hid in the shadows until Lumea appeared. She was now dressed in a green mantle, and on her back she had the bag and the waterskin. Another piece of clothing was folded over her arm.

Without speaking, she took a seat on the spot the two men had just vacated. She watched Elion's surprised face with a smug expression. He had obviously not expected her mission to prove so successful. The two men sat down beside her, and she handed Siard a dark blue mantle. Then she passed around the waterskin and handed them some food from her bag.

Siard was the first to speak. "It seems you knew where to go, judging by the success you had."

Elion only nodded, but Lumea was fine with that. She had another surprise for him.

After dinner, Elion made to leave, but the young woman motioned for him to keep his place.

"Despite the... abundance of information... you gave me," she said sarcastically, "I assume we're in for some dangerous times. And although you did not tell me to bring anything else, I took the liberty of stealing some weapons from the Hosts' archive."

From a fold in her mantle she drew a bow and some arrows and handed them to Elion.

"I could tell from your hands that you are an archer," she said.

For Siard she had a straight, two-handed sword. Lastly she withdrew a wicked-looking curved blade. Taking it from its scabbard, she checked the sharpness with her thumb. As she did, she wondered if Elion had expected her to be able to fight. She was not about to enlighten him, but for a moment her thoughts returned to her childhood, and the lessons in swordsmanship that she had received.

As was the custom in Lunadeiron, her brothers had undergone martial training from an early age. Her parents had retained a master swordsman to teach the boys, among other things, the arts of the blade. Whenever she had had the chance, she had followed her brothers and watched them from behind a pillar as they executed intriguing exercises. She had admired the master's prowess as he showed the boys what to do. She had always hoped to possess that same kind of skill, and in the deep of night, when she was sure nobody would see her, she had imitated the master's movements.

One day the sword-master had caught her watching from the pillar's shadow, and when the lesson ended he handed her over to her parents. Her mother's disapproval was obvious, but her father had given her the chance to explain exactly why she enjoyed watching so much, and because he judged these lessons to be harmless, he had talked with the sword-master—much to the dissatisfaction of his wife—to extend his lessons to include Lumea. Her brothers had laughed at first, but thanks to her nightly exercises she had already learned enough to reach their level in no time, and soon she even surpassed them. Now that she also had a master, Lumea had focused on perfecting her technique, and while sparring she had often defeated her brothers.

She returned the sword to its scabbard and tied it to her back. Then she handed both men a dagger, at which point Siard started to laugh again.

"The lady has thought this through. This is more than we could have hoped for."

Even Elion's face showed a smile, an expression Lumea had not seen since they started their flight. Then he turned around and looked at her, asking, "So, which way are we going?"

"It doesn't seem safe to go back to the archive. They're bound to miss these things soon. Let's take the corridor to the left."

They gathered their things and started out once more.

9

The Hosts had congregated in an emergency meeting. Several things had happened on the previous day that they had not foreseen. It had all started with the theft of the Thuranc's hand. Even though the culprit had already been apprehended, it should not have happened in the first place. Nobody should have been able to penetrate the place where the creature was kept. The culprit had been executed, and that put the embarrassing episode to an end. All that remained was to launch an investigation into how the theft had been possible.

Shortly afterward, the Hosts had discovered a second disconcerting disappearance. Three of the guests had not gone back to their rooms when ordered. Troops had been sent out to apprehend them, so far without success. Most of the electricity in Hydrhaga was now to be used exclusively for the ongoing research, and the machines controlling the warm, summer weather had been shut down. The harsh winter conditions that followed made the search that much more difficult.

The meeting had burst into chaos, with some Hosts pleading to soften the weather so as to make things easier for the patrols, while others favored the theory that the three missing persons must have died in the resulting cold. Even though this was the most favorable of all possible solutions, few of the Hosts thought it to be the likely outcome. Ward sat quietly between them, feeling incredibly guilty, because the guests in question had been under his direct care.

Suddenly, the door opened and a worker ran in, panting heavily. He told them of the artifacts that had disappeared from the archive. His tale dispelled the last of the Hosts' doubts. The three guests were still alive, and since they had taken weapons, their intentions were hostile.

The workman's words, as dark as they were, held a silver lining. The only route the guests could take into the archive without being discovered was past the cave with the six stalactites. Likewise, the only safe way out was through there. The archive's building contained too many people for the runaways to remain hidden long, and if they had stayed there, they would have been discovered by now.

With a shock, Ward realized what it was that he had seen in the archive, though at the time he could not put his finger on it. The dust which had gathered on the wooden showcases had been disturbed! Ward cursed himself. Why had he not trusted his instincts and looked around? When he had entered the archive, the intruder must have been there. He knew he had heard something and yet he had gone away without an investigation. Ward was afraid to look up, for he did not want anyone asking about what had happened. Instead, he listened to the conversation which had erupted into chaos once again.

The Hosts decided to send their troops into the cavern depths. Once in the caves, these Swintheri soldiers would split into five groups, and each group would be assigned to its own corridor. The Hosts then went back to their day-to-day business, convinced that it was only a matter of time before the runaways were caught.

Lumea, Elion and Siard continued through the long passage. The dark, unknown terrain hampered their progress, for their eyes could not penetrate the darkness, but they did not dare to make any form of light, and so they had to feel their way forward. The corridor seemed endless. At times it would broaden into a rocky chamber, but they found no cross-corridors or branches.

It was in one of those rocky chambers that Elion first heard the sounds of pursuit. Lumea's heartbeat quickened. She had made sure they had weapons, and there was no doubt in her mind that Elion and Siard would be able to use them. Even though she was trained well, how would she hold up in a real fight? She did not get much time to wonder, however, as Elion told them to each stand on one side of the corridor, just past the point where it widened into the chamber.

"I will be waiting up ahead. We'll let the pursuers enter the chamber, and then attack them from all sides. Wait for my first arrow."

They had only just taken their positions when the pursuers entered. Lumea tried to count the number of opponents they were facing, and thought that there were about eight of them. They had lanterns with them, but still they did not see Elion, who had found a high spot on the rocky walls. Lumea gripped her sword tightly, and her senses were on high alert. When she had spotted the sword in the archive, it had reminded her of those that were used back home. It was not heavy, and the curved blade lent speed to every strike.

Lumea heard the tell-tale creak of a bowstring being drawn just before Elion released, and she moved into action. Before one man had the time to fall down with a surprised scream, pierced by Elion's arrow, she had killed the soldier closest to her with one stroke. Siard also sprang out of hiding. The Hosts' troops were taken by surprise by the trio's ambush. In the ensuing confusion, five men soon lay dead. After a few moments, the survivors realized what was happening and organized their counter-attack. Elion was of no further use in the skirmish, as the Swintheri's lights were weak, and in the gloom he could not distinguish friend from foe.

Siard and Lumea stood toe to toe with the three remaining soldiers. Lumea fought bravely, but this was different from the sparring she was used to at home. Her quick movements parried her opponent's attacks, but when she tried to wound him she always met one of his two blades. Judging by the sound of metal striking metal, Siard was facing the same problem. Then she felt a searing pain in her arm. Full of disbelief, she stared at the blood running down her arm. The sudden realization that this was a fight to the death—that if she did not win, she would die—gave her a burst of strength. Her movements quickened and when her opponent slipped, she took his life. Slowly, the silence seeped through to Lumea. Siard had defeated the other two Swintheri.

They were safe for the moment, so Elion took the opportunity to make some light. The floor around them was strewn with bodies, their eyes staring into oblivion. Where their armor had proved insufficient, their ocher tunics were smeared with blood. The sight was startling for Lumea. She realized that, to a certain extent, she was responsible for this. She had taken lives here without knowing who these men were or what their intentions had been. She fought to keep control of her emotions, but tears still streamed down her cheeks. Siard looked at Elion and gestured for them to rest somewhere else, where Lumea would not be reminded of what had happened.

She followed the men to the next rocky chamber. This one was deeper than the last. It seemed to be a good place to catch their breath after the fight. Lumea shivered as she sat down, leaning against the wall. She dropped her head on her arms, fighting to regain control of her ragged breathing, though she could not banish the memory of the corpses from her mind. Knowing that she had deliberately killed three men without a clear reason was more than she could bear. She gagged and threw up. Elion came to sit by her, laying a comforting hand on her shoulder.

"Was this the first time you had to kill?" he asked.

She nodded, still shivering.

"It will be less terrible next time."

Lumea suspected that he had meant it as comfort, but to her, his words sounded ominous. It meant there was going to be a next time. Elion did not seem upset about the fight, and Lumea felt shock that taking a life seemed so trivial to him.

Elion touched her arm briefly when he wanted to get up. When he saw her flinch, though, he turned back to her, and she avoided his gaze.

"You are hurt?" Elion asked concernedly.

"It's nothing, it'll heal on its own."

"At least let me take a look at it."

Without waiting for her answer, he hoisted up her sleeve and looked at the wound. It ran down the length of her upper arm, but fortunately, it was not a deep cut. Elion searched it intently, after which he took a small bag from beneath his tunic. He took some herbs out of the bag and chewed them, then carefully applied the resulting poultice to the wound. It stung, but Lumea tried not to flinch.

Then Elion took the kerchief from his head and tore off a piece to bind her arm. Lumea looked in surprise at the pointed shape of Elion's ears. He was an elf! She laughed, how many times had he surprised her now? Now everything seemed to fall into place. Elion's new identity fitted him much better than anything she had thought before. The elf pushed his long hair away from his face, suddenly self-conscious. It had been a long time since anyone had found out his secret, and anyway, human reactions were never predictable. Not all of the old grudges had been forgotten, by either race. But in Lumea's far away land, the battle between men and elves had been the stuff of legend, not the account of a cruel past.

"You fought bravely out there, Lumea. I'm glad you were with us."

As if to wipe away the last memories of the fight, he used the rest of his kerchief to remove the bloodstains from her face.

Lumea smiled. "We did it together."

Siard stood up from where he had been keeping watch at the chamber's entrance. Now he took the waterskin and passed it around. "It's time to move on," he said.

10

Lumea, Elian and Siard tried to hurry along so that they would out-distance their pursuers. They had been lucky to ambush the soldiers, but the party knew that in future encounters the Swintheri would be more careful.

The farther they traveled, the colder it became. A howling wind blew through the corridor, drowning out all other noise. It was getting late and they were exhausted, but they decided to press on. They decided that from now on they would travel during the night and try to get some rest during the day. Elion looked at Lumea every now and then with concern in his eyes, but she bravely kept up. The fatigue and their rapid pace made everything that had happened before seem like a dream.

Finally, they reached the end of the corridor and were outside. It was morning, and they looked at the wintry landscape in surprise. Despite the cold air that they had felt in the corridor, none of them were prepared for the sight of several feet of snow. After all, the last time they had been outside, it had still been summer.

To their left were the woods they had seen from a distance while living in Hydrhaga. They decided to look for shelter there among the trees, so they made their way through the snowdrifts, finding a willow which had been surprised by the sudden onset of winter. Unable to shed their leaves, the branches were bowed down and the heavy snow covering them served to create a dry place near the tree's trunk. Lumea and Siard filed inside, and when Elion looked back he saw that their footsteps were being erased by the wind and snow.

As soon as Lumea lay down, sleep overtook her. Elion changed the dressing on her arm carefully, trying not to wake her. Siard was sitting next to her, the exhaustion clearly visible on his face, and Elion nodded at him to go to sleep as well. The elf was used to going without sleep. He had noticed a long time ago that if he tired himself out enough, the nightmares that usually accompanied sleep had no chance to come close. He drew his cape around him and tried to think of what they should do now.

From afar, he could hear the sound of baying hounds, as if a pack of them were worked up into a frenzy. Afraid that he had landed in another nightmare, Elion pinched himself. He had, in fact, nodded off, but the sounds only became louder. The dogs were real.

Lumea woke up as well, and came over to lie down beside him. Afraid of the barking, she looked at Elion questioningly, but he shook his head. He did not know what to think of it either. Then he turned around and shook Siard. Together, they waited, tensed up and with their weapons at the ready. Then the volume of the baying dogs suddenly increased. Something was happening.

The Hosts had been convinced that the fugitives would soon be caught. When one group of Swintheri after the other returned empty-handed, though, they began to lose hope. Two of the groups had yet to return.

The following day one of the groups did come back, and it became obvious that the last group was missing in action. The Swintheri were ordered to search for their comrades in the last corridor. They hurried into the cave and soon found their fellow soldiers, dead. They had suspected that the group had been defeated by the runaways, but faced with the reality of the corpses, they were dumbfounded. How had three simple runaways managed to kill eight trained professionals?

There was not much time to ponder the question. The Hosts were informed and the soldiers continued their pursuit. They were much slower now, though, the large group of men made too much noise, and they were all afraid of another trap. Every now and then an argument erupted about who would lead the troops through the dark. Everyone was afraid to die.

In an attempt to make sure that the fugitives would not slip through, the Hosts sent one group of Swintheri around to the corridor's exit with a pack of dogs. The three runaways would be caught between the hammer and the anvil, and with that all the Hosts' problems would be solved.

The snowstorm surprised the Swintheri while they were waiting outside the corridor. Cursing, they decided to use the corridor as shelter. The dogs tore at their leashes excitedly. They were hard to control; normally locked in their kennels, they now smelled their freedom. The Swintheri's confusion only added to their frenzy.

The soldiers hoped they would soon catch the fugitives, so that they could all go back to the warm barracks. They blew on their hands and rubbed their arms to keep warm. After a long time, they still had yet to see anyone, and they started to feel irritated.

Suddenly they heard some people approaching, then nothing, as if the persons had been startled by something. When the first men carefully rounded the corner, the dogs flew to the attack. However, they turned out to be the other Swintheri who had come from the corridor. The dogs were restrained just in time. The volume increased, and that was what the three fugitives underneath the willow heard.

The Hosts' troops could not believe that the three runaways had evaded them. They had been so focused on finding them that the possibility of their had not crossed their minds. They even looked around, as if expecting two men and a woman to suddenly appear out of nowhere. When they finally realized the truth, they went outside to look for tracks, but the newly-fallen snow made this task impossible. The Swintheri milled about in the snow for some time, not knowing what to do. In the end, they contacted the Hosts and were recalled to the tower.

Lumea listened to the sounds of the soldiers and dogs die away with a relieved smile on her face. The tree protected her group from the weather, and now their enemies were going away.

"Where do you come from?" she asked Elion, half-expecting to be asking a forbidden question. Elion quickly glanced up at her, then looked down at the ground.

"I am from Omnesia, but I lived there when it was still an elvish city called Arminath. My family was driven away during the war between men and elves.

"Is that when you learned how to fight?"

Elion shook his head, though he did not elaborate. For a moment,

Lumea thought she had found an explanation for Elion's strange remark about taking life, but apparently something else had happened to him after the war that had left deep scars. Though she longed for an answer, she did not have the courage to ask him.

"Why did the elves return to Omnesia, then?" she asked.

"Our roots are there, even if there is not much left to remind people of the elven city. It is holy ground to us, and we are drawn to it. Besides, there was work there. The wells had to be restored. They were always the most important thing for the city, those wells. They allowed us to irrigate the dry ground around Arminath so that we could subsist. To us, the water coming from deep underground was a gift from the gods. Now our life in Omnesia is tough. We are poor and live in slums on the outskirts of the city, but it is still very important for us to be able to work on the wells."

"The war happened such a long time ago. The humans obviously need you. Why do you still keep your identity hidden?"

Elion looked at her with a smile, but his tone of voice was bitter. "If only it were that simple."

She tried to lighten his mood with her question. "Isn't it? The world isn't that bad of a place, really."

His answer was exasperated. He said, "What have you experienced that you can judge that? Terrible things happened during that war, Lumea, things you couldn't even begin to imagine. The elves have enough reason to be ashamed, and the humans aren't about to forget that, let alone forgive us."

It did not escape Lumea's notice that he apparently thought her to be ignorant. She tried to banish her displeasure from her voice, for by now she had realized that Elion had not had an easy life. That did not stop her from giving her opinion, though. "There are two sides to every war. Each of them makes mistakes, and acts in ways they would not during peacetime. Apparently you were able to forgive the humans or you would not have returned to help them. Or do you really feel that ashamed about yourselves that you allow them to treat you like trash?"

She touched his hand, as a sign that he did not have to answer her. Then she stood up and walked around the trunk of the willow.

Elion was left with his thoughts. She was right, the elves weren't the only ones who had committed atrocities. The humans were to blame as well. In all his time of living in Omnesia, he had never known the humans to feel remorse about their part in what had happened. They just seemed content that they had come out the victors, with the elves mostly destroyed.

The kings that ruled Omnesia after the elves' departure had rewritten history in favor of their subjects. There wasn't a human alive today who had witnessed the war. They were all dead now, with many generations having passed since, but there were still some elves alive who had known the war. Were they really so ashamed of themselves that they believed only the human version of events?

Elion looked at the other two, but he could not see what they were doing. He drifted off into a deep sleep, awaiting a new nightmare, but instead, unfamiliar warmth enveloped him, keeping his nightmares at bay.

Lumea had tucked Elion's cloak around him and gently stroked his hair out of his face. Then she returned to Siard, who had found some edible roots that were still fresh, since the winter had disrupted the summer so suddenly. He went out again and returned with his hands full of berries and a few large leaves filled with snow. The warmth underneath the willow's branches would melt it and again they could fill their waterskin.

Elion woke up by nightfall. They ate some of fruit Siard had found while they discussed their next step.

Lumea looked a bit shy about a question she had pondered for a while, but she asked it anyway. She had expected her emotions about the fight to have abated, but now that she was rested and more or less safe they had returned in full force. She hoped the two men could sufficiently explain why the killing had been necessary. "Why did you come to Hydrhaga?"

Elion looked at Siard, who answered, "It's hard to explain, Lumea. We hardly know, ourselves. Hydrhaga is supposed to be a perfect destination, and there were so many rumors about this peaceful world where everybody was welcome and life was easy. Many people traveled here, including the elves. In the first years everyone was allowed to go inside.

"Things changed later on, though. The elves had long been used to hiding their identity, but even so, the ones traveling towards Hydrhaga returned, having been refused entrance. Some people, both elves and men, tried to find an alternative route inside, but soon it became obvious that there was some kind of invisible wall around this country.

"There are still many rumors about Hydrhaga, both good and bad, but there is nobody to confirm or deny them. None of the people who ever entered the city came out of it again. Many Omnesians came here, and their families never heard from them again. I've seen many guests disappear without a trace since I got in, and I very much doubt they've gone home. One day, they just vanished."

"But all of that is just guesswork and rumor. There must be some other reason why you came here?" Lumea asked.

Elion took up the story. "Many elves died during the war, but many of the survivors disappeared in later years. The workmen you saw in Omnesia are but a small fraction of the elves who ever lived there. We do know that large numbers of elves came here just after the land was established, and yet none of them can be found anywhere. It's all one big mystery, but it does seem as though something very strange is going on here. How did the winter start so quickly? What is the Thuranc? What is in those lakes?"

"I don't know. My heart tells me that you're right. I haven't forgotten that woman who was killed right before we ran."

Lumea hesitated for a moment, trying to find the right words. Elion and Siard obviously trusted on their instincts, but for her part, she still felt miserable about her actions, without knowing if they had been justified; neither Elion nor Siard had been able to extinguish her doubts. She said, "My heart tells me that we're in the wrong, that maybe we're the evil ones. We don't know what happened to that woman, or what the intentions of those men in the cave were. We didn't give them a chance to explain. Maybe we made the wrong decision... and are guilty of murder."

Her voice was uncertain and a bit wobbly; she was fighting to keep back the tears. Elion tried to catch her eye, but she just stared at her hands lying in her lap, shivering. Elion suddenly noticed just how fragile she looked. "I understand your concerns, Lumea," he answered in a whisper. "I can honestly say that the same thoughts have crossed my mind."

Siard agreed and Elion continued, "If what you say is true then I owe you my sincerest apologies. There is no way for me to undo what happened, or even make it less terrible than it actually is."

He was silent for a moment, but she would not look up. A tear rolled down her cheek.

"I came here with such high expectations. Now I'm a murderer," Lumea said. She blamed Elion for this, though she did not say it out loud.

"I'm sorry I brought you into this, Lumea. In my heart, I know that what we're doing is the right thing, but you deserve better than to fight someone else's battle."

Finally, Lumea looked up. Her tears had dried. "Alright then, we have to decide what we're going to do," she said determinedly. "There is no way back, and crying about it isn't going to help us."

They agreed to explore the woods, because they had not been there before. It was where the invisible 'wall' was. If they could find it, then perhaps they would learn something more about Hydrhaga.

11

Lumea, Siard and Elion left the relative safety of the willow to continue their search. Lumea stopped for a moment, and, in a silent prayer,
thanked the willow for giving them a safety and shelter. At the same
time, she thanked the snowstorm for wiping away their tracks. She
had a hunch that the storm was not quite natural, but this prayer was
nevertheless important to her.

She thought back to her grandmother, a wise woman who had
taught her to respect nature. The old woman had taken her on a walk
once. They had gone through the woods to the north of Lunadeiron.
During the walk, the woman pointed to some plants and told the little
girl their names.

At times, startled birds would fly up out of the trees. Lumea ran
after them, trying to catch them, but the birds were always faster,
which made her grandmother laugh. She would tell her the names of
the various animals in the forest. Then she sat down in the grass and
motioned for Lumea to join her.

"Lumea, there are some things I need to tell you about plants and
animals. Like humans, they were created by the gods, and as such
they too carry within them the spirit of the gods. Always treat the
world around you with fairness and respect. Do not assume, like so
many do, that you are above nature. Rather, be a part of it. Do not
forget to be grateful for the warmth that the sun gives us today, but
likewise remember that without water nothing can live. Thank the
rain, too, for without it the plants, our sisters, cannot survive.

"Our brothers, the animals, can feed our hunger, but you should
not forget to ask them, and take only what you need to survive. They
will give you their meat, but only if you treat them with respect, as
equals. Our Mother, the earth, gives life to everyone and everything,
and our Father, the heavens, will always be there for those who need
him. The sun warms us, the stars show us the way, and the moon
gives us courage. The moon is also very special for women, Lumea.
A woman's body knows the same cycles. Do not forget to be grateful

to your family. And never, ever let go of the child that you are now."

At the time, Lumea had been too young to really understand what her grandmother was telling her, but she had taken the lessons to heart. She had never forgotten them, and only as she got older had she started to understand them. Unconsciously, she had put more and more of her grandmother's teachings into practice.

She ended the prayer, and returned the memory of her grandmother to a place deep within her heart, where it was safe and warm. She hurried to catch up with Elion and Siard.

The three runaways went deeper into the forest, and their path gradually grew harder to follow. The cold that had taken over Hydrhaga was very bitter and there was snow everywhere. Icicles hung down from branches, glistening in the light of the moon as it shone over the white world. In many places the ice and snow was so heavy that the branches had been torn from the trees. Birds were sitting in them, hunkered down and shivering. Their heavy-lidded eyes watched the three travelers struggle past. At times, an owl screeched a call into the night.

The hem of Lumea's dress was soon drenched. She was chilled to the bone, and her limbs were stinging cruelly. She shivered and pulled her hood tighter around her head. Elion and Siard were better dressed against the cold, but even their hands eventually started to tingle. With every breath white clouds formed in front of their faces, and breathing became labored.

The cold dulled Lumea's senses and stiffened her body. The pain in her feet vanished, which relieved her at first, until she started to worry about it. She tried to feel her feet when she put them down, even going so far as to purposefully stamp on one foot with the other just to get some feeling back. She felt helpless and furious with Elion and Siard for not helping her, but the two men seemed to be experiencing the same problems, if only to a lesser extent.

They struggled on through the night. They had to keep moving to keep their body temperature up. None of them had the energy or the will to pay attention to the other. Lumea lost her grip on the world around her and she no longer realized where she was. The owl's calls seemed to come from very far away.

"Lumea..."

The whispered word came from somewhere behind her. She knew the rustling voice, though she could not remember from where. She turned around to see if the caller was standing behind her. She saw a pair of outstretched arms. She let herself sink into them, but they did not catch her. Instead she fell into the snow. The branches she had taken for arms snapped under her weight.

She didn't move for a moment, but the voice called again. She wanted to ignore it, to just keep lying there and not worry about anything else. The snow was soft, and she didn't feel the cold any more. She was only conscious of one thing: the bone-deep fatigue that had taken her over both her body and mind. The voice did not stop, though, it kept calling her, told her to get up, and so she did. Somehow she managed to rise, and she looked around, disorientated. She was alone, lost in the freezing night.

When dawn touched the sky, Elion and Siard finally reached the wall without any more signs of pursuit.

"Where's Lumea?"

Elion was the first to notice her disappearance, and his voice was worried, but Siard shrugged. They turned back to the forest, but darkness enveloped the trees. They could not see or hear anyone. Elion wanted to turn back into the forest immediately, but Siard stopped him.

"If you go back there now you'll die. You're not strong enough. We have to rest first."

"How can we leave her out there?"

"We'll have to trust that she will be alright."

Siard was concerned about Lumea, too, and uncomfortable at leaving her out in the cold, but he knew that staying where they were was the best chance of survival that they had. There was no way he was going back into that white hell of ice. The only thing he wanted was to rest and warm up, but Elion's conscience was strong.

"She's my responsibility, Siard! I brought her into this mess."

"Lumea has proven more than once that she is capable of taking care of herself."

Siard knew that he had to convince Elion to stay. He would follow the elf if he went back into the forest, but the younger man really did not think it was a good idea. Luckily, Elion followed Siard's advice and stayed close to the wall. Siard had said that from the outside it was invisible, but from the side where they stood, there was a strange, oily sheen about it, and it glinted in the light of the rising sun. It made Hydrhaga look as though it was caught in an enormous soap bubble. Nothing moved in the first few feet behind the wall; plants grew crooked and the trees were leafless on the side that faced it. There was a soft hum coming from it, and it gave off a modest amount of heat.

The two men stood quietly together, warming themselves from the ambient heat of the wall. They decided to rest there and regain their strength a bit. They decided that if Lumea did not appear that they would go looking for her later. Their symptoms of hypothermia abated, but they were still utterly exhausted. The elf kept staring at the woods in spite of his tiredness, growing more and more restless as time passed without an appearance by their friend. In the end, Elion got up to look for her.

"Elion, it's not wise..."

The elf interrupted him, saying, "It's my responsibility to keep the group together."

Siard struggled up with a sigh and followed Elion back into the cold.

They found her near the edge of the woods. She was shuffling forward one step at a time, seeking support with her hands. Her eyes were empty, and frozen tears ran down her cheeks.

Elion started running as soon as he saw her, and he reached her first. When he tried to grab her, she just shuffled on without acknowledging his presence. She put one foot in front of the other with automatic movements. With the two men supporting her, they reached the wall, where the men made her lie down on the ground.

The numbness slowly left Lumea's body. She took greater note of her surroundings and of the feeling that returned in her limbs. Her feet felt as though a thousand tiny needles were stinging them. She tried to crawl towards the snow to dull her senses again, but Elion stopped her, forcing her to lie back down.

"I'm so, so sorry, Lumea, but I have to do this."

He pulled her boots off her feet and rubbed her feet. It only made the pain worse, and Lumea raged against Elion for doing this to her. She kicked and lunged at him so wildly that Siard sat down behind her and restrained the woman. She struggled in vain to break free of his grip, weakened as she was, so she yelled and screamed at Elion to stop hurting her. When he did not cease she gave up, mostly out of exhaustion. Siard felt her body go limp as she lost consciousness. The two men lay down on either side of her to keep her—and each other—warm.

Elion whispered an uncertain prayer that day, thanking the gods for bringing Lumea back to him. It had been a long time since he had last prayed, and he was unsure of the right words. He just hoped the gods would forgive him for improvising. After he changed the position of his arm, which he had tucked under Lumea's head, he fell into a deep slumber.

12

At some point towards the end of the afternoon, Elion woke up from a tingling sensation in his arm. Lumea's head was still lying on his shoulder, and it had cut off his circulation. When he opened his eyes, he saw Siard's back disappearing between the trees with their bag over his shoulder. The elf moved carefully, not wishing to wake Lumea, but she opened her eyes in spite of his efforts. Startled by her position, she tried to roll away, though the elf stopped her.

"You don't have to move. It's nice and warm like this. Siard will be back soon with something to eat or drink. We have to leave after that, but for now you can still rest a bit."

Lumea put her head back down and Elion drew their mantles closer about them.

Only a little time had passed before Siard came back out of the woods. He had made a small fire to cook some water, but he had been afraid to start it near the wall. He was carrying a steaming bowl which he gave to Lumea.

"What is it?" she asked curiously.

"It's an herbal tea. I don't know if it's any good, but at least it's warm."

Lumea took a careful sip and passed the bowl to Elion. After they had eaten, they talked about what to do. A few days ago, they had decided that the wall should be their destination because they did not know what else to do. Now that they had reached it, they were still none the wiser, so they decided to follow it in order to see where it led.

Siard helped Lumea get up and she took a few tentative steps. Her feet hurt every time she put them down, and she labored to walk. Elion made her walk on her own anyway, and she gritted her teeth against the pain. It would do her good in the end, and the movement would warm her body up.

The belt of lifeless land near the wall made Siard suspicious, and on his advice they returned to the relative shelter of the trees. There was hardly a path for them to follow, and they had to make their way through bushes and snowdrifts as dead branches slowed their progress. Elion kept a watchful eye on Lumea and was concerned when he saw how her strength was slipping away, until it was impossible for her to go on.

"Come on, Siard and I will carry you."

Lumea wanted to protest, unwilling to admit that she needed help, but with a fluid motion Elion had already swept her up onto his back. She held on, and they went on. The men alternated carrying Lumea, but it slowed them down considerably. Now that she had the chance to rest again, she fell into a kind of half-sleep. Elion noticed her grip on him slackening, and though she became harder to carry, he did not try to wake her.

As they walked, the sound emanating from the wall grew louder, shifting from a hum and into something akin to the screeching of a dying animal. The darker the sky turned, the more foreboding the sounds became. At first, Lumea did not hear them, but slowly they drove the sleep away until she woke to the sound of screams filling her ears.

When she opened her eyes, they went very wide at what she saw. She quickly closed them again, hoping that the vision would go away. Through her eyelashes she took another look, hoping that it was gone, but there it was. From the wall, a face was looking at her, gaunt, with hollow cheeks. Its piercing scream chilled her to the marrow. She looked away, but there was another face, and another. The whole wall seemed filled with the hollow faces of tortured spirits. Her own cries were drowned out by their screeching.

Elion quickly let her slide off his shoulders and grabbed her shoulders, shaking her. Lumea did not notice, but kept staring at the wall instead. Following her gaze, Elion and Siard were startled as they noticed the faces, and in unison all three of them started running. The fear that Lumea felt for the faces was stronger than the pain in her body. Elion held her arm as they ran. As soon as they stopped running to catch their breath, though, the faces were there again.

Afraid that their pursuers were watching them from the wall and that they had been discovered, they began running again. They ran on and on until their breath came in ragged bursts and they had no choice but to stop. Lumea tripped over a hidden tree stump and fell to the ground. Elion and Siard sat down beside her, breathing hard. They turned their backs to the wall so that they would not have to see the faces, though they could not keep out the sounds.

They were relieved to find that with the dawn the screeching transformed back into the soft hum, and the faces disappeared. In the daylight they had the feeling that the sights and sounds of that night had been nothing more than a dream, so unreal did they seem in the light of the sun. The oily sheen on the wall had returned, and it resembled a giant soap bubble once again. All they heard was the hum.

They followed the wall for some nights, and always the faces returned. By now they were satisfied that whatever was in there could not get out, but it was still frightening and emotionally draining. Every morning, when the sun rose, Lumea and Siard would tumble into a deep and dreamless sleep, but Elion was afraid to close his eyes. The wall seemed to intensify his nightmares tenfold.

Since they had reached the wall, his nightmare was the same. It began with the memory of his parents' death, a common enough night terror for Elion. From the safety of his hiding place among the bushes he watched as enemies cruelly cut down first his father, and then his mother. His mother stared at him with obvious panic in her eyes, and she screamed at him to help her, but he did not, he stayed hidden. His mother's cries came to an abrupt end as their enemies slit her throat. The new part of the dream was that her plea for help did not stop there. It was taken over by a dozen different voices, and they gave him no rest, whether he was asleep or not.

Elion wondered how he could help these voices and what they expected from him. Every time, he woke up more tired than when he had gone to sleep, confused over the meaning of it. The nightmare did not portray the way things had really happened, o so long ago. The farther they followed the wall, the stronger his nightmare became, though he tried to keep this hidden from the others in his group.

Lumea found out about it one day, though. Elion was tossing and turning, and she crawled over to him and drew his cloak tighter about him. This time the gesture did not help; he remained just as restless.

She wanted to help, so she did what her mother used to do when as a little girl she had nightmares: she put her hands on his brow and sang a soft tune. Her mother had been able to take over the night terrors in this fashion.

Now it was Lumea who watched from the bushes as Elion's mother was murdered, Lumea who felt powerless when the one voice was replaced by a dozen others. She wanted to draw her hands away, but she forced herself to sit still. Elion's sleep became more peaceful, though Lumea was awake for the rest of the day, shivering and unable to sleep. Instead, she went to look for food, and even melted some snow to replenish their water supplies. When Siard woke up, she offered him some fruit.

"How did the two of you meet?" Lumea asked him.

"Elion was working near my house. Unlike most Omnesians, I did not look down upon the workmen. I met him once in the forest, and later we started talking."

"But did you know about the workmen being... elves?"

She felt that she should have chosen a better word. She hated the way it made Elion seem somehow different from herself and Siard, while she did not feel like that at all, as the question could make it seem as if the difference was more important to her than it really was.

"No, I never would have guessed."

"But how did you know about Elion, then?"

Lumea realized just how curious she sounded, and she watched Siard's face to see if her questions annoyed him, but the answers that came were calm.

"I met him again in the forest one day. Apparently, there's a hot spring there, though I didn't know about it at the time. Elion did, and he had just taken a bath when I stumbled across him. He hadn't fully dressed yet; he was still holding his kerchief in his hand. He actually seemed almost frightened to see me."

Siard was quiet for a moment before continuing his story.

"I was surprised, of course, but it somehow seemed fitting, so the discovery wasn't too much of a shock."

Lumea agreed and Siard went on.

"Not for me, anyway. He, on the other hand, quickly disappeared between the trees. We did talk more after that meeting, though, and as it turned out, he shared my distrust of Hydrhaga. We made plans to come and investigate what was going on here. I never mentioned his elvish heritage, and I think he appreciated that. But to be honest, I just had no idea how to bring it up."

By the time Elion awoke, it was late in the evening. Lumea avoided looking at him, afraid that the elf could see that she knew about his dreams. He always seemed so strong and independent, and she was fairly sure he would not appreciate her glimpse behind his mask. When he had eaten, they continued their journey. The noises and images on the wall were already going strong.

Eventually, they reached a set of thick cables that ran up to the wall, and where they touched it, there was a noise like a herd of horses galloping past. The wall shimmered from the energy being pumped into it, and there was no sign of the faces here. Siard suggested they follow the cables, and the other two agreed. Despite the ominous feeling that all three shared, they wanted to know what was feeding energy into the wall.

On their next stop, Elion made a small fire, not so much for its warmth—as there was enough of that coming from the cables themselves—but more for the sense of security that the flickering orange flames gave them. The crackling of the wood brightened their moods.

Siard was staring into the flames with a happy expression.

"What are you thinking about?" Lumea asked him.

He looked up. "One time when I was still a little kid, my father took me and my brother out into the desert. We'd brought warm blankets and we were planning to stay the night. I was so excited! My father picked a good spot and built a fire, just like this one. Then he tucked me and my brother in under the blankets. It slowly grew darker and one by one the stars appeared. My father told us that gigantic stilt walkers were going through the heavens, lighting the stars. I remember looking up into the sky, hoping to see one of them.

"Then my father showed us all the different zodiacal signs, and he told us their story. The one that most impressed me was the one about the Lady with the Shining Eyes. As he told the story, I saw her appear, and her eyes did shine brilliantly, high above our heads."

"What's her story?" Lumea was curious.

"The Lady lived in a dark time, full of turmoil and grief. Her mother died giving birth to her second child while her father was far away at the Eastern Horizon, fighting a war. Years went by while the Lady took care of her brother as well as she could, though food grew scarce and the world ever darker.

"One day, a man knocked on her door and chose her for his wife, though he refused to adopt her brother as a member of his family. The woman protested. She warned the man that if he took her as his wife, she would die on their wedding day, and yet he persisted. In the end, she was forced to accepted the man as her husband, and they left together, but she promised her brother that she would always be there for him to show him the way.

"Events unfolded as the Lady predicted. On the day the man married her, she died. That same day, a new sign appeared in the heavens. With a sad heart her brother decided to follow the stars. After a long journey he arrived in the east, where he found his father.

"When the Lady appears in the sky, you can see the Horse Warriors in the east. As time goes by the two approach, until finally they meet."

Lumea enjoyed Siard's story, which told of bravery and hope. But she sympathized with the Lady as well, who had fought against the fate that had been forced upon her, and lost.

"Is your father an astrologer?"

Siard seemed insulted. "Most definitely not! He was an astronomer. He didn't believe in all that nonsense about stars determining the course of people's lives. My father was a talented man, a scientist who mapped out the heavens. He devised the Armillary Sphere, and he invented the telescope. Using it, he realized that it was the earth that circled the sun, not the other way around like people believed not-so-long ago. He built bigger, more advanced telescopes and eventually even the Omnesian Observatory. He was a genius, and other astronomers learned a lot from him."

Siard's voice was proud, but his contempt for astrologers had not escaped Lumea's notice. Astrologers were a very important aspect of life in Lunadeiron, and Lumea had felt good about them. The stars and planets were not objects to be studied, they were spirits whom you could work with, whose powers could be of benefit to you. The stars were a way of the gods to send their message, but she refused to go into that, asking instead, "What about your brother? What happened to him?"

Siards eyes suddenly looked sombre, and Lumea regretted having asked the question.

"Like the Lady looked after her brother, I have to look after mine. He's the one that brought me to Hydrhaga. Twenty years ago, he decided to come here, and I know that he was determined to go back home some day. He never did, though. He was fourteen years older than me. As a little kid, I used to sit by the window, hoping to see him walk up our street. I never heard from him again, but in my heart there was always the hope that if I came here, I would find him and he'd be all right.

"A little voice in the back of my head told me that he was gone forever. My distrust against Hydrhaga and what was going on here slowly grew."

Siard shook his head with a sad sigh. "He was not here when I came, and nobody seemed to remember him. There was only one man who remembered him, and he disappeared the day after I spoke to him."

"I'm sorry for bringing him up, Siard."

"No, it's okay. It's nice to talk about him with other people. It makes him come alive again, if only a little bit."

The young man poked between the burning branches with a stick. For the rest of the evening, they talked about their families, bringing back memories of their childhood. Elion did not speak much, but he listened to Lumea and Siard's bickering with an amused expression on his face. There were moments when they recognized themselves in the words of the other person, but at other times their opinions were polar opposites. The heavy discussion that followed never lasted for long, because both of them knew that these differences were too hard to overcome in one night, as stubborn as both of them were. They would never be able to make the other come around to their own way of thinking.

13

The first light of dawn touched the sky when Elion, Siard and Lumea reached a glade. In the middle of it stood the building where the cables originated. At the top of a high flagpole a blackbird was singing, though no other bird answered its call. The low building seemed impenetrable. It had no windows and only a single simple door. The snow was slushy and brown from the trample of too many feet. Elion suggested that they sit in the shadows for a while and watch the entrance of the building. By doing so, perhaps they could find out something important.

"I'll be the first to keep watch. When the sun reaches above the treetops, I will awaken Siard."

Lumea and Siard agreed. Elion picked a spot where he could sit with his back to a tree. He was planning not to sleep at all. They might have left the wall behind, but he was still afraid of his dreams. He did not want to scream and betray their location.

The sun had already come above the treetops when Lumea awoke. She went over to sit beside Elion.

"You should get some sleep," she said.

"I'm not tired."

Lumea looked skeptically at the dark circles under his eyes. She was not sure what else to say, so they were silent for a moment.

She decided to tell him. "I know about your dreams."

It was the last thing Elion had expected, and he looked at her with wide eyes.

"I woke up a few nights ago, and though you were sleeping, you seemed restless. I looked into your dreams and took them away. You can sleep now, you know. If you have any more dreams I will take them away again. I will stand guard."

When Lumea spoke in that commanding tone of hers, like she did now, there was no denying her.

"Lumea, I was nine..." Elion's voice sounded panicky as he realized what she had just said. "That's not how it happened!"

"It's okay, Elion," she answered. "Of course it didn't happen like that. Nightmares have a way of showing your worst fears to you, they're not real. I do not judge you for your dreams; if you want to tell me what happened, I will listen, but I won't force you. It's up to you."

Elion was relieved, and he went to lie down, but after about a quarter of an hour he got back up, and came to sit by her again. He kept his eyes shut as he started talking, and she knew that he was trying to play down the emotions that would inevitably come to the surface.

"I lived with my parents at the edge of Arminath, in a house among the trees. When the war approached, we were told to go to the city center for our protection. My father quickly threw some things together, and my mother told me to hurry. I began to realize just how serious the whole thing was, so I struggled to keep up with them. My father picked me up to carry me.

"We didn't get very far. Men were screaming behind us, and I looked over my father's shoulder, terrified. My parents exchanged a knowing look, and my mother took me in her arms and hid me in the bushes. I held onto her and refused to let go. She kept telling me to stay hidden until everything was safe, no matter what happened. I was shaking when I nodded, but still my fists clutched at her dress, so she tore herself loose from me. That was the exact moment I knew that she would give her life for mine. Can you understand that?

"My parents made that decision without even discussing it. If we ran, we would be killed, all three of us. I wasn't fast enough to escape our enemies. I am convinced that they knew they were going to die, but they accepted it, because it meant that I would live.

"They hurried on, leaving me in the bushes, but the men quickly gained on them. One of them grabbed my mother's arm and turned her around. She screamed and screamed in an effort to drown out my own cries. All that time, she looked at me with begging eyes to stay put, but oh, how hard it was.

"I wanted to run out of the bushes and help them, and to this day I wonder if I should have. But, somehow, I knew that there was only one possible outcome. If I did try to help them, I would be killed, too. What could one nine year-old do against a group like that?"

Elion's voice faltered for a moment, but he went on anyway.

"When my mother's throat was cut she stopped screaming, and so did I. Our eyes had been locked to the last moment, and her love for me blossomed in her eyes one last time, just before her last breath. My father met the same fate. I stayed where I was, totally numb, trying to shut out the overwhelming grief that was washing over me. I've never quite been successful at it, even to the present day. I don't know how long I lay there, but it was dark by the time I dared come out to continue on my way."

Heavy tears made their way down his cheeks. Lumea was crying, too. She wanted to wipe away his tears, but he turned his head away. He felt uncomfortable crying in her presence.

"It's okay... Elion, it's okay," Lumea whispered.

He didn't answer, and lay back down. He didn't want her to touch him. Lumea rubbed her hands over her own cheeks, angry at him for being so hard on himself.

She didn't want to think too much about it though, so she focused her attention on the building and kept a constant watch. That was how she discovered that there was a second entrance. She watched a man walk towards one side of the building, and a short time later he disappeared, almost as if he had been swallowed up by the ground. After he was gone, nothing happened for the longest time, until more men came out. They were talking loud enough for her to make out bits of their conversation, and while she overheard that the three of them were expected, she could not determine how many of the Swintheri were guarding the building.

When night fell, she woke Elion. He looked much better, well rested, though his eyes were still swollen and red. Lumea almost said something, but thought better of it and instead turned around to wake Siard. The young man was indignant that they had let him sleep for so long.

During breakfast, Lumea explained what she had overheard. Since Siard was the better sneak they agreed that he would go and take a closer look at the building. After he left they lost sight of him within moments, even though they knew he was out there. On every corner of the building, bright lamps drove away the darkness, though just outside their reach the shadows seemed that much more impenetrable and deep by contrast, covering Siard as he sneaked toward the building. For Luma and Elion, it was comforting knowing that the Hosts' troops could not see him.

Elion asked in a soft voice: "What's Lunadeiron like?"

The question elicited an immediate smile from Lumea. "Ah... Lunadeiron. It's a beautiful country, nestled in a valley between the Velvet Rocks and the Dragon Mountains. Nature there is wild, untamed. The gnarled trees reach deep down with their roots, and the bushes have vicious thorns, but on them grow the most beautiful flowers you've ever seen. Rapid rivers hack their way through the mountains and fall down in clattering waterfalls before continuing their journey through the valley.

"Here and there nature forms bridges over them, often they're the only possible way to cross. The waters flow too quickly to swim, or even row across. Narrow paths bend upward between the steep cliffs where no plant grows, except for dozens of mosses, giving the Velvet Rocks their names.

"The Dragon Mountains are full of caves and grottoes, and rumors of mythical creatures living there abound. Every year many people disappear in those mountains.

"The contrast between this wild nature and the fragile buildings of my people is stark. The villages are small, but the houses are built with high, soaring towers. I love the contrast. I used to go out into the mountains in the morning. When you look out over the valley, you can just see the towers reaching out over the trees. It's so beautiful to behold, especially when there's still a bit of morning mist. The sun casts its early light on the colorful mosaics that make up the rooftops, while birds sing to their heart's delight."

Lumea's voice was happy as she described her country. Her eyes stared off into space.

"Your people... they sound very special."

Lumea looked at Elion for a moment without understanding his words. She had not considered her people in that light for a long time. Of course, she had noticed that the Omnesians were different, but in her own country, too, people were forgetting the old traditions, and many held themselves in esteem above the natural world.

Elion continued, "Not everyone knows how to take away dreams. My people did, once, but with the deaths of so many, the knowledge has since been lost. You have a great respect for nature. Did your parents teach you this, or are you the only one of your people to live life this way?"

Lumea realized that Elion must have seen her prayer back at the willow.

"My love for nature comes from my grandmother. She taught me many things, but my parents also had more faith in nature than most in our village. That's why my brothers and I were brought up within the safety of our house. They taught us the old values and traditions. But outside of our house, much of our culture has disappeared."

Elion heard the regret in her voice.

"It sounds to me as though your house is one of the last safe places in the world, where the old values are kept alive, a kind of place I was looking for before I returned to Omnesia. Why did you leave?"

"Perhaps you're right. Now that I'm here, I realize that Lunadeiron is a unique place. It's a very large part of me. The old Lunadeiron, that is, the one my grandmother knew, not the one I grew up in. For a long time, we had only ourselves. But with the coming of the airships, new ideas began to enter our lives. The new ideas were easier to live by, and many of the young people adopted them. They stopped respecting nature, because they began to believe that it couldn't defend itself. They don't even listen to the elders any more, so there is nobody to stop them.

"Possessions have become far too important lately. Animals are killed for the thrill of the chase and their coats worn as trophies. Their deaths serve no other purpose. Sometimes their meat is traded with crews from the ships for trinkets, beads and mirrors. My generation murdered its own brothers." The tone of her voice was bitter.

Lumea continued, "My family saw this change earlier than I did, but since going away I have grown to realize it more and more. Only now I remember—and more importantly, understand—my grandmother's words. My parents kept me inside the house, they gave me old scrolls to read. They were boring, of course, and I blamed my mother especially for taking away my freedom. I heard my brothers' stories, and I wanted the same things.

"I was angry with my parents for not trusting me to make my own decisions, and I still haven't quite forgiven them for that. They held on too tight to old ways that I didn't feel comfortable with. If I would have stayed, I would have never been able to lead the life I wanted to."

Lumea remembered all the times she had cursed her parents for the way they had raised her. Since arriving in Omnesia, she had begun to appreciate her home country more and more. Most of all, she realized, she was happy that she could fall back on her upbringing. Ever since they had started running from the Hosts, she had lived according to her parents' values and her grandmother's teachings. It had kept her standing during the darker moments. Only a little while ago she would not have believed it possible to think like that, but there it was. She looked at Elion and smiled.

"They let you go in the end, though," Elion said.

"Yes, and it brought me much pain and trouble. We argued about it endlessly. I don't think my mother ever really agreed that it was a good idea, but my father knew that he could not keep me from going, so he decided to let me leave with their blessing rather than without it. He even wanted to send someone with me, as a guide and protector, but I was annoyed that he thought I could not take care of myself. I realize now how much I hurt them by leaving, but there's not much I can do about it."

"So how did you get your tattoo?" Elion asked, changing the subject.

Lumea's right hand unconsciously touched her cheek, and her eyes shone with pride. "I earned it with my Ankéabi."

The elf looked at her, though he did not ask.

She continued, "It's a rite of passage, which you go through the moment you are ready to enter adulthood. A Council of Wise Women, the Kunci, decides when the time has come. They come and take you to a place deep in the mountains. Only they know where this place is, as you are taken there blindfolded. It is a simple temple built on one of the highest mountains. Really, it's just a columnated roof with a bell. They leave you there without food, and with only a minimum amount of water. You sit in the temple and can look in any direction you want.

"The duration of each Ankéabi varies. From the moment the Kunci leave you, you are at the mercy of the gods, who send you a message, a vision. When it is over, you ring the bell, and that is the signal for the Kunci to return and get you. You are brought down to the village, only this time you're not blindfolded, but rather wrapped up in black cloth and carried by the Kunci, which represents your death. They take you to their monastery, where you tell them about your vision from the gods, and they interpret its meaning for you. During the ceremony that follows they give you a tattoo, so that you always carry your vision with you.

"Finally, they give you a new name, dress you in white and take you outside. The feast that follows celebrates your rebirth."

Elion was impressed. He said, "That is a very special tradition. Your tattoo must mean a lot to you, and you wear it with such pride. What did you see? But no, you probably can't tell me that."

His face turned red, though Lumea did not see it.

"No, you're right, it's not usual to share your vision with someone else. You're also right that I'm very proud of my tattoo. My Ankéabi was far from easy, and it earned me the name Lumea Ouinwred, which means 'Bringer of Peace Among the People'."

"Thank you for telling me. It's a beautiful name. It suits you."

Lumea looked pleased, but her voice was earnest when she continued, "Unfortunately, few people actually undergo the ritual these days. The older generations all have the Ankéabi tattoo, but my own generation feels fear gnawing in its heart. The roots of our faith don't grow deep enough any more. Many of the younger people ignore the Kunci when they come to get them, hoping that the call of the gods will pass them by. Most of them do get a tattoo, but they do it out of vanity and isn't holy. The inks that are used are different, thankfully, so the difference is quite clear. The light of sun and moon is only reflected in the tattoos created by the Wise Women."

The rest of the night was spent in silence as they anxiously awaited Siard's return. They kept their weapons at the ready in case of trouble, though they tried not to think about the possibility of violence.

They heard people talking every once in a while as they came outside in spite of the late hour. Then suddenly, as if appearing from out of nowhere, Siard was standing beside them. He looked pleased by the things he had discovered.

"Ward is in charge of the people here. They are, in fact, expecting us, but they've been ready for some days already and the soldiers think that we're not going to show up. They're getting careless. Ward doesn't know that they're using the side exit to get a breath of fresh air. He'd be furious if he did, because he's afraid that they'll give themselves away."

Elion laughed. "I don't blame him!" he joked.

Siard laughed, too, then said, "The side entrance is opened with a code. I don't expect anyone to be guarding that entrance because Ward assumes nobody is using it. They're working in shifts, with many people guarding the place both day and night."

They decided to try and enter the building the next night, so that the darkness would afford them some cover while they sneaked closer. Until then, they decided that they would rest. Siard would not stand guard, as he was tired from sneaking around. During the approach to the building, his would be the hardest task of the three. In order to ensure that they remained undetected for as long as possible, he would be responsible for wiping away their tracks. Siard agreed under muttered protest, though secretly he was glad that he would be able to get some sleep.

Elion did not tell him about his nightmares, or his fear that they would return. Lumea would take them away privately, which was something that Siard could not do. For Elion, it was a comfort knowing that she would be the one standing guard while he slept.

14

The sky was blue and cloudless that day. While her two companions slept, Lumea watched the building and the men going to and fro. The knowledge that she was close enough to the enemy to see them felt strange to her, for it meant that the Swintheri could also see her, provided that they paid close enough attention. Luckily, they were too busy to notice.

Suddenly one soldier looked in her direction. Lumea quickly looked down and dived to the ground. Had he felt someone staring at him? She carefully rose up and looked between the frozen leaves of the bush in which she hid. With a relieved sigh, she noticed that he was no longer there. She hoped that he had gone back inside, together with the other soldiers.

Just then, she heard the snapping of a twig. He had gone toward the trees instead, he was somewhere to her left, mere feet away from their hiding place!

Lumea's brain worked at top speed. What could she do? Wake up the others? She dismissed the idea quickly; Elion and Siard were too far away and she did not want to lose sight of the soldier. Besides, he was too close, and if she moved, he would certainly see her. Her muscles tensed as the man took another few steps in her direction. Her sword was drawn and ready, but just as she was about to attack the solider, his friends, appearing from the side of the building, called out to him.

"What's the matter? Saw the enemy?" they teased. "Or did you see a wee wittle wabbit?"

The man laughed along with them and turned back toward the building, though he kept looking back over his shoulder as he went.

After they had disappeared into the building, Lumea allowed herself to fall sideways. She began to shake now that her muscles could relax. That had been a very close call! She knew that they had almost been discovered, and she was deeply grateful to the other Swintheri for distracting the man. She silently moved to another place to keep an even better eye on the building. She half-expected the soldier to convince some of his friends to come out and search the edge of the forest, causing her heart to pound nervously. Lumea waited for that moment, but no more soldiers came out of the building.

The evening sky was as clear and cloudless as the day had been, and Lumea could see the glimmer of stars and the full moon. As it often did, the moon gave her the courage she needed, but it not only shined upon her soul, it also lit up the world around her to a silvery sheen, reflecting off the snow. With that kind of light, the three intruders would be spotted with ease.

Lumea spoke a quick prayer. Within moments, dark clouds covered the light of the moon, and with a proud smile on her face she ended her prayer. Again she remembered her grandmother's words. The old lady had been proven right once more. "Remember, Lumea, if you trust in nature, it will help you, no matter where you are."

She stood up and woke Elion and Siard.

After a quick breakfast, Lumea Elion and Siard started across the snowy glade. The men were terrified that the clouds would break and reveal the moon, and despite Lumea's assurances that they would not, Siard was obviously uncomfortable during the time they were exposed.

The utter darkness hid them effectively, and they slowly approached the building. Lumea carefully put one foot in front of the other. She tried to do what Siard had explained, feeling with one foot for a twig, and if she felt one she quickly turned her foot aside. She could not entirely avoid the twigs, though, and as they snapped in two they sounded like a thunderbolt. Every time it happened, the three of them would stand stark still for a few moments, wondering if someone had heard them and if they would come to investigate.

After a while, they reached a stretch of snow with fewer twigs, so it was easier to move. Just before Elion entered the circle of light, he lay down on the ground and crawled forward, and Lumea followed him. Siard came last, erasing their tracks as he went to make sure nobody would know they had been there.

When they reached the side entrance, Siard spoke the code that he had overheard. The ground disappeared in front of them, revealing a staircase. They went inside and the opening closed above their heads without a sound. The entrance had not been open but for more than just a few moments. They descended the stairs until they reached a dark, empty room with a door. On the other side of it they could hear the sounds of footsteps and voices as some workers passed. Lumea looked around for a safe place to hide, but luckily the sounds died away again.

Siard opened the door carefully and peered into the hallway. When he saw the last worker disappearing around a corner, he motioned for the other two to follow him. They quickly crossed the hallway and went through a door a little farther on. They continued deeper and deeper into the building, and though occasionally they saw other people, each time they had quickly found a place to hide. They did not want to engage anyone as the chance that they would be discovered would become too great.

As they continued on, they saw fewer people. The power plant appeared to work without much supervision, and Ward had not expected the fugitives to come back into the building. The workers were not forewarned of the intruders, so Elion, Lumea and Siard had little trouble reaching the central part of the building. The same loud noise that they had heard in the place where the cables met the wall could be heard here, so they knew they were close to reaching their destination.

The last obstacle that they met was a door which only opened via a hand-scanner, and for a moment they were unsure of what to do. Not even Siard would be able to force open this lock. Luck was on their side, though, because the door slid open and a worker stepped out, not expecting the fate that lay in store for him. He stopped in his tracks when he saw the three intruders. Elion quickly knocked the man unconscious while Siard held the door open. They stepped inside, and the elf dragged the unconscious worker behind him. Then they stopped dead, and Elion let go of the man, whose head banged against the floor. The door closed behind them.

The three of them could not believe their eyes as they stared around the room. In the middle of it there was a conical object, shaped like a volcano. Instead of spewing lava, however, this volcano emitted pulsating waves of light-blue energy. Above it, there was a sphere bobbing up and down, seemingly suspended by the waves of intense light. It was so bright that it was impossible to determine the materials from which it was made. From the sphere, numerous cables snaked out in every direction. Their eyes automatically followed the cables to their termination point, and Elion began to shake. Lumea put a comforting arm around him.

Against the walls, there were dozens of reclined couches, and within them, horribly, lay creatures. The beings were so weak and emaciated that one could count their ribs, and their arms and legs were like brittle sticks. Their skin had no color at all. Their eyes had sunk deeply into their sockets, but in them, Lumea clearly could see pain and fear. It was almost unbelievable that these beings could survive this ordeal, but their chests rose and fell with each labored breath. The creatures were so thin that it was hard to tell their gender, but one thing was obvious from their ears: they were elves.

At first, Elion remained quiet, silently staring at the chairs in abhorrence. Then he screamed in desperation, "Stop it! Stop talking to me! I was hoping that you were nothing more than a nightmare, but you're real! You're real! What do you want from me? I can hear your words, they're filling my ears, begging me. What do you want?!"

Elion pressed his hands against his ears in an attempt to shut out the voices in his head. He fell to his knees, unable to watch his brethren in this condition. He felt as though his whole world was being destroyed. The look he directed at Lumea broke her heart.

Elion whispered, "Why is this happening? I saw bodies during the war, dead elves and men, some of them horribly mutilated. It hurt me deeply, but at least they died for a cause they believed in. To some extent, that justified what had happened to all of those victims. It made the pain I knew as a boy just a bit more bearable."

Lumea sank down next to him. She had trouble keeping her own tears at bay. From the dreams, she had heard the elves' voices, too. She shared Elion's pain, holding him firmly, but she had no words with which to soothe him. She listened to his whispered words, but when he looked at her, she was deeply moved by the hurt she could see in his eyes.

Elion continued, "This is different, Lumea. These elves came to Hydrhaga without any suspicions, hoping for a better future. Instead of an easy life, they were connected to infernal machines and sucked dry of their ancient powers, which are woven together to form that terrible wall around Hydrhaga."

Elion's blood felt like acid burning in his veins. His fury had no valve with which to escape, and it turned inward, paralyzing him. He felt pain in every cell of his body and his muscles contracted. It felt as if all of the emotions he had hidden away through his long life were finally bursting out at one time.

The first thing Siard did when he recovered from his own horror was to walk over to the control panel and figure out how it worked. His eyes scanned over the various controls, and after few moments he went back to the others. Lumea helped Elion to stand, but his muscles were still tense, his fists balled tight, and he stared at the floor.

"You can end this abomination, Elion," Siard said. "Just one push of a button, and you free these elves from their suffering."

Elion looked up with empty eyes. "Then they will die..."

Lumea, still holding the elf tightly, whispered, "They died a long time ago, Elion, but someone stopped them from going peacefully and without pain. You can help them. You *have* to."

Lumea stroked his cheek and her fingers grew wet from his streaming tears. The elf was unsure how to handle the burden that had been placed upon his shoulders. On the one hand, he wanted to stop the voices in his head and end their suffering, but how could he kill his own kind?

"If we tear down their wall, the soldiers will know where we are," Elion said.

"And if we don't, we'll remain undetected? That's an illusion. Sooner or later they will know we're here anyway. The time to act has come. Isn't this what we came here for? We'll see what happens afterward. At least, if we die, we will die with honor." Lumea's tone of voice was determined. The events that were unfolding had nothing to do with her, and yet she was prepared to die for these miserable, trapped elves. She had her doubts earlier, but upon entering this room it had become obvious to her that Elion and Siard's suspicions against Hydrhaga were well-founded.

"She's right, Elion," Siard said quietly.

The two of them led Elion to the control panel. Siard took Elion's hand and put it on the button that would end the suffering of captured elves. Then, they waited in silence for Elion to make his decision. They feared the consequences, but at the same time they were prepared to face them.

Elion felt the burden on his shoulders. Who was he to decide the elves' fate? Where could he find the courage to stop the machine, end their lives and put the three of them in danger? Ultimately, he knew that Lumea was right. He pressed down upon the button decisively, afraid that he would lose his nerve if he waited any longer.

He listened to the sounds of the machinery in the room die away. When all was quiet, the voices grew calm. They thanked Elion for releasing them. He went around the room quietly, saying goodbye to the elves in as dignified a fashion as he could. As they died, they seemed to regain a portion of their former beauty. He closed their eyes and disconnected the cables from their bodies, and as each elf passed Elion became more serene. He stood still for a little longer next to some of them. Lumea wondered if he had known them in his childhood.

After his tour around the room, Elion turned to the two waiting humans. He saw the pain and compassion in their eyes, and he tried to nod encouragingly. He walked over to Siard and gave him an awkward hug, unsure how he felt about the man. The hug he gave to Lumea, though, held far more sincerity. He felt that she understood him better than anyone else ever had, possibly including himself, and he was glad that she was with them. She had no part of all this mess.

"We have to go," Elion said. He appeared as calm as one of Hydrhaga's lakes on a windless day. "The soldiers will be here any minute now, and they'll be expecting us. We might possibly be able to surprise them if we turn up somewhere else."

With their weapons in hand, they ran into the hallway.

15

The Hosts were worried when they had to inform their leader about the problems they were facing. They were terrified of his reaction, as well they should be. He came striding into the room, livid with rage. Gîsal was a distinguished-looking man, not in the least because of his height, which enabled him to look down upon practically everyone. Around his shoulders he wore a heavy, velvet cape which swept down to the floor, and it was such a deep black that it offset his light skin and made him seem even more pale than he really was. His long black hair, bound up in a ponytail, was starting to turn gray here and there, and his face was lined with deep wrinkles.

"How in the name of all the gods did three people—two of which, I might add, were behaving suspiciously—manage to escape? How were they not captured in the tunnels? They cannot have possibly left Hydrhaga, but whom do I see before me? Surely, not them! Only a bunch of layabouts, who have trouble managing even the simplest of tasks!"

The tension in the room was palpable. Ward sat quietly in a corner, hoping that nobody would pay any attention to him. In vain, as it turned out, as Gîsal turned around to face him.

"And you! You're the worst of the lot! You have been weak. Instead of preventing all of this, you practically showed them the way! You failed to ensure that the man and the woman were both immersed in the Hydrhaga way of life, even when there were clear indications that they could pose a threat. You had your orders, and you failed to follow them."

With Ward carrying the brunt of the leader's rage, the Hosts smirked at each other, relieved that the force of Gîsal's anger was directed at Ward and not themselves. Ward had not been able to hide the fact that he had suspected an intruder in the archive, and that he had ignored his instincts. Also, he had revealed much to the woman, but only because she was interested, and she seemed to believe the stories. How could he have known that she would cause so many problems?

"Let me fix this," Ward said. "Let me lead the Swintheri in the chase, and I will make sure the three of them are brought before you."

Ward had always looked down upon the troops, so he had to swallow his pride to work with them now. He would much rather stay in the safe and comfortable rooms provided for the Hosts, but he had his reputation to salvage. Gîsal accepted the offer.

Ward thought long and hard about how the three fugitives could have escaped from the Swintheri. In the end, he decided that the three must have traveled only at night, for it was the only way that they could have given their pursuers the slip. From the cave's exit, the fugitives could have gone any direction, but Ward's estimation was that they had made for the woods.

A quick search of the forest's edge soon revealed their tracks near a willow tree. The Swintheri wanted to go after them immediately, but Ward stopped them. The three runaways would have too much of a lead by now, and besides, they could not stay on the run forever. None of the monitors had registered anyone touching the wall, so either they were lost or they knew about Hydrhaga's protective barrier. Ward guessed the latter was true. He refused to underestimate his opponents again.

Deciding what to do with this knowledge was easy. If the three fugitives had found the wall, sooner or later they would reach the power cables, and from there the power plant, which was certainly to be of interest to them. The next logical step was to lead his Swintheri to the plant and wait for the unwanted guests. They would be trapped and he would rise in the esteem of the other Hosts. Ward was pleased with himself, because Gîsal would have no choice but to praise him. He could hardly wait for that moment; he looked forward to it with all his heart.

When days went by without a sign of the runaways, Ward started to lose patience. The fugitives were taking their time, though he did not doubt for one moment that they would come his way eventually. As more time passed, however, the angrier the Host became. He had put much of his reputation at stake. Throughout his life he had been the odd man out and had been pestered for not fitting in. Ward had hoped to get away from all of that by coming to Hydrhaga, but even here he had to constantly prove himself. The other Hosts had found in him an easy victim to bully, just like their leader bullied them in turn.

Gîsal was subject to severe mood swings. Nobody knew where they originated, though quite likely it had to do with the pressures he felt to complete the Thuranc in time. Lately, he had even become physically aggressive.

The Hosts took the opportunity to blame Ward for this change in Gîsal's mood, and they had made his life even more difficult. What little reputation he had left was destroyed when the three *guests* had escaped. He amused himself by imagining what he would do to them when he finally managed to get his hands on them, and what his life would look like after his honor was restored. No one would ever have the guts to laugh at him again.

Lost deep in thought like this, it took a moment for him to register that something was wrong. He could no longer hear the ever-present sound of the power plant. He jumped up when he realized that the three intruders were in the building already and had stopped the machine. He ran towards the central hall, hoping that he would be quick enough to start the machine up again. Hydrhaga's wall must not fall! He ordered all the Swintheri he met to follow him.

"Follow me! They are here already, don't let them get away again!" he yelled as he quickened his pace.

The soldiers drew their swords and hurried after him as he ran through the corridors.

They met the three intruders close to the core. Ward stopped in his tracks, surprised to finally be face to face with them. He then yelled at the soldiers to get them while he hurried on into the core and to the control panel. With barely suppressed panic he pressed this and regulated that, hoping to restore power to the wall, but it was useless. When he realized that all hope was lost, that the elves were dead and the wall hopelessly beyond repair, he sank down to the floor, where Elion had been sitting earlier.

It did not matter now whether or not the the intruders were caught, for he had failed. None of the other Hosts would ever look him in the eye again and Gîsal would be angrier than ever. He would be lucky to be demoted to the rank of drone, but somehow he knew that Gîsal would have a very different fate in store for him. He would rather die than face that, so he jumped up and rushed out to join the fray that was already underway in the hall.

Elion, Lumea and Siard did not get far before meeting the soldiers. They were just as surprised to see Ward as he was to see them, but the Swintheri attacked the three of them immediately. Lumea and Siard fought side by side, while Elion tried to get some space between himself and the attackers so that he could take better aim with his bow. At first, the number of opponents was small enough that the fugitives could easily handle them, but soon other Swintheri came to investigate the commotion, and they were rapidly outnumbered. The three were beset from all sides.

The door opened again and Ward stood before Lumea. He spit into his hand, pushed back the hair that fell into his eyes, and lunged into the fray, straight at the young woman he was sure had been the source of his downfall. Lumea fought against him with bravery, but the man was larger and stronger, and on top of that he was possessed by monstrous motivation. With one inexorable sweep of his sword he knocked her own sword from her hands, and the weapon clattered out of her reach. Though Siard was too far away to help her, he screamed at Elion. With one look the elf knew Lumea was about to become the victim of Ward's hunger for revenge. In one smooth motion he nocked, aimed and released his arrow, gravely wounding the Host.

The soldiers hesitated when they saw their leader fall. In that one lull in the fight, Lumea jumped up and hit the closest Swintheri. The fight continued, and the woman dodged the attacks and kicked out at her opponents. She turned and jumped without ceasing, and her red skirt swirled out around her, making it hard to judge who her next victim would be. She made good use of the confusion that she provoked.

She seemed to be performing a fiery dance as she ducked, jumped around, and even leaped over her opponents. She knocked the soldiers off balance before finishing them off with a punch or kick. Siard finally reached her and the soldiers that tried to get behind her were slain by him. In the meantime, Elion's arrows made sure that no more soldiers could engage them so that the two fighters could move in the direction of the door.

He waited for them there, picking off one enemy after another so that Lumea and Siard could escape. As soon as he was able, he followed them, and the room in which they found themselves there were three doors. Making use of the confusion of the fight, they managed to slip away from their opponents. Elion had picked up Lumea's sword, and he returned it to her now. They chose a door at random, then moved through a welter of different rooms and corridors, hoping to stay out of the Swintheri's hands.

After some time, they managed to reach an exit. The soldiers that should have been standing guard were instead gambling away their money in a game of cards. An elderly guard hit the table with his fist when the youngest soldier laid down his cards, making it obvious that the younger one had won the game via bluff. The other guards, already out of the game, laughed loudly.

As one of them gathered the cards together, the three intruders rushed in. The guards were completely taken by surprise. They had not been notified of the fight in the core, and now they were suddenly face-to-face with the three fighters. One man had the presence of mind to reach for his weapon, but Lumea was quicker and, in one fell swing, chopped off his arm. Shocked, he looked from the arm to her, but Lumea knew no mercy.

The adrenaline was still rushing through her veins after her melee at the core, and she took out her anger on her opponents. In part, he was responsible for the elves' sufferings, and here he was laughing and enjoying himself as if nothing was amiss. Lumea was livid. Thrusting with the curved sword, she pierced the man's heart, and as he fell down to the ground, her sword slid out the wound, covered in blood. With lightning speed, she attacked the other Swintheri, and they were dead before they even had the chance to rise.

Siard opened the exit and the three of them ran out over the snowy, open space and into the woods. When they were amongst the trees again they saw the Swintheri swarm out of the building. Knowing that the soldiers would not easily give up the chase, Elion led them deeper into the forest. After a while, they turned somewhat to the left in order to stay within Hydrhaga's old boundaries. Dogs had been unleashed, and the fugitives heard the excited baying of the pack behind them. At times a dog would break free of the group and come quick on their heels, and Elion would pause only long enough to take it down with an arrow. The sudden fear of capture gave them the energy to quicken their pace, and they pushed themselves harder and harder, as fast as the uneven terrain would allow.

Finally, the sounds died away. The pursuers gave up the chase, called back the dogs and returned to the power plant. Lumea found an abandoned wolves' den, and they crawled inside it to rest.

After a while, Siard made his way out of the den carefully, and discovered that the snow was melting. Everywhere, water ran in rivulets, creating a myriad of glassy sounds. The man found a few big leaves and, fashioning a makeshift bowl out of them, he caught some of the running water. The animals had also awoke from their sudden hibernation, and with Elion's bow and arrow Siard managed to shoot a rabbit. There was enough dry wood to be found within the den, so the young man got a fire started without waking the others, and he carefully began to cook the rabbit.

The smell of the roasting rabbit woke Elion and Lumea. They enjoyed the taste of warm meat, after having gone so long without it. Somehow, against all expectations, they had survived the fight in the power plant.

Elion was the first to speak of it. "Thank you for supporting me back there," he said to both of them, referring to the hard choice he had to make in the core. "I'm proud to have you by my side in this fight against whomever has done this to my people."

Then, to Lumea, he said, "It's almost surreal the way you fought those Swintheri. It really was quite terrifying, and I'm glad you're on my side."

Siard agreed with a nod. "Where did you learn to fight like that?

You were like a wildfire, burning everything in its path!"

Lumea looked down at the ground, abashed. While in the power core, she had gotten the confirmation she needed that something was amiss in Hydrhaga. She had felt many emotions bubble to the surface because of it, but most of all she had realized that if she did not act, she and her friends would be the next to fall. Still, her own strength had surprised her, and she was almost afraid to think about it. She shrugged and answered, "What else was I supposed to do? It was fight or die."

They grinned at her answer, but she had spoken the truth. They were starting to realize just how serious this situation was.

"We've come far, the three of us, probably farther than any of us had expected. Who knows what else we will find on our path? I, for one, would like to know what it is that they are building here in Hydrhaga."

Elion looked at the others again and got up. They wanted to get as far away from the power plant as they possibly could, now that the Hosts' fury would increase. They would travel every waking moment from now on. They would also leave the forest behind. They had a feeling that there was nothing more to be discovered there.

In the following days, the three fugitives exhausted themselves as they ran. Every time they heard faraway noises of pursuit, signifying that the Swintheri had taken up the chase again, they pushed themselves even harder. They had to be careful all the time, and there was not much time to rest or find food.

The speed with which Elion led them away from the power plant was grueling. They crossed between the trees, dodging branches as they went. At times, Lumea or Siard would pause for a moment to catch their breath, but every time Elion would call out that there was no time to rest. Every step she took, Lumea thought that it would be her last. First the fight in the plant and now the unrelenting pace at which they ran and stumbled through the forest was becoming too much for her. She needed time to rest, and try as she might, she could not get it. She cried at the unfairness of it all, though her tears served only to make her angry. She did not want to give in to the exhaustion.

They went on and on.

After a long time, something drew Siard's attention. To their right, two small lights were danced erratically in the twilight. He told the others about it, but unlike Elion, Lumea could not see what he was talking about. The two men had a whispered conversation.

"Do you think they're Swintheri?" Siard asked fearfully, trying to find cover.

More lights appeared, and at last, Lumea noticed them too. Elion looked at them intently, but then he suddenly started laughing.

"Alright, let's rest here. We don't want to miss this."

Siard looked at the elf's suddenly-cheerful face with a surprised expression.

"What is it?" Lumea asked, but Elion told her to stay quiet.

"Shh... Just wait."

He had hardly said it before the number of lights multiplied. Fireflies! The yellow dots danced in the air around them, and they stood quietly together, enjoying the sight and the rest. A sigh of admiration escaped Lumea at the sight of this enchanting dance, for it was comforting to know that such beauty still existed in this land. Hydrhaga had not been completely abandoned by the gods, after all! The show was over too soon, and they were left again with the reality of their situation.

They moved on again at the same speed as before, but somehow the fireflies had given Lumea a new burst of energy and hope, and the hike did not seem nearly as tough as before. They went on, full of purpose now.

16

Eventually, Lumea and her two companions reached the edge of the forest. Before them they saw a wide, sloping landscape dotted with lakes and houses in the distance. Between the houses and the three of them there was a windmill farm, and the mills' sails were spinning nearly out of control.

They saw that winter was losing its grip on the land, and the effects that the wall's failure had on the weather. The sky was inky black and heavy rains slashed across the plains, limiting their visibility. A gigantic, dark cloud roiled across the sky, almost rotating as it went. Squalls whipped across the landscape, leaving a trail of destruction behind them. A hellish noise accompanied it all.

They found shelter near some trees and a well, and while Lumea freshened up, the men talked about what to do next.

"It won't be easy crossing this plain. I don't know if we'll be able to fight the force of that wind," Siard said, as a threatening rumble punctuated his words. "Listen, there's a thunderstorm brewing. It isn't safe to stay under these trees, but going out there on the plain without any shelter, that's just stupid. Judging by those clouds, that storm won't go easy on us."

Elion disagreed. "I have the same concerns, but do we really have a choice? We have a chance so long as the storm is far away. I think we should leave these trees behind us as quickly as possible."

Just as Lumea rejoined them, a lightning bolt flashed across the sky, immediately followed by a heavy thunderclap. The woman instinctively flinched and put her arms over her head, as if they could protect her from the force of nature. The two men looked out over the plain with serious expressions on their faces. The wind tore everything in its path, and flashes of lightning illuminated the world in short, violent bursts. Small tornadoes reached down from out of the clouds, and as soon as they touched the ground they ravaged the landscape. Windmills were uprooted and thrown back down, turning them to splinters. The noise accompanying the destruction was drowned out by the rolling thunder.

Lumea had turned around towards the plain as well, staring at the nature's fury with a mixture of awe and admiration. Endless lightning bolts flashed through the sky, the tendrils branching out as they neared the ground. The windmills, as tall as they were, were hit time and again, and some of them caught fire, but the driving rain quickly doused them again.

"Look over there!" Lumea called, pointing at a solitary building. "That building is closer to us than the rest, and it looks a lot different too. Let's try to reach it."

The structure stood at the edge of a lake. Elion nodded approvingly.

"If we walk in between the windmills, we can reach it. The mills reach higher than us, so we should be safe from the lightning among them. Let's go."

Siard's said angrily, "Don't be stupid. Those mills attract lightning, and as soon as the electric charge reaches the ground, we're toast. There's no real safe place at the moment, but the safer option is to stay put."

Elion grumbled. "So what's your suggestion then?"

"I do think it's a good idea to investigate that building, but we have to wait for the weather to change. You see that hill there, halfway out on the plain? With this wind, we'll be lucky to reach that in one night and going farther is completely out of the question. Once there, we can rest in relative safety. It's the only possible route, but not just yet. First, we need to wait."

Lumea agreed with Siard's assessment of the situation, but Elion looked doubtful. "Elion, Siard's right. If you decide to leave now, I don't want to follow you. Even if I wanted to, I couldn't. I just don't have the strength left. Our flight these last couple of days has utterly exhausted me; I won't be able to win against the wind."

Elion reluctantly agreed. He was tired as well, but he was also afraid of their pursuers finding them. Still, he abided by the decision of the group.

The sun broke through the clouds above the forest where they stood, but on the plains, the deluge poured down unabated. Rainbows showed themselves in between the flashes. Any other time it would have been magical to watch, but under the circumstances the phenomenon had a sinister quality to it.

Siard was the last one to say something. "If this weather is artificial as well, we might be able to deduce patterns in it. That would increase our chances."

Elion nodded, and Lumea heaved a sigh of relief, giving in to her body's fatigue.

"So how are you feeling?" Lumea asked Elion.

She sat down next to him. They had yet to speak about the elves in the power plant, even though the emotional impact on him was obvious. She look at him worriedly.

"I did what I had to do," Elion replied soberly.

"That doesn't mean you're not allowed to have feelings. Anger at those responsible, sadness for the loss of even more kinfolk..."

Elion interrupted her. "Don't make it worse than it already is," he snapped.

Lumea hung her head. "I'm sorry... I didn't mean to make it worse," she said.

The elf took her hand and gave her a sidelong glance. "I know you didn't, and I shouldn't have snapped at you. It's just that... I don't really want to let it sink in. Humans are apparently still targeting my people."

Elion looked over to where Siard sat, and his look was cold. When Lumea followed his gaze, she was shocked to realize what he was thinking.

"Siard has nothing to do with this! He's on your side, remember that."

Elion shrugged. Everything that had happened had only served to increase his distrust of the humans in this region. "He's Omnesian," Elion finally said.

Lumea shook her head. "He's your friend. You can trust him."

Elion looked at her. "I know that. But it doesn't always feel that way. That's why I told you I'd rather feel nothing at all. It's easier not to feel."

112

"What happened to you to make you think this way, Elion?" Lumea asked with a sigh.

The elf thought about her question for a moment. When he started talking, he had his voice entirely under control. "All right, I will tell you.

"My past has been filled with loneliness. As you know, I was nine when my parents were killed, and not long after that, the elves were forced to flee Arminath, and we hid in the woods. The land around the city was greener then than it is now, but we still had very little living space. It was a time of fear, hunger and persecution. At the same time, though, there was this feeling of belonging. We were all up the same tree, so to speak. We had to rely on each other, help and protect each other. They were uncertain times.

"It was then that I killed my first opponent. It was either him or me, there was no middle way. Survival was most important, and I learned that from a very young age. I did not have the luxury to dwell on it.

"When I was about thirty, I decided to leave the other elves. There didn't seem to be anything else to be learned from them. They were stuck in a vicious circle, and their moods were turning ugly. For years, I wandered through strange and faraway countries. My past was like a burden and I tried desperately to escape it.

"Finally, I reached some desolate region, quite nearly inaccessible. The rocks were colored red and orange, the earth was sandy and of the same color. For centuries water and wind had ate away at that landscape, until all that remained was a labyrinth that only a few creatures dared to enter. I was sure I would be safe there, from both humans and elves. I remember thinking that if there was any place I could forget myself and my past, it was right there."

Elion was silent for a moment. When he continued, the slight change in his voice betrayed the emotions that were awakening, despite himself. "But how can you forget your parents, when you expect to see them around every corner? How can you forget what happened when every morning, before even opening your eyes, you pray that it was all just a bad dream?"

In the silence that followed, Elion got a grip on himself and the rest of his story was spoken with near-indifference. Siard had moved a bit closer and was listening, as well.

Elion continued, "I did not succeed in forgetting, in that land. On the contrary, every day my memories seemed to become more vivid and alive. It was a land of scavengers, and vultures always circled above me. They were anxious for me to die, and thus feed them. Those scavengers were my only means of survival. Sometimes I would kill a hyena, and I would share it with the vultures, but most of the time, I ate nothing."

Elion remembered the hyenas visiting him in the early morning. Even in his sleep, he heard the shuffling gait of the animals; they were curious whether there was any food to be had. He had often wondered what would happen if he just kept still, how it would feel if he let them attack him and rip the flesh from his bones, however he had always roused himself and chased them away.

He did not tell Lumea this, of course. He really did not expect her to understand that death would have been a release. The scavengers showed him the truth: they all waited for his death, but it never came. He carried the genetic trait for elven immortality, and that everlasting life had become a burden for him. He knew that the only way for him to forget would be to die, but that path was closed to him.

"Finally, after a few decades, I left that land behind and decided to go back to Omnesia. On my return travels, I heard that more of my people were returning to their old home. I had also heard the first rumors about Hydrhaga. It felt good to be back. I could barely recognize the city any more, but it still felt like a homecoming. The elves organized many parties, and the depression that had chased me away had made way for happiness and a sense of purpose. My people had taken their lives into their own hands again, and the time that followed was lovely. Strangely enough, now that I was no longer determined to forget it, the past receded into the background. I went to Hydrhaga, but when I arrived, they would not let me in. I had almost accepted that, until you came along."

He looked at her, and the cheerful light in his eyes did not escape Lumea's notice. She was convinced that there were still things he was not telling her, but she let them slide. The important thing was that he did not feel too terrible after the events in the power plant.

The three fugitives stayed near the well for another night and day, but they could not discern any sort of pattern in the quickly-changing weather. The storm blew all that time, though by the end of the second day the delay between the lightning and thunder seemed to increase. Siard softly counted the seconds between each and and he looked more content all the time.

"The storm is moving off. It will be a lot safer to cross the plains now. The wind will be our biggest problem, but at least we won't have to worry about getting electrocuted."

As night fell, they began the trek across the windswept plains. At least their scent would be blown away, so the dogs could not follow.

Staying close together, Elion, Siard and Lumea moved out of the shelter of the trees and into the full force of the wind. It drove them to the left as soon as it had a grip on them, and they had to fight against it to keep going in the correct direction. Just when they were used to this, the wind turned without warning and they fell over. Siard was the first to get up and he helped the other two back to their feet.

With the wind in their backs, they made good time, going so fast that their legs could hardly keep up. Then the squall blew in their faces and made breathing laborious. They could hardly move a step as the biting wind and pouring rain tore at their faces. There were times when Lumea felt that the wind would soon pick her up and carry her away like one of Aeron's kites, and sometimes she had so much trouble that she would not mind if it did. She forced herself to go on. Progress was slow.

At times the wind fell away entirely, leaving the three fugitives dazed and lost as to where they were. When the clouds would break apart briefly and the moon shone down on the landscape, Elion could always determine which way they needed to go, and in turn, that gave Lumea new courage.

Worst of all were the twisters which ravaged the land. They would appear unpredictably, knifing down at the ground from the roiling clouds overhead. The three of them had some resistance against the wind, but if they ended up in one of the tornadoes, they knew their lives would be forfeit. When one formed nearby, they would run to get out of its path.

By morning they reached the hill they had seen from the edge of the wood. They fell down, exhausted, and huddled underneath Lumea's cape together. In all this grass, the green of her mantle was the best camouflage. Lumea prayed that the storm would leave them alone, and that they would not be discovered.

There was still an audible rumble in the air, and lightning flashed far away, but the thunderstorm did not near the hill. The fugitives fell asleep, grateful for the warmth they shared with each other. At times, one or the other were awakened by the raging wind, but the twisters miraculously left them alone during their cataclysmic dance.

The following night, in spite of the unpredictable weather, the three made their way to the building. They came past tree stumps that had been burned to charcoal by the lightning. They looked like hands outstretched to the heavens in a desperate plea to the gods. It was spooky going past them, but eventually they reached the building.

They trusted their luck when they went into the building as the howling wind prevented them hearing anything through the door. They stepped into a hallway with many doors, behind which they could hear people talking. Sounds were coming from above them as well. To their right there was a spiral stair, which they quickly descended, since they could hear nothing from below.

17

Gîsal was furious when he heard about the fall of the wall. He paced lividly up and down the room. Some Hosts cowered, waiting for him to stop raging and actually tell them what to do, but others were loud in their disapproval of Ward. Suddenly, Gîsal stopped pacing and straightened his back, towering above them all. In an icy voice he said, "Silence."

Although it was hardly more than a whisper, every Host shut his mouth immediately.

"I don't want to hear one more word about Ward. You are all responsible for this mess. All... of... you..." He pointed at each of the Hosts in turn. His signet ring glinted, displaying the symbol of the Thuranc engraved upon it. The contempt in his eyes was obvious.

"Useless creatures!" he spat. "If you don't act quickly, Hydrhaga and all that it stands for will disappear. This is not the time for self-pity. Any other day, I would have you drowned in the lakes, or better yet, thrown in front of the Thurancs just to see how far they've advanced."

Gîsal looked around the room to measure the impact of his words on his audience. Most of them cowered, trying to make themselves even smaller under his gaze, but the ones who had protested the most about Ward looked indignant. What was he yelling at *them* for? They hadn't done anything. Their leader's next words taunted them.

"You haven't done anything... That's right! That's the whole problem, you're doing nothing! What do you think? That the situation is going to solve itself while you're sitting here, feeling important? From the very first moment all of you made the wrong decisions! Now, what will be our next move? Will someone tell me or do I have to hand the solution to you upon a platter yet again?"

The silence that followed was so heavy that nobody dared break it, until one small, quavering voice in the corner spoke up: "Perhaps we needn't do anything... With the wall destroyed, the weather has become uncontrollable. Hydrhaga is being torn apart by heavy and unpredictable storms. In such extreme circumstances, surely the escapees cannot survive for long. Perhaps our problem is solving itself as we speak?"

Gîsal hit the table with his hand. "Have you learned nothing at all? Those three won't let themselves be beaten that easily, not by the Swintheri and most certainly not by the weather. Waiting here for their dead bodies to show up is out of the question. If they're struggling through this weather, then our troops will have to go after them. I don't care about the consequences."

A dramatic sigh escaped him as he sat down.

"Is there anyone here who has a plan with some virtue to it?" he asked.

Nobody dared answer any more of his questions.

"Well then, let me enlighten you..."

At that moment a worker burst into the room.

Gîsal spoke to him in a friendly manner. "How goes the research?"

The worker reported that the Thuranc was improving. They still did not have him entirely under control, but they were making fast progress. Gîsal told him to speed up the research even more. "Use all the guests who are now in Hydrhaga. If you run out of guests, you're free to use some of these Hosts. They're have outlived their usefulness for anything else."

When Gîsal coldly looked in the direction of the disapproving murmurs, the protesting men shrank under his gaze.

"Good. We're all in agreement. You, gentlemen, will be going with the Swintheri to find the fugitives. Double the guard on the laboratories, and woe betide the one who lets them get away this time. I swear to you, that person will wish he shared Ward's fate."

Without waiting for a reaction, Gîsal got up and strode out of the room. He made his way down the the hallway, passed through the last door on his left, and walked into the hospital. Ward was lying there, terribly injured. He had been hit by an arrow, but worse than that, his mind had broken. He babbled nonsense all day long, though when Gîsal entered he grew quiet and trembled with fear.

"To think that someone like you could manage to destroy the things I have been working on for so long. Do you have any idea what your actions have cost me already?"

"I'm sorry, Lord Gîsal... I did my best..." Ward whispered.

"Your best, was it? Well, that was obviously not good enough. But then, perhaps, it was my fault for expecting more of you."

The tall man seated himself on the edge of Ward's bed and lost himself in thought. Unlike the story that the Hosts told the guests, the Thuranc was not really an archaeological find, preserved by Hydrhaga's soil. The first Thuranc had been a robot, though that was already some time ago. Right after the war with the humans, Gîsal had gathered some researchers and given them the order to create a highly-destructive robot. If it functioned like it should, they could create more, and Gîsal would have an army of inestimable power.

Hydrhaga had yet to exist at that time and the laboratory had been hidden deep within a forest. When the robot was finally finished, it proved to be no more than a paper dragon; it could not function independently and it was defeated with ease.

Gîsal then proceeded to gather scientists from other fields to help with the development of the Thuranc. For decades the only work on the robots was on paper, and Gîsal grew more impatient all the time. Finally, though, the day had come when the scientists had agreed on a way to proceed.

"That was the first moment I savored the sweet, sweet taste of revenge. My laboratory grew larger, and under the cover of the darkest nights a group of people were kidnapped. They were the first test subjects for my scientists. Parts of their brains were implanted in the robots."

Gîsal sounded almost happy at the memory, but soon his voice turned dark again. Ward reached out a shaking hand to put on the leader's shoulder, as a gesture of comfort, but before he could do so, the man grabbed his wrist and pressed it back down upon the bed. Ward groaned in pain, but Gîsal ignored him as he continued his story.

"The research continued slowly. Soon, the scientists were out of test subjects, and everyone agreed that it wouldn't pay off to abduct a second group of people—too many disappearances would make the townspeople suspicious. Already there were nervous whispers in the streets of Omnesia. I could not have curious townsfolk poking their noses into where they had no business, so I built Hydhraga."

Finally, Gîsal let go of Ward's wrist, and he rubbed the painful spot unconsciously. The leader's voice was cold with contempt for the Omnesians.

"I never understood those people. They were nervous and suspicious about what was going on here, but, if you build a nice gateway, spread rumors about an easy life, then they come voluntarily. It is apparently very hard to resist the temptation of investigating a closed door, which makes it all the more easy for us, of course. More than enough test subjects, and nobody lifts a finger to prevent it."

The man laughed at his own inventiveness.

"My scientists were soon able to devise a second draft of the Thuranc. Unfortunately, there was a new problem. Where the old Thuranc had been too dependent, the new one had too much free will. It realized what kind of monster it was, and refused to obey orders. There was no use in punishing it because it loathed itself. All it wanted was to die."

Gîsal shook his head in disgust.

"At the same time my guests seemed to be waking up to their life here. They started looking around, noticing that some of the guests were disappearing. Many of them vanished overnight and the ones who remained were not given clear answers by you Hosts. That's when I had the brilliant idea to drug the guests. Inconspicuously, of course. Not only did it free us from inconvenient questions, but it also led to a great leap forward in our research. The scientists were now able to use the drugged guests for the robot, which came closer to the obedient soldier that I originally had in mind."

His voice was euphoric as he looked at the man on the bed. This Omnesian that had almost ruined his entire life's work was, in his eyes, just as despicable as the rest of the human race.

Still, the helpless man was fascinating to look at. When he bent forward, Ward shook, and the human hid his head under the blankets. In one swift motion, the leader pulled them away and dropped them carelessly onto the floor. While Ward tried in vain to cower away from his master, Gîsal tenderly stroked his cheek. Slowly the fear and confusion in the Host's eyes made way for hope. In his confused mind, the cold fingers meant that the leader had forgiven him. He calmed down.

Gîsal was not about to relinquish the power he had over the Host. On the contrary, with the wounded man looking at him so gratefully, that power had never been greater.

"My dear little Ward," the leader said in a deceptively soothing tone, "you do know that, eventually, I will kill you for what you have done to me?"

With those words, he put his nail to the man's cheek and scratched down, drawing a red line of blood. Ward immediately shrank back into his pillow. Tears stream down his face in silent witnesses to the unbearable pain he endured.

In the following days, the activities in the laboratories were increased at the orders of the leader. The research on the best way to produce the Thuranc continued without any complications.

All other facilities on Hydrhaga functioned on minimal capacity. Most of the workers were required in order to conduct the last phases of the Thuranc research. The gates were sealed against the outside world. The guests were brought into the labs in large numbers, where the scientists divided them into two groups.

Those guests that protested—in spite of being drugged with calmatives—were held separately. The protesters would be taken out of their cells when the Thuranc's strength needed to be tested. Most of the guests were obedient, though, and the scientists removed the organs of those guests so that they could be implanted into the Thuranc. Those guests who stayed behind in the houses were given a higher dose of the drug so that they did not realize that more and more people were disappearing. They would still go willingly when they were needed. Ever since the summer had ended, the drug that kept them docile had been spread through the water supply.

18

The spiral stair that Elion, Lumea and Siard took ended in a great hall. To one side of it there was a huge wall of curved glass, and it held the dark water of a lake at bay. Algae clung to the glass, but the water was so impenetrably dark that nothing could be seen anyway. The other walls had paintings covering them. Lumea noticed the horrors that were depicted in them, the most prominent of which was the Thuranc.

Not all of the paintings showed human figures, but on the ones that did they had a different purpose. Some of the pictures depicted hospital-like rooms where Thuranc were being treated, but on others the humans were being attacked by several of the creatures. The largest of the paintings showed countless Thurancs assaulting a city.

Siard was the first to recognize the city. "They're planning an assault on Omnesia!"

Neither of the others reacted to his disconcerted words, as a large symbol in the middle of the wall had caught their attention. Elion walked towards it and followed the lines of the relief with a finger. His look was one of dismay.

"What is that?" Lumea asked. She stood by the elf, giving him an inquisitive look.

"It's the insignia of Senator Gîsal," he whispered.

"I don't understand."

With a stiff face, Elion closed his eyes. "Gîsal was one of the most important elves in Arminath. That's his seal."

"So he's the one behind all of this."

"No, no, it can't be," Elion denied.

He turned around and strode to the other side of the hall, where there was another staircase, and they descended this one as well. The stair creaked with every step they took, and the sound echoed off the smooth walls. It seemed deafening in the silence.

They proceeded carefully, trying to make as little noise as possible, afraid of being heard. The stairs seemed to go on forever, but eventually they reached the bottom, where they found themselves in another large room.

The spacious area was filled with copper kettles of varying size, and they were all connected to one another with a network of pipes. The walls were hidden behind countless monitors and control panels full of buttons and lights. Siard was immediately attracted to it. Only a few of the indicator lights were lit.

Lumea walked over to a table full of scales and conical glass flasks, broader at the bottom than at the top. In between those, she found labeled bottles, so she read what they said. By far, most of the bottles contained mandrake. She called Elion to show him the bottles.

"Do you know what mandrake is?"

"It's a plant belonging to the nightshades. It's poisonous, especially the root, it causes paralysis and dulls the senses even in small doses. In and of itself, mandrake isn't lethal, though it can lead to death."

Lumea realized that she knew this plant as well, though in Lunadeiron they called it lûffah. She suddenly remembered her first night in Hydrhaga, and how she had struggled for breath and could not move.

Siard announced another discovery, saying, "There's some kind of sluice-gate here. It seems to be working in conjunction with a drain system. That glow we saw in the lakes must have come from a place like this one, Elion."

Elion nodded. "It looks like they've been sluicing the mandrake into the water. That's why those other guests were so obedient."

The two men were right. During the summer, the guests had been drugged in this fashion. Most of the mandrake had been taken to the room which regulated the water running through the guest houses, though some of it remained here.

Elion and Lumea looked through the rest of the room together, and they soon found a small amount of antidote. They decided to take it with them, thinking it might come in handy.

Other than the antidote, the place was otherwise empty, so they went through the next door. To their relief, all of these underground rooms were deserted, so they could rest and regain their strength without fear of being caught. They had not been this relaxed since the winter had started. Food had been left behind down here, and there was even a kitchenette where they could cook it. With the materials they found, Lumea and Elion made new arrows and mended the rips in their clothing.

"Tell us about Gîsal," Lumea said. She had noticed how Elion's thoughts had turned inwards from the moment they had discovered the insignia on the wall. She could only guess at the confusion in his mind upon seeing it.

"Gîsal was a rich man, I believe one of the richest in Arminath, and the city owed a lot to him. He put himself and his riches into service of the city and its inhabitants. That is why he was chosen as senator time and again. The people loved and respected him."

"Did you ever meet him?"

"Just once, though my mother often spoke of him. Not a day went by that she was not grateful for the opportunities he gave her."

The lines on Elion's face softened as he recalled his youth.

"You should know that my mother was a very gifted weaver, and it was Gîsal who made that possible for her. Her fabrics were the most prized in the whole city and she was well-known for the complicated patterns that she could coax out of her loom. But if her life had run just a little bit differently, nobody would have known about it.

"You see, my mother came from a family of blacksmiths, and it was usual for a craft to be handed down from one generation to the next. Gîsal changed that, because he wanted the things my people produced to be of even higher quality than they already were. So he ensured that the schools not only paid attention to the sciences, but also to creativity. Instead of a system where a skill was handed down from parent to child, he let the masters of a craft choose their own apprentices.

"My mother was one of the first children to join one of these new schools. When her talent became obvious, Gîsal personally made sure that she was taught by one of the best weavers in Arminath. If she had been a blacksmith, she would not have been nearly as happy as she was being a weaver. I used to watch her sitting behind her loom, working away and beaming happily. She was proud of her work."

Lumea liked watching Elion when he was this way. The shadow

that was usually present on his features disappeared completely, and his natural beauty emerged in full. He suddenly looked years younger.

"When did you meet Gîsal?"

"About a year before the war began. He had just become engaged, and he and his fiancé came over to our house to see how far my mother had come with the fabric she was weaving for the wedding gown.

"My mother sent me away, but as I ran past, Gîsal caught me in his arms and put me on his lap. I looked at him, full of admiration. He had a friendly face, I remember, and his eyes smiled. He talked to me in a soft voice as he praised my mother, and told me to always be proud of her. I felt him to be sincere, and when he told me about his wedding, I knew how important it was to him."

"Did you ever see her in the wedding gown?" Lumea asked.

Elion shook his head sadly. "Nobody did. When the war broke out, she was one of its first victims. They were never married."

"His heart must have been broken," Lumea whispered.

"I'm sure it was. I remember the way he looked at her, while she stood next to my mother's loom. She was admiring the fabric, but every now and then she looked over her shoulder and gave her future husband a brilliant smile. Every time she did, his eyes would start to shine. When they left, he placed his hand on the small of her back, and the love between those two spoke as much from that single gesture as from the unconsciousness with which it was done. I'm convinced she was his whole world. Loss like that must be a terrible thing."

Elion's story clarified many things for Lumea. "That explains why he built Hydrhaga, and why he wants to attack Omnesia," she said.

Elion became angry. "I refuse to believe he's behind any of this!" He stood up and towered above Lumea, but she looked up at him fiercely.

"Then how do you explain his insignia on the wall?" she said.

Elion hesitated for a moment, but then he said, "I don't know. All I know is that an elf could not have done that to his own kin."

"Unless he thinks he's acting on their behalf as well."

Though Lumea was close to the truth, Elion still refused to believe her words.

"Elion, think about it." She raised her voice in an attempt to get through to him. "The war has been over for centuries. All that time he lived alone, among his enemy, remembering all the wrongs they did to him. He wants revenge. That's the only part of him left."

"How dare you claim to understand what happened!" he said, furiously. He turned around and strode away. When he was close to a wall, though, he stopped and stood with his head bent for a while, his jaw clenching and unclenching. When he turned around again, he muttered, "You're right. During the war he lost everything he had. His city was destroyed, his beloved murdered, his people made into pariahs of society. He's had more than enough reason to do these terrible things."

The elf came back and sat down with a sigh. "But then who am I to take that away from him? If he's taking revenge in the name of all the elves, shouldn't I be following him?"

Lumea quickly shook her head. "This is a personal matter that has cost too many innocent lives already. You have already picked your side. You have to remember why you came to Hydrhaga!"

"You said it yourself, he also acts in the name of those elves in the power plant," Elion said.

"I said that is what he thinks, but you could see the fear and the pain in their eyes. Do you really think they would have begged you to stop the machine if they believed in him?"

Elion put his head in his hands and shrugged.

"Just give yourself the chance to think things through," Lumea said.

The elf did not say anything, until he angrily swept the arrows from the table.

"I should have never come back. Why couldn't the hyenas have just killed me?"

Though she did not entirely understand his words, Lumea was startled by their sincerity. She got up to put a comforting arm around his shoulders, but he shrugged her away.

"Maybe it was your destiny to come back. Perhaps the gods have something in mind for you."

Elion rose again and for the second time looked down at her.

Though his voice was furious, his eyes showed more confusion than anything else. "The gods? What do I care about them? They've never lifted a finger to stop the elves' fate, and now all of a sudden they choose me to somehow make everything right? Thanks, but no thanks, Lumea, if it's all the same to you."

"Don't you believe in the gods?" Lumea was shocked. The gods were very important to her, and she had always assumed that the elf felt the same way about them.

"How can I believe after everything that has happened? How cruel can these gods exist if they allowed it to happen at all? If they are responsible for all of the bad things that I've seen, then they don't deserve my trust."

"But the gods give you direction! You're never alone if you believe in them." She was trying her hardest to convince him, but Elion snapped at her.

"I've been alone all my life, Lumea, except for the first nine years."

"When did you turn away from them?" She was concerned.

"Me? I wasn't the one that did the turning. They left when my mother was killed in front of me."

Tears burned in Lumea's eyes. She could understand why Elion had started to think that way, but it was still difficult for her to accept. She wanted to put a hand on his arm, but with an angry gesture he turned it away and left the room without another word.

19

In the time that followed, the three fugitives created some private space. They had been together for so long that a little privacy was more than welcome. The sense of safety they all felt made them less careful of their surroundings.

Lumea had found a small room with eight corners, and it greatly reminded her of a chapel. To four of the eight walls candelabras were affixed, and the candles—once she had lit them all—gave off a warm, yellow light. Wax had dripped from the candle holders and was lying on the floor in small heaps. The floor tiles made a mosaic of intertwining branches, though the center had been left bare of an image. It was a comforting place, and Lumea often found herself retreating there to meditate. Thanks to the rest she received, her body healed quickly, while her meditations provided a different kind of medicine for her spirit.

She often used these meditations to pray to the gods about Elion. She was worried about the elf, and if he did not seek help from the spirits, then she would do it for him. She prayed to them to forgive him for the way he talked about them. She hoped that they would not turn away from him now, but that they would help him in his choices now that he most needed it. It was clear that he did not wish for her help, but maybe in this way she could do something for him.

Usually she was in such a deep trance that she took no notice at all of her surroundings. Thus, she did not hear the creaking of the stairs. It was only when the door abruptly opened and the subsequent cold wind blew out one of the candles that she looked up at the stranger that stood before her. A wisp of smoke drew a wily image in the air, gone within seconds.

Lumea jumped up, startled by the man's entrance. He was young and his face was open and friendly. It was obvious from his greeting that he was surprised to find anyone here, and he did not seem to realize that she was one of the fugitives. Lumea took a step back, her mind working at full speed. He was standing between her and the exit, and she wondered how was she going to get out. He reached out his hand, just like Aeron had once done. He did not seem frightened, and most certainly not threatening. Lumea hesitated about what to do.

"What are you doing here?" he asked in a light tone of voice. "Are you lost?"

He seemed to want to help her. The realization was a relief, and she relaxed. Before she could answer, though, Elion appeared behind the man and ran his dagger into the man's back. The one emotion that registered on his face as he slid to the ground was surprise. He looked up at Lumea with questioning eyes as she watched him fall. She felt her stomach turn.

The worst thing, however, was the glow of pride that she could see in Elion's eyes. Blood dripped from his dagger and onto the floor. Lumea screamed and pushed the elf aside, running out of her improvised chapel. Elion called after her, but she did not stop. She grew dizzy as she made her way to the room where Siard had made his own camp. When she opened the door, he saw the paleness of her face. She blindly tried to find support from the wall. Siard was with her in two steps and helped her to sit down.

"What happened?" he asked.

The question released a floodgate of tears, making it impossible for her to tell him. All she could do was shake her head. Finally, Siard lifted her from the floor and carried her to a couch. Then he left her for a few minutes to fix her a cup of tea. With each sip she became more calm.

"He's a monster..."

"Who is? Lumea, who are you talking about?"

Elion chose that moment to come into the room. He had disposed of the body, hoping that if anyone found it they would think that the fugitives had already moved on. Lumea looked at him with eyes filled with loathing. His clothes were drenched with the man's blood.

"You killed him! He only wanted to help me and you murdered him, and you were proud of it, too... You monster!" She spat the words at him.

Siard got up and took Elion to the next room.

"What happened out there?"

The elf told him the whole story, while he showed the weapon that he had found on the man.

"All I want to do is protect her..." He sighed deeply. "Why doesn't she understand that?" Then he suddenly became furious. "How dare she think those things about me? She detests me, and I don't deserve that!"

"You're right, Elion, but why not give her some time to get over this shock?"

Elion nodded thoughtfully, looking at the young man in shame. "She was right, you know, I was proud when I killed that man. I felt powerful and that scares me. But it's not for the reason she thinks. I was proud because I was able to protect her."

They were silent for a second.

"What else could I have done?" he asked hesitantly.

"Nothing. You did the right thing, and I will tell her that. In the meantime, I think it would be best if you stayed here while I try and talk to her."

The young man walked back to the other room, where he knelt next to Lumea to show her the weapon that Elion had found.

"That man was carrying this thing, and I'm sure he would have used it, too, if Elion hadn't been there. He did what he had to do. He saved your life, Lumea."

As his words sank in, she became calmer. He made her some more tea, and she held the cup in both hands, as if she were cold. She was terribly tired, but every time she closed her eyes she saw the eyes of the dead man and the way they had looked up at her from the floor. She wondered who he was, if he had a wife and kids who would now miss their father.

The other eyes she kept seeing were Elion's, and the look they had held at that moment. How could he just kill the man? Had there really been no other way? And how could a murder make him feel pride like that? Confusion, anger and sadness fought for emotional primacy in the whirlwind of her emotions, but in the end, sleep won out.

The next day she could think more clearly and she remembered everything that had happened. Her anger had not completely abated yet, even though she knew he had killed the man to protect her. His actions went against everything she had ever learned. When she sat up, she saw Elion smiling at her uncertainly. He got up, and she smiled back at him, though with less enthusiasm than before. Not knowing what to do with the situation, the elf sat back down.

"I hope you're not expecting my apologies, because I can't offer them," he finally said.

Lumea shrugged. "I have mourned all the dead people we have on our consciences, but I know why they had to die. This man was different, though. He did not seem like a threat. I was shocked to see you stab him."

Siard had also gotten up and came to stand next to her. Lumea looked at him.

Lumea said, "I know you were right, it was him or me. But that was still not the right way." Then she spoke to Elion again. "I will never forget him. Under any other circumstance he could have been a good person."

Elion nodded. "I will always remember him as well, Lumea." Getting up again, he walked over to the couch and stopped next to the woman. "I only wanted to protect you, and I was proud that I had done just that."

"I know, and I'm sorry I called you a... that I insulted you." She lightly touched his hand. "Thank you, Elion."

Even though the conversation had closed this episode between them, the tension did not dissipate so easily.

During breakfast they discussed their next course of action. They had been safe enough up until now, but the chance of getting caught had grown exponentially. Siard decided to go out and explore again, hoping to discover something that would be of some help them. As he wandered through underground rooms, his eye fell upon a large metal object, suspended from the ceiling with long cables. Walking around it, his hand drew a trail in the deep layer of dust. At the front of the thing there was a window, so he quickly wiped away the dust there to peer inside. In the dark he could just discern some instrument panels.

Walking around it again, he saw that it was shaped somewhat like an oblong fish. He concluded that it was a submarine, so he happily called the others to share in his discovery. They soon figured out how to open the door, and Siard climbed in to study the controls. He was confident that he would be able to make it work.

Some days earlier they had found a map, which they thought depicted a network of underground waterways. It had explained why Lumea had not felt the ground under her feet when she'd taken a swim on the first day. They had disregarded the map at first, because it did not have much use in the tunnels, but now they took it up again in order to try and decipher its meaning.

There were no words written upon it. All they could see were curved lines in different shades of blue. Here and there were numbers paired with arrows that pointed in different directions. There were also some green areas that seemed to indicate land, and each held symbols of varying sizes within. Lumea assumed that the size of the symbol had something to do with the importance of the place, but none of them knew what the symbols actually meant. Elion gave up, and Siard went to study the control panel again, but Lumea kept looking at the map. She had never been able to let a puzzle go unsolved, so she spent hours pouring over it. There were times when she folded it and tucked it into her belt, but it never left her thoughts for very long.

At the same time, Siard tried to get the submarine going. Studying and pressing buttons, he made lights turn on and off, or produced a buzzing noise, but otherwise he could not make the machine move.

Sometimes Elion sat with Siard in the cabin, though most of the time he walked around in the room, not knowing what else to do. He was often lost in deep thought, and Lumea assumed it still had to do with Gîsal. Once, when Elion withdrew into a different room, Lumea walked over to Siard.

"I'm worried about Elion. He seems conflicted by this Gîsal situation."

Siard shrugged, saying, "He has to judge Gîsal by his deeds, not his origin. For a long time he suspected that humans masterminded Hydhraga, but that was no reason for me to..."

Elion walked back in and Siard stopped talking.

"Oh, don't stop now, I've already heard enough." He sounded irritated.

Lumea walked over to him. "Siard is right, though. And it won't hurt to talk about it. I want to know whose side you're on, next time that we're in a fight."

"I think I've already proved that I'm on your side. You hardly thanked me for it last time."

Lumea closed her eyes. "That's not fair."

Siard spoke up in her defense, saying, "Then tell us what you're thinking, Elion. Do you think Gîsal is right to seek revenge or do you disapprove of his actions?"

"Gîsal should not have used those elves to his own ends. Now that he has, I don't feel connected with him in the least. He is my enemy."

"So why are you still thinking about it so much?" Lumea asked.

Elion turned to Lumea with an annoyed look in his eyes. "Why can't you ever just be happy with my answers? You seem to live in some kind of delusion that talking solves everything. Well, guess what, it doesn't. You're too young to realize that it only serves to rip open old wounds."

Now it was Lumea who could not hold back her anger. "Okay, so wallow in your grief and pain that you claim you don't feel. Try to solve everything by yourself, and, by all means, treat me like a child if that makes you feel better. I'll tell you what, though, as much as you keep telling me that I don't know anything, you don't know the first thing about me either. So I will forgive you for still despising me, even after everything that has happened here. I thought that I had proven myself worthy to you by now, but apparently I was wrong, since you're obviously still looking down upon me. I hope that one day you really will be as wise as you think you are now."

She turned on her heel furiously and left the room. Though she had gotten used to men thinking less of her because of her gender, it still rankled her that Elion was one of them. The elf looked at Siard questioningly, but the young man shook his head disapprovingly.

"She doesn't deserve your contempt, Elion. You need to decide who your friends are. Thinking about that might help you forget about those other things."

20

Lumea was hanging around in a corner of one of the rooms when she suddenly had an idea about the map. Grabbing a lamp, she got up and opened the door. Elion turned around and looked at her with raised eyebrows and a question in his eyes. She hesitated for a second before motioning for him to follow her. As usual, they had not spoken about their disagreements, and just as usual the tension between them remained palpable. On the other hand, she did not want to be alone after what had happened with the worker. Siard looked up to watch the door close behind the two of them. Then, he turned back to the control panel and hesitantly pushed a button. Nothing happened.

Lumea led Elion through rooms and stairways and into the large hall they had entered first, the one with the drawings on the walls. With the lamp held in between them, they studied them anew, closer than the first time. With one hand, the woman took a corner of the map, and when she waved it around, it unfolded. She pressed it against the wall and looked at Elion.

"I suspect that these drawings hide the key to the map. I think they were both created by the same person, or at least around the same time."

She turned back to the paintings and let her eyes wander over them. At times she was distracted by the image as a whole, but soon she found a symbol. On the biggest painting, the one with all the Thurancs, banners were depicted. One of the map's symbols matched the one on the banner, so she pointed it out to Elion. "That's where the Thuranc is."

The elf nodded in understanding, but as it turned out when he tried to help her, he had no aptitude for this kind of thing. He was distracted by the sight of her as she examined the wall, inch by inch. The lantern illuminated her face and her green eyes had an animated quality about them. It made the golden glow in her irises and the sheen of her tattoo more noticeable.

Now that she understood the way the map-maker thought, it did not take her long before she had deciphered the meaning of the other symbols. She discovered where the three of them were now. When she looked up from her studying, she noticed Elion looking at her with a smile on his face.

"What?" she asked, suddenly shy and self-conscious.

Elion just shrugged. He did not say anything. They walked back to Siard, where Lumea explained what she had discovered. Using the map and Lumea's explanation, they decided that they would go to the place where the Thuranc was. There was probably a dock there for the submarine, but when Siard suggested that there might be too many people there, they decided to land a little bit farther away.

Elion and Lumea remembered from the time they had seen it, that, next to the building, the forest stretched out towards the lake. They hoped to land where the two met without being seen. That's as far as their plan went, though. They were afraid to make any other plans, because for one they did not know what the weather was like out there, and for another they were probably expected, and the building was likely to be heavily guarded.

They were a bit hesitant to leave the safety of the mostly-deserted building behind, considering the danger they were certainly walking into, but there really was not much of a choice. They could not stay there forever, and the task they had in Hydrhaga was not yet finished. They decided to leave soon, because Lumea was not the only one who had solved her puzzle. Siard had figured out how the submarine worked too.

That same day, Elion and Siard moved every useful object they could find near the boat, and Lumea stacked them inside. They did not know how long the journey would take, so they took all the food that they could find. All of the bottles of antidote went in the stack, as well as the weapons that Elion had found somewhere. Lumea looked at them and chose one for herself, remembering how Ward had disarmed her back in the power plant. This way she would at least have a backup, just in case it happened again. Elion took a sword as well, because fighting with just bow and arrow was not always the preferred option.

They tried to postpone their departure as much as possible, but finally there was nothing left to do but to board the submarine and leave. Siard started the engines and opened the sluice gates, and they were pulled into the airlock by the cables that suspended the craft.

As soon as the gates closed behind them, water filled the chamber. Siard looked around expectantly. He had repaired the submarine here and there, but only now could he really find out if it was watertight. As the pressure on the hull increased, the boat creaked ominously. Lumea's heart drummed a frightened beat against her chest as the water level rose excruciatingly slow, but the hull held together. All the while, Siard kept his hand on the button that would stop the pumps.

When the room was filled to the rafters with water, the three passengers heard the muffled snap of the cables releasing. The second sluice gate opened and they silently moved out and into the depths of the lake. Siard maneuvered a bit to get the hang of the controls, and then they explored the silent, watery world around them. Lumea seemed to have interpreted the map correctly, so they steered toward their destination.

The vessel had a few windows, but the murky depths of the water let little light through. Lumea fell asleep to the soft rocking and monotonous buzzing of the submarine.

As soon as Siard picked out their course, Elion walked to the small room in the back of the boat and made a soft bed out of their mantles. Then he came back, lifted Lumea off her chair and carefully put her on it. She mumbled something in her sleep, but she did not wake up. The elf tucked her in and stood looking at her.

"Sleep tight, Lumea. You mean more to me than you realize."

Siard looked at Elion with a meaningful smile playing around his lips, though his companion studiously avoided his gaze.

"You're finally beginning to appreciate her," Siard said.

At those words, Elion did look back. He said, "I think that, deep down, I have for a long time. What you said really made me think, and when we were looking at the painting I remembered the first impromptu party she organized. She was positively aglow, and suddenly she began to sing. Everyone was listening breathlessly. It was... enchanting." Elion smiled. "You know... it was in that moment that I decided that I couldn't leave her behind."

"It's good that you didn't. She has played a big role in the way our search has gone."

"Yes, I'm finally beginning to realize that." Then the elf pointed at the buttons in front of them. "Now, suppose you tell me how to steer this thing."

When Lumea woke up, she was surprised to find herself tucked in among the cloaks. Since it was comfortable, though, she refused to get up. She suspected that Elion had placed her there. He always took care of her as much as possible, including that day he had killed the worker. For the first time, she really knew why he had looked so proud. He had been relieved that he had been there in time. She had not considered that he might have been afraid for her, back then. Lumea was ashamed to admit that she had hated him for his actions, and he had not been furious about that, just... disappointed. They had never talked it through, and all they seemed to do was to add insult to injury. And now she had no idea how to bring it up again.

When she realized how a warm feeling of affection spread out from her heart when she thought about the elf, a slow blush crept upon her features. The thought took her by surprise, because he had many exasperating traits with which she found hard to come to terms. Nevertheless, she understood those as well. Despite everything she had learned about Elion, she could still only guess at some of the horrors he had experienced. It had made him seem indifferent, hard, and even callous. She knew that he fought for the things he believed in, and he protected everything that was important to him. She was proud to know that she belonged in that category.

This new feeling made her uncertain, though. They still had a battle left to fight here in Hydrhaga. Giving in to love would make everything harder. What if something happened to him? Lumea knew all too well that the lives of all three of them were at stake here, so she quickly shoved the thought out of her mind.

Her thoughts would only keep mulling around in the same circles if she stayed in bed, so she got up and made her way to the fore of the submarine. Siard was bent over the controls, and Elion half-turned toward her. She nodded as a sign that she had slept wonderfully, so he turned his attention back to Siard, who was explaining the last things he needed to know about the control panel.

It had taken Elion quite a while to really get the hang of steering the submarine. To Siard, who had been interested in mechanics since childhood, it was second nature. Elion, on the other hand, could barely remember even the most simple things about the craft, and the young man had despaired of ever teaching the elf the ropes. After a lot of practice, though, Elion could at least keep their course steady.

Siard steered the boat towards their final destination, which was relatively simple by this point—just keep going—so he left the task to Elion. He walked to the back room, and Lumea, who was afraid to be alone with Elion, followed him. The feelings that had awoken within her were still too fresh for comfort.

"Can you tell how long we'll be underwater?" she asked, more to break the silence than anything. Then she realized how stupid of a question it really was.

"Probably about two days, though I'm not entirely sure."

They were silent for a moment. Then Lumea continued, "Are you afraid?"

"Yes, of course," Siard answered, a bit uneasily. "We've been through a lot already, but I think the path ahead is still fraught with danger." He took a moment to gather his thoughts, then said, "When we first met, we hardly knew each other. Even Elion and I were more of acquaintances than friends. Now, I think we are closer. That doesn't make any of this easier."

Lumea stared at him. Had he just read her mind or did he really mean what he said?

Seeing her expression, Siard laughed aloud. "Of course, it might make things a bit easier, as well. We have an added impetus to fight."

"Losing you would be unbearable."

"Losing both of us? Or just Elion?" Siard asked.

Lumea looked at him with wide eyes. "Siard, I would be horrified if you died!"

"I'm just teasing, Lumea. I'm glad you're not angry with him any more. I know he's not always the easiest person to live with, but he really does care about you."

"I know, and I appreciate that."

"So why don't you tell him that? This fight between you has been going on for long enough. The trust between you has been lost, to a certain extent. But it would do him good to hear you say it."

"I don't know what to tell him."

"There's nothing wrong with just saying what you feel for him. His answer might surprise you."

Lumea blushed and looked down. "Is it that obvious?"

Siard laughed again. "It is to me." He placed an arm around her shoulder. "But to return to your first question... We'll be all right."

He was not sure if he could believe his own words, though. Taking some more food, he walked back to Elion and gave it to him. Lumea took a seat behind the two men.

As the days went by and they came closer to their destination, they became more nervous. They were expecting a fight pretty much as soon as they set foot on land.

Siard decided to explore the surface above. Using the periscope, he calculated their position. He could see the place where the forest's edge touched the lake, but there were no humans in sight. The weather was still rough and unpredictable, the waves coming up high and crashing down, and he spotted several waterspouts.

The submarine rocked dangerously, so they had to hold on tight. On the horizon, Siard could see clouds racing past, fluctuating in shape at an tremendous speed. The sun was hidden behind them, but he guessed that it was late afternoon.

Suddenly, the wind changed direction and the boat made a sharp turn. Lumea was thrown across the cabin. Waves were pulling at the submarine as if to lift it up out of the water. Siard dove back down into the depths, where they were safe from the waves.

Lumea scrambled back up. Looking at her, Siard said, "We will stay at this depth until we reach the dock, then we go straight up. I hope we will come out just right. Then we'll unload our gear and hide it. It will be difficult with this weather, but..."

It looked like he wanted to say something more, but he did not.

Lumea could guess his unspoken words, though. There was a very likely possibility that as soon as they reached the surface, the waves would catch them and smack them against the shore.

"I think you had better get some rest, then, Siard. You'll have enough to do when that time comes. I'll manage the submarine for now," Elion said.

Siard nodded and disappeared into the back room. Lumea got up as well and sat down in the chair next to Elion's. He kept staring through the window, into the dark of the water, as if all kinds of interesting things were going on there. Now and then he looked at the control panel, but never at her. It had been like that for days, and Lumea hated it. She remembered her conversation with Siard, but she was still hesitant.

"Elion..."

He looked at her without any change of expression. She still did not know which words to use that could summarize her feelings. The tension between them could be sliced with a dagger, though. When Lumea didn't continue, Elion turned back to the control panel.

With a treacherous catch in her voice, Lumea said softly, "I hate the way we're treating each other..."

There was so much more she wanted to say. She wanted to impart how grateful she was and how she felt about him, but the words would not come. When Elion looked at her again, his eyes showed the relief he felt.

"You were avoiding me so much, I was afraid you were still angry with me."

She shook her head. "Quite the contrary."

He watched her thoughtfully, until his look turned suddenly ashamed. "I couldn't even blame you, you know. I said many things that you didn't deserve, Lumea. You stood up to me and forced me to acknowledge my feelings. After everything that has happened here in Hydrhaga, though, so many more emotions came to the surface. It was far easier to be angry with you than to feel them. I know it wasn't the right way, but maybe the fact that I let in that one feeling says quite a lot already." Silence followed his words, until he whispered, looking the other way, "This is coming out all wrong, like usual."

Lumea shook her head. "I know exactly how you feel. It's easy to be hard on the people closest to you because you know they will understand. You don't have to hesitate around the people you love, you can speak your mind. At least, that's how it works for me. I said more than I normally would, but that's because I like you, very much. I thought we were more than friends. We know we can depend on each other, and with everything else that has happened... I thought we were equals."

A smile lit up his face. "We are, Lumea."

Another silence ensued, but then Lumea shyly looked up at him, sighing a little. "Why is it so much easier to blame than to give a compliment? Why can't I just say that I think you're special?"

Elion's eyes shone. "You really think so?"

She nodded.

He tenderly touched her cheek. "I think the same of you."

21

Once the submarine reached the place where they suspected the dock was located, Lumea rose to wake Siard. He took the controls again and brought the ship to the surface. The higher they rose, the more the waves tugged at the submersible. Lumea grabbed hold of her chair. For a moment it seemed as though the lake's depths refused to surrender the submarine, but then it shot to the surface like a cork, where a wave caught it and dragged it a few yards to the side. Siard started the rotors and tried to find hold on the water.

The dock was about a hundred yards to their left, though the heavy rain prevented Siard from seeing anything. He had to trust to his instincts and his instruments. He fought the water for every turn of the propeller, but the engines were powerful enough. They slowly moved towards the dock, that is, until the storm intensified in a matter of moments. New waves pummeled the submarine, but in spite of Siard's efforts to try and dive back down, it was too late. A large wave caught the submarine at its crest and tossed it forward into a gale. For a brief moment the ship seemed to float like a feather, and then the wind died down again as quickly as it had appeared. The boat smashed onto the dock, tossing its passengers across the cabin and ripping it open by the sheer force of the impact.

A sharp pain dragged Elion back to consciousness. With difficulty, he sat up, and the pain in his side flared. The cabin was in a jumble, what was left of it, anyway. They had stacked as much of their stuff as they could in the small back room, but the fall had thrown everything forward and damaged many items. Everywhere around him he could see wood and metal. Plates from the ceiling had come loose and thick glass windows that could withstand the pressures of depth were dashed to smithereens. Lumea lay not far from him, trapped beneath a heavy metal plate. He helped her out from under it before checking on Siard, who was lying motionless, his head resting on the control panel. He had a large wound on his forehead. Elion carefully lifted him and carried him outside, and Lumea followed with their mantles.

Not far from the lake they found a deep pit that was mostly covered by the roots of a tree. Elion brought Siard into it and started tending his head wound. Lumea stood watching for a time, but as there was nothing she could do to help, she returned to the wreck and attempted to salvage as much gear as possible. Everything that had even a remote chance of usefulness she took to their hiding place. On her last trip she put aside a large piece of canvas which had at some point been used in the construction of the submarine. Then she started to clean up their landing place. She threw the wreckage back into the lake, even the biggest parts she towed towards the water and pushed into its depths. All that was left when she was done were a few pieces of wood and metal, which looked like they had been thrown onto the dock separately. Hopefully, anyone who came past would think that the sub had been wrecked while out on the lake and that the three of them had drowned. Lumea was satisfied with her work.

The last thing she did was to wipe out thier tracks. The rain had intensified, and the streaming water had turned the ground into mud, which helped her task tremendously. Then she took the canvas and made her way back to the tree under which they were hiding, wiping out their tracks as she went.

Elion was still busy taking care of Siard, who had yet to regain consciousness. Lumea was afraid to say anything, but the elf looked at her and silently shrugged his shoulders, the uncertainty clearly visible in his eyes. The rain began to seep through the tree's leaves, so Lumea took the canvas and spread it out over the top of the pit to provide at least a modicum of shelter against the elements. In an attempt to make the canvas less conspicuous, she littered the top of it with branches and leaves. There were more than enough of those, having been ripped from the trees by the raging winds. She stayed near their hiding place, afraid of leaving tracks which could lead to their discovery. Still, she hoped that it would be enough to keep anyone from finding their shelter unless they knew what they were looking for. Drenched to the bone, she went back inside. She stripped off her wet clothes and wrapped her cloak tightly around her in an effort to get warm.

Elion was sitting on the ground next to Siard. There was nothing more he could do. Lumea sat down opposite him and shivered.

"Are you cold?"

She nodded. Elion took his own cape and put it over her shoulders. He then looked up at the canvas and nodded approvingly.

"You were gone for some time, that last time you returned to the wreck."

Lumea told him about her attempts to make it look like an accident on the lake.

"Oh, that was very clever," Elion said. "Well done!"

The compliment made her blush, and she was glad that the canvas colored everything green, sparing her embarrassment from scrutiny. She was sure Siard would have done the same thing with their shelter, but since he could not, she had taken the duty upon herself. Looking at his still form, she hoped that they would not be found. He was going to need time in order to recover.

Taking turns, Elion and Lumea guarded the young man's body. As the days passed, the weather seemed to quiet, though there were still moments when it stormed heavily. Siard's condition did not improve.

During the lonely hours while it was her turn to watch, Lumea relived the time she had spent with her grandmother in her imagination. She managed to forget for a little while where she was when she heard the woman's voice again. "A very, very long time ago, when there were no humans, the world consisted only of water. The Creator rose up out of the depths and shaped the land and the sky, the animals and the plants, and finally mankind, first the woman and then the man."

The memory was so real that the old woman seemed to be sitting next to her, and she listened to the familiar voice. Of course, she knew the story. It had been the first story the woman had ever imparted to her, explaining how the world had been created. It was the first story that Lumea could remember, though many more had followed. Lumea listened attentively, when she suddenly realized that the voice she was hearing was her own. Lost in the memory, she had unconsciously imitated her grandmother's voice, dusting off the old words as she retold the tale. She suddenly laughed aloud, but Siard, her only audience, remained still.

The Omnesian, as down-to-earth as he was, always approached things scientifically, like his father had. He said the earth had started because of something he called the big bang, after which matter evolved into the world they knew. Animals, and even humans, existed purely because of chance. Lumea did not understand his viewpoint. The concept of chance did not play any part in her world, whereas Siard did not believe at all in her concept of destiny. A long time ago, or so it seemed now, when they had sat around the campfire, she had noticed how their views on the world were quite almost polar opposites, and here she was, telling him the story of Creation, and he could not talk back. If he had been conscious, he would have never taken her seriously.

Her laughter passed, making way for grief. She realized that, like Siard, she herself had not always shown respect for the lessons that her grandmother had been trying to teach her. She had not immediately taken to her grandmother's faith, and she had not always respected the old woman's opinions. Only now did she realize just how valuable those lessons had been, and how she turned to them for support in such a chaotic world. She was sure she had hurt the old woman very much, but that knowledge came too late. Her grandmother was many years dead.

Lumea had been upset by her passing, because she had really loved her grandmother. She hoped that if the wise old lady could see her now that she would be proud. The young woman felt the tears stream down her face, but when Elion woke up, she quickly wiped them away, even though they probably were not visible in the darkness.

Some time later, Lumea decided to tell Elion about her Ankéabi vision. Much had happened here in Hydrhaga that she was uncomfortable with and she hoped that the elf could help her straighten out her thoughts. The primary reason for telling him, though, was a need for him to understand her reaction on the day he had killed the worker. They had more or less made up after that fight, but she still wanted him to understand her anger.

"Elion."

The elf looked up immediately at the earnestness that her voice carried.

"I would like to tell you what I saw during my Ankéabi."

"I am honored. I know you wouldn't tell me if you didn't trust me."

Lumea nodded and Elion waited for her story.

"The day the Kunci knocked on the door of my parents' house, the weather was lovely. It was a warm, spring morning. From my room, through my open window, I could see how my father opened the door for them. When I heard them talking about me, my heart filled with joy. I had been waiting for this day for a long time, the day my Ankéabi would begin. Soon enough, my father opened the door to my room and I followed him without a word. When the Wise Women took me between them, I did not look back, though I knew that my mother had come to stand beside my father. She had some trouble accepting that I had to go. She thought I was too young.

When we reached the edge of the village, I was blindfolded, and we started the long trek to the temple. It's really harder than it sounds to trust the people who are guiding you, if you can't see the road ahead with your own eyes. I tripped over roots and stones, but my guides never let me fall, and they warned me when the terrain became rough. I felt helpless, like a newborn babe who depends solely upon others to care for it, a whelp whose eyes have yet to open, for whom each and every sound is new.

"When we came to the temple, the blindfold was taken away. Before my eyes had time to adjust to the bright light, the Kunci had left. I looked around. The temple was built upon a rocky outcropping, jutting out severely from the mountainside. There was no path from there to the top, because the side of the mountain was too sheer. I turned my back to the mountain and looked to the right. The forest that spread out over the mountain started almost next to the temple.

"The edge of the forest was close by, and under the trees it was dark and foreboding. I didn't like the look of it, so I looked before me. There was a wide vista there. I walked to the edge of the rock and looked down. Far down below, I could see a river. The sky was clear and the view magnificent, but though the landscape fascinated me, it did not feel like the right direction for my Ankéabi.

"Then finally, to the left, I could see the mountain sloping gently away. Its base was littered with rocks, and here and there were bushes growing among them. It was a neat, tidy view, and it comforted me, for some reason. I sat down, facing in that direction.

"Immediately, a strange feeling came over me. This was the place where my future would be decided. I was excited, but at the same time I was incredibly nervous, afraid that I wouldn't understand the message of the gods, or worse, that they would not send a message at all. I tried to bury that feeling and put my trust in the gods, but I still couldn't help thinking that maybe my mother was right and I was too young for the trial."

As she talked about the landscape, she tried to think of the right words to use. She wanted to describe it as best as she could, for as unbelievable as the events were, they were completely real to her. How would Elion react when she explained her vision to him? She took a drink and continued.

"It was around noon on the second day when Wolf came to me. I did not feel afraid when he approached me. He sat down in front of me, and I knelt down to him. He licked at his coat, and I waited, not moving. Then, he spoke, and I could hear the authority in his voice.

"'Girl, I brought you a present. Sit down and listen to what I have to tell you.'

"I obeyed, and when I sat down again, I saw the sword that Wolf had put down in front of him. I looked into his golden eyes and waited for him to speak. He chose his words carefully, and because of that he spoke slowly.

"'Girl, it is not safe to be out tonight. There is a demon on the loose and he wishes to destroy our world. You are part of this world, and therefore you will be subject to the same fate. It might be wise to turn around and flee. You have that choice. Not a soul would blame you, because it is likely to be the best choice. Should you choose to stay, however, I give you this sword, so that you may defend yourself.'

"Then, he stood up and calmly left the rocky outcrop, and I saw how his thick fur waved with every step that he took. I stayed behind, alone.

"When the sun had set and darkness fell, I felt decidedly uncomfortable. I had the feeling that a thousand eyes were watching me. Bats kept swooping down over my head, and in my fear I remembered that bats were omens of death, but I forgot that they were also a sign of a new beginning. What was I to do? Go back and not finish my Ankéabi, or stay and defy whatever came to me this night? I decided to stay. If I went back now, I would never get another chance, and I wanted this more than anything. I banned the fear from my heart and just waited for whatever would come."

The young woman sighed.

"Suddenly I heard a snarl, like that of a wild animal, and I saw a creature—half-man, half-beast—come up the mountainside. I don't know how else to describe the thing, as any animal that I could compare it with would be insulted by the association. I felt his malice; he had no purpose but to destroy. His bloodshot eyes peered at me and I felt a cold chill shoot down my spine. I decided to kneel again. The demon laughed at me.

"'You came to honor the gods, and instead you kneel to me? You fool, soon this world will be destroyed and my own will overtake it. Your Ankéabi is meaningless. You should have left when you had the chance, for now it is too late.'

"The thing attacked me, with claws outstretched and its maw opened wide. I dodged the attack and drew the sword that Wolf had left for me. Again he came at me with agile movements, attacking unpredictably, because one moment he moved slowly and the next he was as quick as lightning. All the time he spoke, telling me how he would destroy the world, and how he had the power to do so. His voice was calm, controlled, hypnotic. What had I gotten myself into?

"That question made me realize that all this had been my own choice. Wolf had warned me. I could have rung the bell. I had chosen not to do that, so I had to bear out the consequences. I had to stop this demon or I would die. His next attack missed, and he stood with his back turned toward me, so instead of waiting for him to come at me again, I attacked him instead, and my sword found the mark. I managed to wound him, though he dodged most of my follow-up attacks. The fight was slowly draining me of endurance, whereas my opponent showed no sign of tiring. He flung me backward, and I felt the air rush from my lungs when I slammed against a pillar of the temple."

In the moment's pause that followed, Lumea swallowed audibly. Elion was listening attentively.

"In that instant, I knew it was over. Fear of death crept through my body, paralyzing me. The demon approached slowly, and his grin was wide enough to bare all his teeth. He bent over me and pushed me against the pillar. I smelled death in his breath, a musty stench like stagnant water. It made me nauseous. I felt his teeth pressing into my neck, I actually heard my skin being pierced and felt hot blood running down onto my shoulders. He was going to rip my neck open like the lions do with their prey.

"How long would the Kunci take before they came for me if I didn't ring the bell? And how would they find me? Would I look maimed or would it seem like I had passed away from hunger and thirst?

"I felt panic at first, but then my head cleared suddenly, and I regained control of my body. Using all of my strength, I pushed the demon away, braced against the pillar. He rolled back to the edge of the rock. I used his momentary confusion to grab my sword. The battle had suddenly turned in my favor. I was the one bending over him, my sword at the ready. All I had to do to kill him was lower it. He dared me to do it, and the contempt was clear in his eyes. Instead of killing him, though, I took a step back, though I didn't lower the sword. He sat up, hesitantly, and I said, 'Tell me, why do you want to destroy this world? Why can't there be a place for you to live alongside everything else? There has to be a way for everyone to live together.'

"It said, 'Kill me. If you don't, you will die in shame and you'll be responsible for the demise of the gods. You have the fate of the world in your hands. Kill me, or I will kill you.'

"'No, you won't. I'm not afraid of you.'

"I felt a new kind of power rise within me. I knew he could not harm me.

"I told him, 'I will not kill you, and most certainly not because you're telling me to. Nobody will die tonight. This world will be like it once was: a peaceful place, with room for everyone.'

"The demon laughed at me, but then the tone of his laughter changed."

Lumea's voice changed as well, it sounded proud now, full of awe.

"Its voice sounded chipper. Before me, in the blink of an eye, Eagle was sitting where once had been a demon. It took me by surprise. Eagle is the most important messenger of the gods. I bowed to him and didn't dare move. I felt his hand lift up my chin. It was warm and soft, like down, and when I looked into his yellow eyes I saw the proud glow in his deep, black pupils. He had changed form, and instead of a bird I saw a man, though wings came from out of his back and his legs were still those of a bird's.

"He said to me, 'Sit down, my lady. I want to look into your face. You did a good job here. It required courage and faith, faith in the gods, but more importantly, faith in yourself.'

"I sat cross-legged and looked at him. I couldn't keep my eyes off of him. There was such a sense of... calm... emanating from him. Different hues of blue swirled around him. The movements of his hands punctuated his words, while his wings rustled in the wind. His voice was like the lulling sound of the sea. Calm and soothing.

"He said, 'I am glad of the choice you made. If you had killed me, you would have learned a different lesson, but now you can learn something truly valuable.

"'You chose the way of peace, and that is often the hardest way. It may seem like soldiers have courage, because they go out to fight, but they hide behind their weapons and other people's orders. The truly courageous one is the person who approaches the other with an open heart, because they dare to work to change the world into one where people can live together, in peace.'

"I felt so proud about the compliment that Eagle had bestowed upon me. I had passed his test. I listened to his words very carefully. After a while he stood up.

"He said, 'Come, Bringer of Peace, climb on my back. I will show you this world.'

"He changed back into a bird and I did as he told. As the rising sun painted the skies, he showed me the world of the gods. It was marvelous. A warm wind caressed my face and I could see fields of flowers and fast-flowing rivers stretching out below us. Sometimes other birds flew with us, and every creature we came across greeted us warmly. Eagle gave me my new name, 'Bringer of Peace Among the People', and it was repeated everywhere, by all of the animals. We flew during the days and nights, and I saw Wolf nodding proudly at me. At the end of the fourth day, Eagle flew up to great heights and there, hidden amongst the clouds, on the top of the biggest mountain I had ever seen, stood the palace of the gods. I can't begin to describe how beautiful it was to behold. Then, Eagle brought me back to the temple, bid me farewell and flew away without me. It was then I rang the bell."

Silence followed the end of her story. Not knowing what to say, Elion took her hands. During her story her voice had changed its pitch all the time. When she talked about the demon, it quivered, communicating the fear she had felt during that moment to the listening elf. Then she told him about the flight on the Eagle's back, and she had started talking louder, in more of a sing-song and rapid tone. Not once had she looked at Elion, and even now she was still staring off into space. After a moment she did look at him, and a shadow passed over her face while tears welled in her eyes. She tried to swallow back the tears.

"Everything that happened here in Hydrhaga... did I do right?" The words came out like a stutter. She clenched her fists, closing her fingers over Elion's hands.

"The gods showed me a path, but am I still walking on it? Or did I get lost somewhere along the way? Do I bring shame to my name? Is there something I could have done to stop all those people from being killed? Am I disappointing the gods? It's so hard to fulfill their expectations, and most of the time I'm not even completely sure of what they want from me."

Her head dropped, and her shoulders began to shake as she cried. Elion let go of her hands to put his arms around her. He drew her close.

"Lumea, I don't know the answer to your questions, but I can tell you what I know, what I've learned from experience. There are times when you just can't do without weapons. These people blindly follow their leader. They won't be swayed by any passing opinions. The demon in your vision only started listening when you had power over him. That was the moment you pulled back and left the choice to him. It will go exactly like that here. As long as this world exists, the people will hold on to their own ideas and values. Things can only change when their leaders no longer makes their decisions for them."

Elion stroked her back as he spoke. "You're wondering if you're not taking the easy route of which Eagle spoke, but from the moment we fled, your road has been anything but easy. I forced you to follow me. You didn't come blindly, without asking questions. You doubted what Siard and I were doing up until you saw the proof that we were right. Only then did you decide that my path was worth fighting for, dying for.

"I'm convinced you are following the path of your vision. Eagle's lesson is obvious in every step that you take.

"And now I really understand why you were so angry with me when I killed that man. I wonder now if *I* did the right thing. Perhaps we could have convinced him and he would have helped us. It was a reflex. I've been hunted for so long that violence is the only way I know to protect the people I love. That's still no excuse for the way things went. I can't turn it back, but your sharing your vision with me is a gift, because you taught me the lessons you learned."

Lumea was relieved that he understood her.

Elion felt her calm down with every breath, and he continued, "Do you remember what you told me underneath the willow? About why the elves had forgiven the humans, or why else would they allow themselves to be treated like that? It's that same peaceful road. That is not something the gods taught you, it's always been inside of you. The gods only clarified it for you."

He was silent for a moment, but when she kept crying he tried to find more words to comfort her.

"And here I was, thinking you couldn't teach me anything because I was far older than you and so much more experienced."

This made Lumea laugh. She sat up and looked at him. He had

told her what she wanted to hear, even though she had known it all along.

"Thank you, Elion."

"I should be the one thanking you. It's very special that you wanted to share your vision with me."

While they talked about Lumea's Ankéabi, she noticed how he kept rubbing over the scars on his hand.

"Do they bother you much?" she asked softly.

He looked at her uncomprehendingly.

"Your hand..."

He studied it for a moment, because he had not realized that he had been rubbing it. "It's stiff, and there are times that it hurts quite badly. Usually I use an ointment to keep the tissue flexible, but unfortunately I don't have any with us."

Lumea took his hand carefully in hers and massaged his wrist. When she was done she ripped a bit of cloth from her skirt and drenched it in water. She secured it around his hand and wrist. The coolness alleviated the pain only a little, but it was all she could do for the moment.

22

Lumea left their hiding place late in the afternoon in order to seek out some plants that she thought must certainly grow in the area. She had seen Dark Cranesbill growing under a nearby tree, its buds on the verge of bloom. It had miraculously survived the sudden shifts in the weather. Plucking off the buds, she muttered, "Cranesbill, please give me your buds, and let me help Elion with their healing power."

She made sure to leave enough buds on the plant so that it would survive to bloom again. Once she had collected them, she decided to go farther from the hiding place than she had dared before. She had to if she wanted to find the other plants that she needed, which she knew grew on open plains. Before leaving the safety of the trees and stepping out into the field, she looked around carefully, ready to turn back at the first sign of their pursuers. There were no humans in sight, though, so she took the risk. She kept a watchful eye on her surroundings, while the other eye scanned the different plants growing in the field. At times she bent over and rubbed a finger over green leaves, but they were not the plants she was seeking.

Then her heart leaped when she spotted a few Aloe Vera plants growing close to each other. That was exactly what she needed! Again she asked the plants for their permission, like her grandmother had taught her, before cutting a couple of the fleshy leaves. The juices immediately dripped out, so she quickly turned them upside down in order to preserve the precious liquid. Then her eye fell on a low plant growing next to the Aloe. When she rubbed it, it spread out an overpoweringly fresh scent.

It was the last ingredient she needed, a mint, so when she had picked it and added it to her growing supplies she turned back towards their hiding place. It was nearly nightfall by the time she got back. Elion made a remark about how he had hardly seen her all afternoon. She answered that she had needed some breathing space, though she did not tell him exactly what she had been doing.

That night, while Elion was asleep and Lumea was watching over Siard, she squeezed the juice from the Aloe leaves into an empty bowl that she had salvaged from the wreck. When they were empty, she added some of the leaf tissue and created a paste that could be used as a poultice. She chewed the buds of the geranium and the leaves of the mint to a pulp, adding both to the paste. Rubbing it between two fingers, she nodded, satisfied with the result. Then she ripped another band of cloth from her dwindling underskirt, neatly rolled it up and put it next to the bowl, in a corner of the hiding place that the lantern's light did not reach.

When Elion woke up the following morning, she reached out and took his hand. She noticed how he hesitated, though he did not pull back.

"Please be careful, it's really hurting again."

She nodded comfortingly and took up the bowl with the ointment. She applied a thick layer of it on the scar tissue, covering it so that it had a chance to soak in. Elion was obviously surprised.

"Where did you get that?"

"I made it last night, from the plants that I gathered yesterday. It's made mostly from Aloe Vera; it will make your skin less dry and tight."

"It's soothing, too."

"That's because of the mint I added. And the geranium buds will hopefully make the stiffness subside. It's the best I could do, considering. I hope it works."

The ointment proved powerful, and around the same time, Siard's status began to improve. His wounds were healing, and every now and then he moved. Lumea was relieved that he was not lying so motionless any more. They started talking to him, but it was some time before his situation improved further.

One morning, Lumea was awoke by Elion, who was talking loudly. When she sat up, she saw the elf sitting on his knees next to Siard, addressing him earnestly. The woman came closer and saw that the young man's eyes were open. He looked dazed, Elion's words did not seem to register and his eyes were glazed over. All day long Lumea and Elion tried to get through to him, but improvement was slow.

At one point he actually seemed to see them, but he did not really react. Sometimes his eyes were closed for a while, but only when he was slept did Elion and Lumea stop talking to him.

After a long time he was able to sit up by himself and eat, but he remained in a fugue-like state. Lumea was glad that he was improving but she had not imagined that things could be quite this bad. She was worried about how they could go on. How much more would he improve? Their quest was hard enough without an injured man, and yet they could hardly leave him behind, could they? She tried to find clues about what they were to do in Elion's face, but it was etched with worry as well.

Then, unexpectedly, the healing process leaped forward. As Lumea sat in the dark, she heard a voice.

"I'm... thirsty."

The voice startled her, it was not Elion's and it had been ages since she had last heard Siard speak.

Only when she heard "thirsty..." again did she jump up and light the lantern, quickly grabbing the water bag. Siard was sitting up and he took the bag with a grateful nod. Lumea watched fearfully while he took a sip, as she held the bag for him.

"Do you know where you are? Who you are?"

He thought for a second, but his answer was certain. "Siard. I'm in Hydrhaga."

"And do you remember what happened?"

"Boat... smashed... on shore."

Convinced that everything would now be all right, she laughed exuberantly. She gave Siard a hug. Still not fully recovered, he could only put a weak arm around her shoulders.

"Is there anything else I can do for you?" she asked.

He shook his head and lay back down. The woman tucked him in and soon he was asleep again. Then Lumea turned towards Elion, wondering what to do. He was sleeping peacefully, but he had been worried about Siard as well, so she woke him up. Elion was relieved when she told him what had happened.

From that moment on, Siard's condition improved rapidly. He refused help, though in the beginning he was very shaky on his legs. He wanted to know everything that had happened after the wreck, and though there was not much to tell, he praised Lumea's inventiveness. He was also the first to remark that it was a pity they had lost the boat as he had hoped to use it during their probable flight, but that was out of the question now. Elion and Lumea had not thought about that yet, for they had been too worried about their companion.

Not long afterward, the majority of Siard's strength was regained, and they decided to move through the forest. As soon as they reached the forest's edge, on the side of the Thuranc's building, they would decide what to do. At the same time it was a test to see how hard Siard could push himself. There was no trouble, and he seemed to be very much like his old self again. All there was to remind them of his condition was the bright red scar on his forehead.

The following day they stood at the edge of the field that they had to cross to reach the building. Gulls had taken over Hydrhaga, showing off their acrobatics as they floated on the howling wind, which muted their screeching calls. In front of them they saw the heart of Hydrhaga rising up from the plane. It looked vaguely like a fortress, with a large central dome, on top of which a tattered banner flapped in the wind.

They saw the building as the sun set behind them, stretching their shadows on the path before them. The afternoon was running on its last legs. They decided to risk the crossing since the first part of their journey would be concealed by the greenery.

Night had truly set in and a veritable choir of crickets was producing an entire symphony by the time they reached the lower grass. As they neared the building's perimeter, they were startled by a guard dog. The animal barked once but he was quickly silenced by Siard's dagger. The three of them stayed quiet for a while, tensed, as they expected a guard to have heard the noise, yet nobody came. They pressed on, only this time they were more cautious. Behind a stained glass window they could see the silhouettes of men moving about. They angled left in order to avoid passing too close to the window. Their nerves were stretched taught, slowing their movement to a crawl.

Finally, they reached the building proper, near a large, unlit window. Elion quietly opened the window and slipped through. He soon returned and helped the other two inside. The first part of their mission was a success.

23

The Hosts were extremely worried when they failed to find the fugitives. Some of them struggled through the worst possible weather for days on end, while others pretended they were too busy perfecting the Thuranc. They were slowly starting to believe that the three really had died out there. The Swintheri were growing exhausted, so Gîsal pulled them back before they became completely useless. He increased the amount of guards around the laboratories, certain that at some point the three would show up near one. The rest of Hydrhaga was slowly cleared of all activity, so it did not really matter to him what they discovered there. His priority now was to make his army. He wanted his revenge.

Host and soldier alike were relieved when they heard the new orders. They had not relished being out there in small groups, where they could be ambushed at any moment. Now the Swintheri could just sit and wait for the runaways to come to them, and they felt safer in the large group. The Hosts returned to their easy lives.

The number of guests in Hydrhaga rapidly dwindled as well. Large groups of them were led to the laboratories for all kinds of tests. Gîsal could be found there every day, although he did spend a lot of time with Ward, who seemed to know whenever his visitor was there. The leader's presence confused him, and the fear was evident in his eyes. There were times when he had tried slipping out of bed, which only resulted in his crashing to the floor, screaming in fear and pain. Gîsal usually enjoyed the enormous power he had over Ward's mind, but today, he was in a great mood. After all the worries from the past few weeks, the tide was turning in his favor, and that made him happy.

"We're almost ready, Ward. The researchers tell me that the Thuranc is greatly improving. It looks as though, very soon now, it will be the soldier that I had in mind. Although there were times when it seemed like all of this would amount to nothing, my army is now reaching its completion. Maybe it was meant to be, after all."

Gîsal bent towards the Host and whispered, "There were many times I regretted having to find my stock from elsewhere, but the Omnesians grew too suspicious. They didn't want to come any more. Perhaps my decision to send invitations to the more eastern countries was not such a bad one after all. This Lumea woman started all of the trouble, but now I feel that I should be grateful to her. Without her, the Thuranc would not have been finished so soon."

When he sat back up, his cheerful laughter bounced around the small room.

"To think that the day I've been living towards for so long is finally at hand!"

He then looked back at Ward. The man had admittedly made many mistakes, but in the end those mistakes had sped up the research more than any other variable, and now he was lying here in a hospital bed, with his gaunt cheeks and dry lips. Gîsal put a careful arm around Ward's shoulder and helped him into an upright position. The Host started to panic, but Gîsal shushed him.

"It's okay, I won't harm you. Let me help you."

As soon as the man was sitting up, the leader took the glass of water that stood on a side table and brought it to Ward's lips. The Host drank deeply. When the glass was empty, Gîsal put it back and tenderly wiped the spilled water from the man's chin. Then he helped him to lie back down and tucked him in.

In a confidential tone of voice he continued his story. There was no bitterness as he looked back on his past.

"All I ever wanted in my life, I had in Arminath. I wanted it to be a city that the elves could be proud of. A center of knowledge, where every skill reached its apex of potential, a place where everyone could develop as the gods wished. That was my dream. As magistrate, I was closely connected to the daily governance of the city. My riches made many changes possible. In turn, the elves thanked me by electing me to the office of senator, time and again. I could complete the reformations that I had started. Whenever I walked through the streets I saw the prosperity that I had brought to my people. They surrounded themselves with things as beautiful as they were."

He was silent for a moment as he stared into his memory.

"But there was nothing more beautiful than her. She meant everything to me, my fiancé. I was overwhelmingly, intensely happy
whenever she was near. We knew so many beautiful moments together. With her, I could forget the world around us. She was the
most beautiful creature I had ever known, and not just physically.
Her heart was pure, and it had chosen me to love. I saw her every
day, and we'd meet near one of the fountains and dream of our future
together. We walked through the streets of the city and barely noticed
the rain falling upon us."

With a smile playing around his lips he looked at Ward again.

"Very soon now, everything will go back to the way it used to be.
Once Omnesia falls, I will find the right place to build a new city. I
will try to capture my love's beauty within it, so that this new city will
be even more beautiful than Arminath ever was. The elves will be able
to gather there and restart their old lives. They won't have to hide any
longer. They will prosper once again and recover their pride. I don't
think I will ever forget everything that happened, but the younger
generations have a right to the future that only I can give them."

Gîsal stood up and straightened the blanket that had slipped off
Ward's shoulder. He left the Host there, lost in confusion.

In the following few days, the Thuranc underwent test after test.
Groups of drugged guests were repeatedly brought for the tests, but
still, he was not perfect. Gîsal stood in the middle of one of the laboratories, satisfied with the news he had just heard. The workers had told
him that development was in the final phase. He had ordered one last
test to be completed, hoping that it would be the last. If the Thuranc
passed the tests, production could begin in earnest, and then it would
not be long before he had his mechanized army.

Through a window, Gîsal could see into the testing room, where
a group of unsuspecting guests was led inside. Gas was released into
the room that neutralized the effects of the drug that kept them docile. The prisoners looked around, blinking in a daze. Some of them
tried to find a way out, eager for freedom. They were not given much
time to wake up, though, because Gîsal pulled the lever that opened
the doors to the Thuranc's chamber. The humans gathered together,

as if they knew what was about to happen, and then there it was, the Thuranc, more life-like than the first model, less mechanical in its movements and so much more threatening. It looked like a living monster as it stepped into the test room, and that was just the result for which Gîsal had hoped.

He could not help but be satisfied with his creation. The effect it had on the humans was spectacular. At first they huddled together, utterly frightened. Then some of them fell down on the floor, begging to be let out. Others ran about the room, banging on doors and windows, but it was to no avail.

This was the first test with humans who were actually awake, and the creature did even better than Gîsal had dared hope. It walked through the room at great speed, killing everything in its path in great, sweeping blows.

Within moments there was not one living soul left alive in the testing room. Gîsal's laughter echoed throughout the laboratory. It was just perfect! Omnesia did not stand a chance against his creations. Soon now, there would be nothing left of the city but ash. All of the humans would be dead, doomed to the same fate as Gîsal's people had been so many years ago.

He turned around to the researchers and cried out, "Revenge!"

Then he ordered the immediate commencement of mass production. The sooner his army was ready, the better. He had almost forgotten about the three little fugitives running amok in his land. He felt invincible, and he was convinced that there was nothing anyone could do to stop him, not now. The Thuranc was invincible, and as a consequence, Gîsal was too.

The complex of factories where the army would be produced was tightly sealed and heavily guarded. Anyone left outside would have to fend for themselves. An alarm sounded through the building to warn all the workers to hurry if they did not want to be locked out of the factories. All of the energy generated in Hydrhaga was to be directed solely for the production of Gîsal's army of Thurancs.

24

There were many people working in the building. To either side of long, straight hallways were the offices of workers and Hosts alike, and people were constantly coming and going. Time and again the three intruders had to dive away into some dark room to avoid detection. They could proceed at nothing more than a crawl. Behind wooden doors they could hear voices, excited talk about some test or another that would soon take place. It made Lumea and her two companions uneasy.

Suddenly, the door at the end of the hallway in which they stood opened. The three barely had time to flee into a side room that was, luckily, empty. Nobody had seen them.

Through a small window in the door, Elion could see workers walking by, leading a group of groggy guests, who followed meekly. Many doors opened throughout the hallway and workers spilled out in order to watch the procession. Some of the Hosts yelled at the prisoners, whose only reaction was to hunch their shoulders slightly, otherwise they did not give any sign that they were being screamed at. When the prisoners had passed and nothing more happened for a while, Elion, Siard and Lumea came out of their hiding place and went carefully on their way.

They decided to take the door that the prisoners had come through. After walking along the hallway for some time they suddenly heard a loud alarm. They dived into a new hiding place and prepared themselves for a fight, convinced that they had been discovered, but the only thing that happened was workers hurrying past their door. Not long after this, the lights went out. Sitting in the dark, the three looked at each other with doubt in their eyes.

"What's happening?" Elion had not directed his question to anyone in particular, but none of them could answer it.

Again they went on very carefully, but the building was deserted, where earlier there had been so much activity. Siard lit the lamp that they had brought with them, and after searching the now-empty building they found row upon row of cells. Most of them were deserted, because the guests that had been held there had all been taken to the laboratories.

Some of the cells still contained prisoners. They had been left there in an obviously weakened state, staring up at the ceiling, unmoving. Though their doors had been left unlocked, the guests were not physically capable of leaving. The sounds of screams echoed from some of the cells, the inhabitants there sounding as if they were being tortured beyond their endurance. Most prisoners were only partially dressed, and some had poorly-healed wounds where their organs used to be. None of them even noticed the visitors.

The three walked passed the cells, horrified at what they were witnessing and yet not knowing what to do. They had the antidote for the drug, but that drug was all that kept these people from feeling the tortures that they had endured. Unable to help them, the three fugitives had to leave them to die.

A bit further on there was a group of guests left together in one cell with a locked door. All of them had been terribly injured. Nothing had been done to cleanse their wounds, and some had even died. The manner in which they were wounded must have been terrible, and all had been left here to die. Once they had served their purpose, they had been discarded like trash.

Siard looked away, disgust evident in his eyes, but Lumea kept looking at the prisoners, unable to keep her eyes from these bodies and their testament to an incredibly cruel fate. Her emotions were not really involved though, because her mind refused to process the reality.

Then she stopped dead, covering her mouth with her hand.

"Oh gods..." she murmured.

In between the bodies she could see the harp player that she had met all those months ago. His hands were horribly mangled. The reality of the situation made itself known almost like a physical blow to the stomach. These people had been living with her, and like herself they had the same dreams of living their own lives, hoping to see them come true in Hydrhaga.

Just like me, Lumea thought, overcome with horror. It could have been her in there, lying between these mutilated men and women, and the corpses, next to the man who had played his harp so beautifully.

Elion, who was walking behind her, almost bumped into her when she stopped so suddenly. He followed her gaze and recognized the man as well, so he gave Lumea's shoulders a soft squeeze, providing a reassuring presence in the face of the tragedy.

"Siard, could you open this door please?" Elion asked quietly.

The young man looked at him with questioning eyes, though he did not ask it out loud. Instead, he took out some small metal bars from his pockets. Trying them out on the lock in the thick glass door, they made a tinkling noise as he turned them.

"Lumea, could you make some space over there, perhaps you could try and make a few beds?"

Elion was pointing to the room where the guards had once sat, and Lumea nodded and started to work on it immediately. She found some more lamps, which she lit, and blankets and clothes that she used to make makeshift beds for the prisoners. Elion kept a few of the blankets aside in order to tear into bandages.

Before long, Siard managed to open the cell door. Together with Elion he lifted up the survivors and put them on the blankets that Lumea had spread out. Most of them hardly noticed, though some moaned. In the meantime, Lumea prepared bowls of warm water and started washing the prisoners' wounds. At times she recognized faces from people she had met during the summer. She never stopped talking to them, trying to comfort them and keep them awake.

Pretty soon, the whole room was full of people who were only barely alive. Elion and Siard put the dead bodies together in the cell farthest away from the living patients and covered each one with blankets.

When they came back, Elion started binding wounds, assisted by Lumea and Siard. They also used the antidote on the injured, which greatly improved their conditions. At least it was clear now that they were alive, even if they were in great pain. Siard prepared a light meal, after which Lumea helped them to eat, which lifted the spirits and atmosphere in the room tremendously, their chances improving even with only meager sustenance. Others, though, died even as El-ion battled to save their lives. They were placed in the cell with the other bodies, where the stench of decay hung thick, though the mias-ma was kept from spreading by the closed door.

One of the prisoners was called Almar. His injuries weren't too grievous and he healed quickly. He proved to have a lucid memory of what had happened to the other guests, though the others had been too drugged to have more than the vaguest memory of the nightmare they had endured. Almar told the them about the day they had been taken from their cells.

"They led us through hallways. I had no idea which way we were going, or for how long, but finally we came to a large, dark room. All I could see was that it was roughly octagonal in shape. We were pushed in through a small door, and on another wall there was a sec-ond door, this one larger and taller. In the other six walls there were windows. I felt like I was being watched, even though I couldn't see if there was really somebody standing behind them.

"When the guards left us, a buzzing sound filled the room. Lights went on, one after another, suspended from the ceiling. They were bright enough to blind me, but I heard the larger door open. When my eyes had adjusted to the light, I saw the monster that walked through the second door, and when I close my eyes now, I still see it, so tall and thin... and so strong. I still feel the fear that gripped us all. It was strong enough to overwhelm our drug-induced minds, and that fear took possession of every fiber of our bodies.

"The creature started fighting us immediately, and most of the time it hit what it aimed for. There were times, though, when it seemed un-certain, or it missed its target. That alone gave us the courage to gath-er together and fight back. It was a tough fight, but even with the lot of us it was impossible to defeat it, no matter how much we wounded it. It seemed as though it had some kind of armor protecting it, and we could only fight with our bare hands. I never saw anything like it, or even knew it existed. I knew they had found some kind of creature in Hydrhaga, so they must have been able to bring it to life.

"Then suddenly, the door opened again and the monster left. We fell down on the floor, exhausted, and we were taken back here and locked in a cell. They left us here to rot." Almar was silent for a moment. "Your coming was like a miracle."

During his story, Zephyr had joined them. She was a lanky young woman who nodded at Almar's last remark.

"I ran and ran, just to stay away from the thing. I dodged most of his attacks by running," she said.

The three were impressed by his story, and they kept interrupting him to probe for further details. When it was done, they mulled his words over in silence. He in turn wanted to know of their adventures, but they told him very little, and mostly avoided his questions. They thought about all the things that had happened here in Hydrhaga, and tried to decide what Almar's story meant for the rest of their mission.

That night, Elion, Lumea and Siard had trouble falling asleep. They sat in a corner and talked about what they should do. Elion put his thoughts into words.

"We already know that Gîsal is planning an attack on Omnesia, that's why he's raising an army. But I don't think he found the Thuranc and brought it to life, like Almar suggested. It's what the Hosts would have us believe, but I think it has to be some kind of mechanical creature, created by men."

He looked at Siard, who elaborated further.

"That would fit in with what Almar told us. I think you're right. These people survived some kind of test, which suggests that the test was not successful. Since then, though, they must have improved on the creature. Those people we saw in the hallway, just before everything went dark, they probably underwent the same thing. Didn't we hear some people talking about tests?"

Lumea stared ahead, sad. She could not fathom the cruelty behind it all. The things she knew about Gîsal did not justify murder. A woman started coughing in her sleep, and the conversation was paused, as all three waited to see if she would wake up. They heard her turn over and settle back into sleep, though, so Lumea broke the silence.

"So what are we going to do?" she asked.

Elion answered her question. "We wait for these people to regain some strength. Then we find out how far Gîsal's plans have come, and perhaps find a way to interrupt them. I'm afraid we can't lose too much time before we attack."

"Should we go back to Omnesia and gather an army there?" Siard asked, but Elion shook his head.

"We would lose too much time doing that. The journey there and back again would take twelve days, not to mention the time it would take to gather an army, and besides, the king might not even believe us. In the meantime, Gîsal's army grows stronger, and they can use that time to prepare for their attack. It's a long shot, but I think we should try and defeat Gîsal with the people we have here."

They accepted Elion's seemingly-unattainable plan and decided to inform the others accordingly. Lumea also suggested sending one prisoner to Omnesia so that the city could at least be warned, should their mission fail.

"All right, that's the plan, then," Elion decided.

It was quite some time before most of the guests regained their strength. Zephyr and Almar helped Elion and Lumea to take care of the injured while Siard scavenged for anything that might be useful. On one of these expeditions he found another wing of cells, but the people there had yet to be tested upon. They only lacked food and water, but otherwise they were fine. Elion was happy when Siard brought them back with him. Lumea joined them, and said what Elion was thinking: "Our army is growing."

She recognized someone among the new joiners, and she made her way quickly to the kite-runner, relieved to see a well-known face that was not too injured.

"Aeron, you're alive!"

The man was equally glad to see her.

In the meantime, Siard in walked over to Elion.

"I found a Thuranc as well. Come on, I'll show you."

While Lumea took care of the new arrivals, the two men left the room. Siard led Elion through some laboratories built entirely from cold steel, with nothing in the way of ornamentation.

"It's so strange that all these rooms are deserted. I fear this means that Gîsal is further along with his plans than we had hoped. He might even be done already, if you take into account the number of people he had no use for."

Siard opened a door and lit the lantern he had brought for just this purpose. The light revealed a small room stacked to the rafters with objects of some kind. Parts of robots were carelessly thrown into a corner, and their resemblance to human body parts, in conjunction with the poor light from the lantern, gave the place an eerie atmosphere. On those robotic parts, the artificial skin still clung to the metal in some places, but mostly it hung down in loose slabs. On top of the pile of parts there was one complete Thuranc, and Siard dragged it off the pile with Elion's help. They put it in the center of the room.

"Do you think this is the Thuranc that Almar and the others fought?" the elf asked.

"I hope so, because that will give us a lot of new information."

Elion shrugged. "What information? It's just a bunch of scrap metal."

Siard laughed. "More information than you'd think. In these rooms they built the Thuranc to its most recent form. That means that I have access to the same instruments that they used. That gives me the opportunity to discover some of the Thuranc's secrets."

"I will leave you to it then, Siard, I'd only get in the way."

Siard did not react to Elion's words, for the young man was already busy removing the Thuranc's skin and revealing the metallic skeleton underneath.

25

In the meantime, Lumea told the people about the plans that the group had made, as well as some of the adventures she and her two companions had undergone before they had arrived in this building. After some deliberation, everyone agreed to fight. Then she had taken the women aside and given them some sticks to cut to the lengths of swords. She figured if she was going to fight beside these people, she might as well teach them how to hold a sword. The women followed her, but they were hesitant because fighting was done by men, not by women.

She tried to convince them otherwise. "As a woman, you have an advantage. Men tend to underestimate you, and surprise is often the greatest advantage you can have in a fight. The Swintheri won't know what hit them, and by the time they do, it'll be too late and you'll have already won."

She tried to keep her voice light, but she could see the women looking at each other with uncertainty. She said, "I will show you how to defend yourself and from there, defeat your opponent."

One of the women in the back of the group spoke up. "Fighting's reserved for men."

Lumea shrugged. "That's what they believe in my country too. It's not going to help you one bit once you're standing face to face with a Thuranc. Swintheri might be sensitive about the fact that you're a woman, but a robot most certainly is not. In any event, you had best know what you're doing or you're going to die."

Now most of the women were nodding. When Lumea looked up she saw Elion leaning against the door frame, watching her with a proud expression on his face. He had returned after Siard had showed him the Thuranc. She smiled at him and beckoned him over. "I will show you that a woman does not have to be inferior to a man when it comes to fighting," she said.

She took one of the sticks and gave it to Elion.

"Don't let me win too easily!" she teased him.

The elf laughed. "If there's anything I've learned in the time we've been together is that you wouldn't forgive me if I did!"

He had not stopped speaking before he came at her with the stick, but Lumea dodged his attack. They circled each other, their sticks hitting each other in quick succession, until Lumea's 'sword' shattered and she lost her balance. Elion turned away to claim his victory, but Lumea regained her feet and pushed the elf to the ground. He lay there with a surprised look on his face. He had not expected the sudden attack. Lumea took his stick and made a motion as if she had killed him. Elion laughed and she helped him get up. Then she turned back to her pupils.

"Don't give up too easily. Elion underestimated me, but the fight's not over until one of you is defeated. In the upcoming fight, that means when one of you is dead."

Lumea saw the shocked reaction the women had, but she decided that it was better for them to understand that point now than after the fight had already begun. Then she suddenly realized that she was being as casual about death as Elion had been after their first fight, but she pressed on nonetheless.

She said, "Never forget that if you spare your enemy, you will be the one to lose your life. The Thurancs will most certainly not show any mercy."

She showed the women how to use their swords. She enjoyed the lessons, for they reminded her of the training she had received back in Lunadeiron under the tutelage of her sword master. At times she even forgot the future battle that lay ahead of them all. They trained every day, and as others healed from their injuries, the group grew in size.

Following her example, Elion had also found a group of students to whom he taught the basics of the bow. Now it was Lumea's turn to watch while she sharpened her sword. With controlled, even strokes, she drew the whetstone she had found in the guard's room over the edge of the blade. Elion gave a woman some instructions on how to hold her arms, then he came over to sit next to Lumea.

"Why did your parents allow you to fight? That doesn't really fit with the things you have told me about them."

"That's right, but my father didn't have a problem with my learning, and he knew how much I wanted it. Luckily, Master Archivald didn't mind teaching a woman. I believe that he was even proud of me, sometimes."

"If he could see you here, he most certainly would be."

Lumea nodded. "I think he understood how much I wanted to learn. What more could a master want than an eager pupil? My brothers just did what he told them to do, but I went beyond that. At the end of the lessons my brothers would leave the room, almost relieved for it to be over, but I stayed to practice that one move until I really got the hang of it. At first I did it alone, but it wasn't long before Archivald stayed as well to help improve my mastery over the weapon."

Elion called something to one of the archers, making Lumea look up.

"What attracted you to it so much in the first place?" he asked.

"I loved watching Master Archivald. There was so much raw power in the way he handled his sword. But most of all, it was the control of the weapon that attracted me, and the peace that comes from that kind of control. Once I realized I had achieved that, I was so proud of myself.

"But the biggest acknowledgment that I received from Master Archivald was when he gave me my own sword. That was after my Ankéabi. It looked a little like the one I have here, though this one is nowhere near as nice. It was made especially for me, and it bears an inscription that gives me strength. If only I had it with me here, I would be even stronger."

She took a bit of sandpaper and wet it. Elion watched as she concentrated on her fingers gliding along the edge of the sword. He held his tongue, as he did not want to interrupt her concentration. Then she checked the blade's edge with her thumb and noted with a satisfied tone in her voice, "Since I don't have it here, this one will do just fine."

Thanks to the time in the cell wing the group was well-prepared for the upcoming battle, but it was Siard who gave them the biggest advantage for the fight. He had spent his time examining the robot which they had found, and he had discovered the one flaw that the researchers had left in its design, in spite of all of their improvements. There was a place in the back of the creature's neck where the transmitter was located, and it was ill-protected. The scientists had never taken the trouble of reinforcing that spot because they assumed that the creatures were invincible, and that the Omnesians would never attack them from behind

Aeron had often gathered the Omnesians and together they had figured out how to combine their respective skills into an effective force. When Lumea joined the group, Aeron was building a large kite. Just like back when Hydrhaga was still peaceful, she helped him by holding the different parts of it while he worked. He then looked around in deep thought, and then mumbled, "Now for something to make the wings."

"What are you looking for then, paper? Like for the kite you made for me?"

Aeron beamed at the memory.

"Yes, or some similar kind of fabric. Light but strong. The kite itself will be pretty heavy already."

Lumea thought for a minute, before saying: "Do you think my skirt could help? The upper layer is made of silk, and you could use that."

Aeron touched the silk and tugged it once.

"Yes, that's perfect! If you don't mind..."

Lumea was already tearing the silk from her skirt. It was this layer that had been painted with the depiction of birds, and Aeron looked at what was left of the dress.

"It doesn't suit you, a plain dress. It's too boring for someone as vibrant as you."

Lumea smiled. "Never mind that now. Just make a good kite out of it."

"Oh, I'm planning to. This is going to be another eagle! I'm going to use the fabric's patterns to make him seem really alive. You'll be present in more than one place during the battle, Lumea. This might prove to be a deciding factor!"

Though Lumea assumed that he was talking about the mysterious thing he and Siard were making, his comment made her blush. "How are you going to make it fly? I assume there won't be any wind..."

Siard came into the room just as she asked her question, his arms full of things he put on the table. He proudly held up one of the transmitters that the Hosts used as communicators.

"We're going to build a motor into it that will be steered from a distance," he explained, almost casually.

Lumea shook her head, not believing her ears. Elion joined them as well and picked up one of the objects that Siard had been working on. It was light and small, no bigger than his thumb, with small wings and a pointed head. Elion turned it over between his fingers while Aeron and Siard looked at each other, full of mirth.

"So what is it that you're making exactly?" Elion said.

Siard's response was mysterious. "You'll find out in due time. I could explain, but you would understand it about as well as you did the submarine. Rest assured, it will work," he said.

Elion shrugged and turned around, which made the two men laugh all the harder. Lumea took up Elion's question, but no matter how hard she tried, she could not get an answer out of either of them. In the meantime, Aeron had started painting the bird, and Lumea looked on in admiration as the small brush strokes made the kite more and more beautiful. Grayish-blue lines emphasized the feathers on its head, and with a small white dot in its black eyes, the eagle really came to life.

With the refugees engaged in various occupations, the time was spent until most people were healed enough to go into battle. Elion looked at the group sitting around him, until his eye fell on an elderly man.

"Gentil, I'm going to ask you to stay here. We can't leave the people who are still not fully recovered without someone to take care of them. Do you agree?"

The man's initial reaction was one of relief, and after some thought he accepted the task, though with mixed feelings. "I will do what you ask of me, though I feel a deep-seated need to take revenge on these Hosts."

Elion nodded. "I understand how you feel, but you're not strong enough yet to take them on. Plus, I want someone here who knows what to do if the enemy should discover this place."

Then he addressed the whole group. "Is there anyone who will volunteer to undertake the journey to Omnesia? I don't know what it's like out there, but the last time we were outside the weather seemed to be calming down. I also don't know if there are any Swintheri or Hosts left out there guarding Hydrhaga. I think the best way would be through the woods, as there's no wall left there to stop you."

The people looked around, trying to decide where their best chances lay. Fighting against the Thurancs was scary, but they had no idea how they would fare outside, on their own. In the end, one man stood up to take this task upon his shoulders. He would leave two hours after the others. Elion gave the man a sword, so that he could defend himself should it become necessary.

The other weapons that they had scavenged were divided amongst their small army. Despite Lumea's lessons, the women looked decidedly uncomfortable with swords in their hands. One woman's hands were visibly shaking when Siard handed her a weapon. The feel of the cold steel against her skin had made her realize just how close the battle really was. Siard put an encouraging hand on her shoulder. "Elvire, you're not in this alone. You're fighting for something that you believe in."

Elvire nodded at Siard. Her hands stopped shaking. She still bit her lip, which turned white under the pressure, but at least she now had a decisive look in her eyes.

Lumea felt bad for the women, but she did not want to show her own fear to the group, so she quickly walked to a small room. Everywhere there was evidence of the activities from the last couple of days, but now the place was deserted of people. Elion followed her and grabbed her shoulder, turning her around.

"This might be the last time before the battle that we really have a chance to talk," he said.

Lumea nodded tensely.

"I often treated you worse than you deserved, Lumea, and though I do not deserve it, I hope you will remember me in a good light."

She shook her head and said softly, "Please don't say goodbye, Elion. If you do that, I won't be able to fight."

He looked at her with a smile. "You're right. And, you know, I prayed to the gods to give us strength."

"You prayed?" Lumea was surprised. She had not forgotten the way he had reacted when she had told him to have faith in the gods.

"You have taught me many things, my Lady Lumea, more than I have been willing to admit."

She laughed aloud when she heard the title that he had given her on one of their first meetings. She felt proud when she heard his next words.

He said, "The first time that I really prayed again was that night in the snow, when I thought I had lost you, and we found you again. But, because of all the anger I had inside of me, I refused to admit it later. Only when you told me about your vision did I really start trusting in the gods again. I don't have a choice. They threw you in my path, and I have to be grateful for that. At this moment, I honestly feel like they're standing by me."

He pulled her close to him and held her silently. Lumea hid her face in his clothes and held onto him. After a while she reluctantly let go.

"I'm glad I met you in Omnesia and asked you to guide me here," she said.

"Are you, really? Sometimes I wonder if I shouldn't have stopped you. I thought it might be dangerous, so it wasn't fair to use you for my own ends."

Lumea's eyes danced as she smiled. "Don't blame yourself. Everyone told me not to go to Hydrhaga. What makes you think that you're so special that you would have succeeded where they failed?"

Elion laughed. "Fair enough, but I still should have told you about the danger and given you the choice."

"You're probably right, but I don't blame you for it."

Elion hugged her again, before they walked back to the others. During their last, tense meal, nobody spoke a word.

26

"I don't care how much time has passed; I will never forget what the humans did to my people."

Gîsal looked off to the side. Ward tried to appear as if he were sleeping, but the elf knew better. He knew that the man had woken up as soon as he had entered the room, because for just a second he had held his breath. He decided to let the Host think he had been fooled.

"I experienced everything from up close. The war was pretty bloody, but I guess both sides were to blame for that. I can tell you this, though: I tried to calm the elves down. For hours on end I talked to the other senators, trying to convince them to receive the delegates from the human villages, but they refused to listen. Their thirst for human blood could not be slaked, and my pleas for tolerance fell upon deaf ears. The elves shot my words down without mercy."

His voice was cool as he spoke of the events during the war, but it changed until it almost sounded remorseful.

"I blame myself for what happened too, you know. I never foresaw that my riches, and what they brought to the people, would have such an effect, but in hindsight they were responsible for much of the suffering. Now the time has come to put everything right, however."

Then he became furious again.

"But they had no right to kill her! The worst thing about the whole affair is that after it was all over, they dragged her and all of elvendom through the mud. The human kings did everything in their power to give us a bad name. And of all the human cities, Omnesia is the most responsible for the persecution of the elves. It was because of that city that my people were all but slaughtered, and those that survived went from a wise and well-respected people to pariahs of society."

Gîsal grabbed Ward's shoulder and shook it until the man opened his eyes. He wanted him to see the pain, so that this human would understand why the old elf had become what he was now.

Gîsal had not stood by idly, watching his people being trampled.

He had sworn to take revenge, for his family and for his people, who deserved better than they received. For all those long years, he kept that revenge firmly in mind, all because those humans had destroyed his world, everything he stood for and everything he believed in.

"It took decades, no centuries, to build up Arminath. I devoted my life to it. It took the humans nineteen months to destroy it all."

The look he directed at Ward was bitter. He stood up and started pacing.

"You might think this war has long been over, but that's not true. It's still raging, though in silence now. I saw how the humans treated the elves, and I know how my people live now. I've seen the slums. It saddens me to see how a race that used to build such wonderful things is now forced to live in decrepit old houses at the edge of civilization. They barely survive, and despite the hard work that they do, they are shown no gratitude. It's a shameful way to live."

He looked at the man on the bed again. "Do you understand that? The war is not over, yet! The elves are desperately trying to improve their lives. There are regular meetings with song and dance and poetry, but they're nothing like the feasts that we used to organize. The wind blows the sand out of the desert and into the houses of the elves. The women try to clean it, they move tons of sand back into the desert and try to hide the rest, to best forget the conditions in which they now live. But the next day, all the sand that they have dumped outside of the city gets blown back into the quarter. Vermin come out every night and crawl through the streets in search of something edible. My people are living beneath their dignity. They are ashamed of the heritage that they should be so proud of, so they hide their identities. But not for much longer, now!"

Gîsal recalled the sacrifices he'd had to make to reach his goals. Abducting Omnesians had never overburdened his conscience. On the contrary, using them for his experiments had let him taste a small measure of the revenge for which he longed. Some of the humans had allowed him to gain power over them, and they had become workers and Hosts. After a long time of toil beneath him, they had stopped doubting him.

He sat down again and smoothed back the hair out of Ward's face.

Then he put his hand on the man's shoulder and left it there. "Do you want to know why I chose you as a Host, Ward?"

Ward hesitantly shook his head, afraid of getting the brunt of the leader's anger.

"You were afraid of me. I could see it in your eyes, Ward. It was the same kind of fear that I can see inside you now. You were afraid, and because you thought I recognized your talents you became loyal. Don't worry about that, though, that is how I picked all of my Hosts."

Gîsal laughed at the shocked expression on Ward's face. Then he continued in a conspiratorial whisper, "But the truth is, I never felt anything but contempt for all of you. You are fools, you lot. You sold your soul to me, and you thought you were safe. You were so fond of the luxuries I offered that you did not ask any questions, and just danced to my tune."

Each of the Hosts was the kind of man that enjoyed the power that Gîsal gave them. He had left the daily governing of Hydrhaga to them, without much interference. Ward's hair had fallen back into his face and Gîsal smoothed it back again.

"You didn't really serve any purpose. You were always replaceable, just like any of the others. But the knots that you tied yourselves into to meet my expectations were... amusing. For a while, at least. I always knew the day would come that you would have outlived your usefulness."

With that, he left the room, leaving Ward filled with confusion yet again. Soon, the Host would be sacrificed to its creation, but not yet. For a moment the elf thought of the other sacrifice he'd had to make, the deception and torture of his kin. He had needed their strength to reach his goals, and they had helped him to protect Hydrhaga. Their suffering had been a necessary evil, and after all, his revenge would be in their name as well. They were casualties of war, but Gîsal was convinced that his cause was the right one.

He salved his conscience with the thought that, if they had known what he was planning, they would agree with him. He refused to admit to himself that if that were the case, he could have told them instead of deceiving them. He quickly walked towards the huge hall where the workers were completing his army, banning all thoughts of elves from his mind, refusing to think of the core, the power plant that had once kept his wall intact, a place which he had avoided at all cost.

The Thurancs were slowly being completed, and the army grew every day. Gîsal followed the preparations with a satisfied smile. He had waited to march on Omnesia for so long, and now, it was almost time.

27

The group of men and women, led by Elion, climbed the stairs. There was nothing more for them to do on the floor where they had trained and recovered for so long. They slowly approached the closed-off center of the building. They reached a curved hallway, which seemed out of place given all of the straight ones they had passed.

According to Siard, this meant that they had reached the center of the building, around which this hallway ran in a ring. The group of fighters carefully went along the corridor, searching for a door, or any other means of entry. They were all surprised when they returned to the very place where they had entered the hallway without finding any entrances. The wall seemed to be built entirely out of metal plates that gave off a soft glow in the half-light. The plates were decorated with symbols and scenes in relief, with some symbols thicker than others.

They were uncertain on how to proceed. They looked at each other, hoping that someone would provide a solution. Some of them secretly hoped that this was the end of their adventure.

Siard examined the wall, carefully stretching out his hand toward it, almost afraid to touch it. For a moment he pulled back, but then he gently touched the metal. It was slightly warm, and it vibrated. He started walking, keeping his hand upon the wall, and Elion motioned for the others to follow. He was not about to let anyone get separated from the group.

They walked slowly, and Siard stopped for a moment every now and then to listen with his ear pressed against the wall. Finally, he found what he was searching for, and though he looked at Elion, his words were meant for the whole company.

"This is the entrance. It's probably the only one, and we're likely to be discovered as soon as we go through it."

His voice sounded doubtful. The group stood around him, their shoulders slumping. The wall barred their way, and even if Siard managed to open it, death was waiting behind it. Nobody dared to voice what they were thinking, but Elion spoke up.

"We all knew that victory would not come easily, though we might have hoped for it. We don't know what's behind this door, we can only guess. There's a big chance that it will surpass even our worst nightmares. But we are armed, and prepared. Siard, Lumea and I have come a long way already. We have no choice but to go on, unless we want our hardships to have been for naught. Many of you have already fought this thing, and I do not blame you if you don't wish to face it again. I would be glad for the honor of fighting alongside you, but I will not force anyone into something that they don't want to do. If you wish to go now, you may. We will wait for a few hours before opening the door, so that you have a fair chance to escape."

Elion looked around to gauge their reactions. Lumea agreed with him, there was no way the three of them were going to back down now. They would not blame anyone if they lacked the courage to go on. She could see the fear in everyone's eyes. One man, standing to the back of the group, was shaking and had tightly shut his eyes, as if that would shut out reality, but otherwise, nobody moved.

"You will all stay to fight?"

Again Elion waited, but everyone stood their ground. Elvire, Zephyr and some of the others nodded their consent.

"In that case, the time has come to fight for ourselves, for Omnesia, but most importantly for everyone who has suffered and died here in Hydrhaga. Let it never again be repeated!"

Everyone righted their shoulders and lifted up their heads. They had a determined look about them now, in sharp contrast to the defeatism they seemed to carry about earlier. Even if each and every one of them died here, the Hosts and their army would be greatly weakened. The King would be warned as well, so the Omnesian army could finish what they had started. Before it came to that, however, they had the chance to get revenge on the people who had used them for their own gains. Elion nodded, and Siard concentrated on the door again.

Long minutes passed in which a number of possible scenarios flashed through Lumea's mind. Before she could dwell on the bad ones over-long, Siard figured out how to open the door. The group prepared themselves to fight. Siard stood to Elion's right, next to the wall. He held his sword in his left hand so that he could open the door with his right. Elion himself was placed squarely in front of the door, one arrow nocked and another at the ready, and Lumea stood to the left, with her sword raised.

Behind them, everyone else was ready to spring into action as soon as the door opened. They were all determined to fight for their own lives as well as that of the others. Almar, to the side of the group, had drawn his two short swords. Like all Omnesian men, he had received training since childhood, so he knew what to do, but the women stood with their weapons at the ready, too, as if they had done this all their lives.

Siard looked at the group one last time, and then he pressed one symbol after another. He had seen this kind of lock before, so he knew how it worked. There were many different symbols, but the ones that were often touched by human hands betrayed a minimal discoloration of the metal. When he pressed the last symbol, the plate slid to the side with a long sigh.

With only the smallest of openings, Elion could see two men already and he fired two arrows in quick succession. As the men fell, the door opened farther and Elion fired another two arrows, both of them hitting their targets. The workers hardly knew what had hit them.

When the door was open far enough, Lumea and Siard ran inside. The guards, now prepared, tried to defend themselves. One of them managed to sound the alarm, but he was immediately hit over the head and slumped to the floor, unconscious.

A door to the right of the room opened and some workers stormed in. From the left came some Swintheri to the worker's aid, but the small army the three fugitives had put together was still in the majority. Elion drew his own sword and fought his way to the left door, because almost all the soldiers had come from that direction. Lumea tried to follow him, but there was always a new opponent blocking her way.

Everyone fought with grim determination. Lumea tried to give one woman some cover, but she had joined the training late, and was quickly killed. Lumea did not have any time to feel sadness about her death, though, because she was suddenly faced with two soldiers. She fought bravely, but they were stronger than her and they knew it, as was obvious from their taunts.

"Hey little lady, think you can manage the both of us?"

It made her furious, because she had heard that tone of voice too often already. Many men did not see her as a complete person simply because of her gender. That was exactly the reason she had started fighting against that prejudice.

"Too bad a pretty little woman like you has to die."

"Maybe we can just knock her unconscious, that way we get to have some fun with her later."

The words brought her back to reality. "They'll never get me alive!" she swore. She ran forward and turned behind the left soldier. He was the older of the two, and he had obviously not been expecting her move. She mercilessly stabbed him from behind, and followed up with an attack on the younger soldier, who was now the only remaining focus for her fury. They were equally skilled, but Lumea's weapon eventually found its way into the body of this soldier as well.

The moment's lull let her ascertain that Elion had taken up a position next to the door, and his arrows buzzed across the room. Siard saved many people from certain death, and Almar was like a typhoon with his two swords. It was impossible for the Swintheri to dodge his blades. Lumea dove back into the fight, overcoming opponents and sending her own people to the relative safety behind Elion's arrows.

One by one, all the soldiers that had come into the room were defeated, and the workers gave up the fight when they saw the odds. The survivors were quickly bound and gagged. Lumea allowed herself some time to think about the losses they had suffered and silently asked the gods to usher them safely into the afterlife. Everyone was relieved about how well their first fight had gone, despite the sadness for their slain friends.

There was not much time to think about their feelings, though, because Elion immediately led them deeper into the building's center. They passed some smaller laboratories and rooms where the workers lived. The few people that they met were immediately slain. At one point they passed a high window of stained glass. On the other side of the window there seemed to be a chapel of some kind. When Lumea looked through it, all she could see was the shape of a large number of people. She looked at Siard, who had joined her.

"The army?" she whispered.

"I think so," he answered just as quietly.

Behind them, Elion nodded. They proceeded quietly, until they reached a large doorway that was flanked by two bronze statues, which they supposed led to the chapel. The statues depicted slim creatures that looked down condescendingly upon the group. Both of them held spears, which were aimed at the intruders. Next to each statue, two torches burned, and their reflections in the illuminated bronze made the statue's eyes seem threateningly alive. Elvire and many others felt the cold clutches of fear, and everyone huddled together a little closer.

28

Gîsal had retired into his study, where he pored over an old parchment that had yellowed from age. Strewn about his desk, in between candles that offered scant illumination, were various volumes and loose papers. Though his eyes seemed glued to the parchment, he was feeling impatient, as was obvious from his fingers that drummed incessantly upon the surface of the desk. His thoughts kept returning to the Thuranc. Some time ago his creation had finally reached perfection, and since then, his men had been working long hours to build him an army that would be large enough to launch an attack on Omnesia. Gîsal looked up at the painting of Arminath that dominated most of one wall.

"My wondrously fair city," he said lovingly.

When a knock sounded on the door, the leader waited a moment before he opened it. The messenger on the other side bowed low.

"My Lord Gîsal, your army is ready and waiting for you in the Chapel of Justice."

"Wonderful! Tell my body servants to join me and send everyone else to the chapel. This is the moment that we've all been waiting for."

The messenger bowed reverently again and left the room. Gîsal walked over to the wardrobe that spanned the left wall, and opened its doors. From the drawers he withdrew some pieces of armor. Suspended from hangers were soft green robes that were woven with a pattern of gold flowers. As he felt the soft fabric glide through his hands, he had a faraway look in his eyes.

Soon, his two servants entered the room. They helped Gîsal to undress, and neatly folded his sombre black clothes, placing them on the sofa. Then, layer by layer, they dressed him, while he looked at himself in the old mirror hanging on the inside of the wardrobe door. The candlelight glinted off the golden decorations. He could still see the man he used to be, but he had grown old. The years he had spent working on the Thuranc had aged him more than he would have thought possible.

One of the servants placed a stool behind Gîsal, and he sat down on it. From the wardrobe came leather shoes that were reinforced with silver. First one, and then the other were strapped onto his legs. As he stood again, another servant brought his golden armor. It encircled his waist like a corset and ran up to a point across his breastbone. This part closed with straps as well, and one servant pulled them tight across his back. The leader felt the air being pressed out of his lungs and his belly being pushed in.

"Tighter!" he hissed.

The servant tightened the straps until Gîsal's ribs were pushed inward as well. The leader let his hand wander over the metal as he felt the decorations on the armor. Knowing it was time for the next piece, he spread out his arms. His breastplate and plackart would serve to protect his chest. Silver pauldrons were fastened to his shoulders and upper arms, and the gorget forced his head up into a regal cast.

Over the suit he wore a heavy ocher cape, and the outfit was completed by a pair of golden gauntlets. Gîsal looked at the mirror once more, and, happy with the result, he sent the servants away and extinguished the candles with his fingers. His long strides caused his cape to swoosh behind him as he made his way through the corridors and toward the Chapel of Justice.

Moments later, he stood before his army. The Thurancs were assembled in long, neat rows. As one, they saluted their leader. The gesture touched Gîsal's heart, and his eyes shone with pride. Somewhere to the left, a door opened, and Ward was dragged inside. The moment his eyes met Gîsal's, he started screaming, but when he turned his eyes away and saw the Thurancs, he realized just why he had been brought there. With his last ounce of strength he tried to fight the two Hosts that held him. Gîsal enjoyed the show. He no longer needed Ward to confirm the power he had over humans. After all, he now had his creatures of perfection, and the time had come to sacrifice Ward to his creations.

Gîsal gestured at the two Hosts, and they threw the terrified man down before him. The elf bent his knees a little, wanting to smooth aside the mop of hair hanging before Ward's eyes, but the former Host determinedly turned his head aside from Gîsal's touch. The leader smiled affably at the man whose fumbling had been partly responsible for all the recent mishaps in Hydrhaga. He whispered softly enough so that only Ward could hear him, "You've served your purpose. Now is the time to punish you for all of the troubles that you've caused."

Ward felt a shiver run down his spine at the leader's threatening words. There was no time for anything else, because Gîsal stood up and commanded one of the Thurancs to attack.

Ward was torn to pieces, and Gîsal enjoyed the sounds that accompanied the exhibition. The former Host screamed and fought to the bitter end, though it was to no avail. It was surprising to Gîsal how much strength the man still managed to find. It took the Host a long time to die. The Thuranc was utterly silent as it finished the job, but the sounds of tearing flesh and snapping bones filled the chapel. When the robot was done, the corpse hardly resembled anything human. Gîsal ordered the Thuranc to stand down, as a feeling of euphoria washed over him.

The band of resistance fighters had reached the door to the Chapel just as Ward was being ripped apart, and from outside they could hear the horrifying noises. Elion carefully opened the door, just in time to see Ward die, and he watched as Gîsal ordered the Thuranc to cease. Nobody paid any attention to the door, as riveted by the spectacle as they were. The fighters sneaked in and hid behind the statues that lined the back of the hall. Lumea tried to comfort the others. Everyone was shocked by the glimpse of pure evil they had just witnessed.

More than that, though, there was the fact that the Thurancs were tall and strong, while most of their force was inexperienced. How were they supposed to win this fight? They had nearly been killed when they had faced just one of the monstrosities, and that one had yet to be perfected, and yet here was a whole hall full of them. They all felt as though they were about to commit suicide. Just thinking about the upcoming battle made them die a little on the inside.

Rather than joining in the general despair, Elion studied the room for something he could use to their advantage. Siard came up beside him. With gestures and minimal whispered words they discussed what to do. The place, with its high, vaulted ceiling reminded them of a sanctuary, though it lacked a blessed atmosphere that usually accompanied such places. This hall was built with the blood of victims of past wars in mind, and with the promise of more blood to be spilled. The vaulted ceiling was not so much a stairway to heaven as it was a heavy claw gripping all who were inside. The crimson pillars standing in between the statues looked like blood-soaked fingers. In the middle of the hall there hung a huge chandelier that suffused the entire chapel with a cold, white light.

To the left there was a spiral stair running up to a bridge that spanned the space. It was relatively near the group, but with the people standing between them and the stairs, they would be discovered as soon as they tried to reach it. Elion tried to find another way in which they could use the high ceilings. Siard pointed to the right. Along that wall, right next to them, were ropes hanging from beams that ran just below the ceiling. If Elion climbed up, he could use the height to eliminate many of the Thurancs before they could fight back. In any event, he'd be well out of their reach.

There were more archers in the group, so Elion gestured for them to rally to his side. He quickly and quietly explained the plan to them, so that they could decide whether or not to follow. It was a risky business, but they agreed to it, seeing how much advantage they would gain if they managed to succeed.

Aeron had joined them as well, to listen to the plans.

"My kite can give the cover that you need to climb up those ropes. I will let it up as far to the left as possible, so that the attention of the Hosts will be drawn that way."

Siard nodded his agreement. "I will join you. Elion. Wait for the eagle."

The young man made to follow Aeron, but at the last moment he turned back.

"Remember, their necks are their weakest spot," he reminded the others.

Lumea took Siard's place, wondering what the two men had been planning. Elion took her hand, and the two of them waited while tension and adrenalin coursed through their bodies.

Gîsal was just finishing his speech when some workers noticed
Aeron's kite. Everyone started whispering excitedly, trying to guess
at what it might mean. The eagle climbed up to the vaults, then flew
down in a large circle. Lumea could clearly see Gîsal's confusion as he
pondered on the nature of this strange object. Elion pressed Lumea's
hand once before letting go to start up the ropes. The other archers
followed suit. Lumea kept her eyes on the eagle, which was just now
flying in front of the chandelier, so that the light shone through the
silk wings. Aeron had used the patterns inherent in the fabric as much
as possible, but the wingtips were red. It gave the eagle, floating calmly through the chapel, a sinister look.

The animal had a wingspan of a few feet, making it harder to steer
than the kites that Aeron usually used. Siard still managed to make
it fly through the whole room, so that everyone got a good look. It
hovered for a brief moment before swooping down to the army of
Thurancs. When it was near them, Siard flew it right over their heads,
as if taunting them. When there was no reaction forthcoming, the eagle started climbing up again.

At its highest point, it suddenly stopped. Its body opened and
dozens of small objects, made by Siard, flew out. The chapel seemed
suddenly filled with insects, descending rapidly and gaining speed.
Then their purposeless descent changed direction. Attracted by the
signal sent out by the robots, they plunged into the one weak spot of
the otherwise invincible robots.

Where most workers and Hosts at first had been surprised, their reaction now turned into utter shock. As soon as the metal pins plunged
into the Thurancs' necks, the robots fell down, no longer functioning.
Up until that moment, everything had happened in complete silence,
but now Gîsal screamed at his troops to attack. The robots, however,
did not budge. Without a visible target, they stood their ground, even
as large numbers of them fell down, completely useless.

Right then, the archers had reached their vantage points, and
though Lumea could not see their arrows, they added greatly to the
confusion. A robot fell down with a shaft protruding defiantly from

its neck. It told Gîsal and his men that the kite was not all they had to deal with. More arrows rained down on the troops, quickly diminishing the number of robots still standing. Everyone was staring up, but the archers stayed hidden in the darkness of the high vaults.

Gîsal sounded almost desperate as he yelled at his troops to attack. Swintheri hurried up the staircase, but they could not get close enough to Elion and his men to keep them from shooting, and none of the Swintheri carried bow or arrows.

Lumea decided that the time had come to join in the fray. With a deep sigh, she uttered a quick prayer. Then she looked at the other fighters. Not a trace of doubt was left in their eyes, and Lumea knew that she could depend on them. Everything that they had experienced lately had hardened them for this fight. She sent out half of her troop over to Siard and Aeron and kept the other half with herself.

As the second group moved from statue to statue, unnoticed in all the confusion, Lumea and the rest of the warriors pulled down two of the statues and placed their round bases on their side. They rolled them into the fray and followed them in, hopefully taking out some opponents in the process. At the very least, the act would add to the confusion. Their limestone bases were heavy, taking quite some strength to move them quietly.

When Lumea nodded, the fighters pushed the stones, and then everyone emerged from their hiding places, creating as much noise as possible. The rolling bases knocked over some of their opponents, and they were subsequently defeated with ease. The Swintheri ran towards them, but with an agile leap, Lumea jumped up on one of the stones which had rolled to a stop, and she fought the soldiers that stood in her way.

The group reached the army of Thurancs without too much resistance. Because of the two attacks from above, their opponent's numbers were already greatly reduced, and the robot warriors were no longer in the majority. Now, though, the Thurancs could see their opponents, and they immediately attacked. Arrows buzzed down from the ceiling. In a flash, from the corner of her eye, Lumea saw that Siard had come out of his hiding place. With the army concentrating on her group, he managed to surprise them from their flank.

Gîsal was kept off balance, this time by the sheer number of opponents. Even if he had expected the fugitives to still be alive, even if they had the audacity to attack him, he had only counted on three of them. He wondered where all these other enemies had come from.

The robots did exactly what they were made to do. Their attack was aimed to the front, to the people who had first come into their range. They did nothing to defend themselves. Most of them had only their claws and strength for weapons, though some of them carried swords to further extend their reach.

Elvire froze up when two Thurancs approached her from both sides, and she was the first of their group to die. At the same time, Lumea felt a claw close around her waist. She was lifted up as the claw slowly tightened its grip, and the sharp nails tore at her skin. With all her strength, she let her sword descend on the arm, severing the joint. She dropped down with her back against one of the stone bases.

When she saw the next robot making its way over to her, she hid behind the base, trying to get a grip on her breathing. The creature kept coming nearer, though, so she climbed up on the stone and used the advantage of her height to pierce her sword through the Thuranc's weak spot. The thing stopped in the middle of its motion and fell over.

The last arrows having been spent, Elion used the ropes they had climbed up on to get back down into the fray quickly. Another archer followed him, but he lost his grip and landed on the floor, where he was run over by two robots chasing Zephyr. Just like during the test, the agile woman outran the creatures.

Elion, on the other hand, had somehow managed to land on the back of the Thuranc whose arm had been severed by Lumea. From this vantage point he managed to defeat some opponents, and weaken others.

The ragtag group of fighters were having a difficult time. They fought bravely, but the Thurancs were fast, and more often than not they killed their opponent in one stroke. They were also taller than most men, not to mention the women, so it was hard to reach their weak points. During a short lull in the fight when nobody was paying attention to her, Lumea looked around, noting that her group had suffered many losses. Farther on, she saw a group of women bringing their training into practice. It made her proud to see that they were standing their ground against the robots. Something caught her attention, and she noted a robot as it renewed his attack. As it drove one woman back, its sword swished through the air.

Lumea could not help laughing when the robot finished its attack. She recognized a pattern in which the creature swung its weapon. Under Master Archivald she had endlessly repeated the same pattern, and apparently the researchers in Hydrhaga had programmed their creations with the same basic techniques.

Overconfident as they seemed to be, they must have thought that the opponents would not survive the first round of attacks. It was another fatal miscalculation that, like the weakness in their necks, would cost them dearly tonight. Lumea had taught her own pupils the same thing, and she now yelled at them what she had discovered. She was thrilled to see that they understood her, and now that they knew what to expect they could easily avoid the attacks and wait for more opportune moments to defeat the robots.

The lull ended when Elion was thrown from his perch by the one-armed robot. Jumping off her pedestal, Lumea landed next to her friend to help him up.

"Follow me! Let us finish this!" she yelled above the cacophony of the battle, as she drew her second sword.

Aiming for the weaker joints of the creature's knees, she brought the robot down. Elion jabbed his sword into its neck, and together, they moved on to the next creature. Seeing how Lumea attacked the robots, Almar followed suit. With his two short swords, he felled the creatures, after which a woman finished the thing off.

The Swintheri and workers were finally starting to join in the fight with earnest, and after some hesitation the Hosts followed their example. One of them managed to surprise and kill Almar, but the Thurancs were built to fight humans, and in the confusion of the battle they could not distinguish friend from foe, so workers, soldiers and Hosts alike fell victim to the robots. They quickly ran for cover again, but in the few minutes that they had fought, many of them had fallen.

Gîsal stood in the middle of the battle, looking on with mixed emotions. The large number of dead enemies made him happy, but the fact that just one kite had managed to finish off so many of his army—without anyone capable of stopping it—was rather disconcerting. This whole fight should not have been happening, anyway. He was mad that these people were weakening his army in a battle that should have been raging in Omnesia. The anger morphed into white-hot fury when he realized that his plans had just received another major setback.

On the other side of the chapel, Gîsal could see a woman in a red dress, who he knew must be the Lumea woman. Her dress was very different from the clothing of the other fighters, as was her combat style. Unlike the others, she appeared to know what she was doing as she felled one robot after the other.

Just as the leader of the robots was watching, one robot grabbed Elion, who struggled against its grip. The creature was the stronger of the two, and Gîsal waited for it to kill the man. After a moment, the robot threw Elion away and turned its attention to another opponent. The man landed against a pillar, but he was still alive. Gîsal was dumbfounded. Why had he not been killed?

Elion soon got up again, and threw himself back into the battle. Gîsal noticed that the man's attitude had changed, somehow, as if he felt himself invincible. Despite his right arm that hung uselessly at his side, he hacked around with the other one as if nothing could harm him. The Thurancs avoided him, but he chased them until they lay defeated at his feet.

Almost as if he felt himself being watched, Elion turned around. Their eyes locked for the briefest of moments.

"Impossible," Gîsal muttered.

He had never even considered that one of the fugitives might be an elf. He had closed Hydrhaga off from them a long time ago, so how had this one found his way inside? As Elion fought on doggedly, Gîsal approached him with measured steps. The Thurancs avoided their leader, as they had been programmed not to harm elves. On his way towards his opponent, Gîsal bent to retrieve a discarded sword.

He had to stop the other elf; he was too great a danger to what little was left of his small army. If Gîsal managed to stop him, he could always restart with the production of the Thurancs, but as long as Elion remained alive he posed too great a threat to Gîsal's creation.

Soon, Elion noticed the leader of Hydrhaga approaching him, and moments later they were face to face. There was no time for pleasantries as Gîsal attacked. With one arm hanging limp, Elion defended himself with the other as best he could, though his opponent was strong and determined. Despite Gîsal's stiff armor and motionless torso, his arms flowed through the air in elegant arcs, never letting up their fierce attack on the other elf.

Although the long journey through Hydrhaga—not to mention the current fight—had had exhausted Elion, he still managed to keep his opponent at bay. Gîsal was more fit and better rested, but by adapting to his fighting style, Elion could fight him off, even with only one functioning arm.

Lumea wondered for a second where Elion had gone, when she saw that Siard had replaced him. She was in the heat of battle, though, so there was no time to really think about it. With the assistance of a few of her warriors, they disabled the last of the Thurancs. All there were left now were humans facing each other. In the lull that came from the Swintheri's hesitation, Lumea had the chance to look around. She saw Elion locked in a battle with Gîsal. She could clearly see that her friend was heavily wounded. He had trouble keeping his balance, and it was increasingly hard for him to dodge the leader's swift attacks. He was quite obviously losing.

Despite her exhaustion, Lumea still found an unknown reserve of strength when she saw the two locked in battle. Quicker than ever, she ran toward them. One Host tried to stop her, but she did not even notice him. Zephyr pushed him out of the way and pointed her sword at his throat so that he could not get away.

With effort, Gîsal threw Elion down to the floor, where he stayed, apparently dazed, and at that moment Lumea reached the two of them. She took Elion's place, effectively keeping her companion out of reach of the leader.

"Give it up, Gîsal. Your army's destroyed. It's over!"

He laughed squarely in her face. "I'm not afraid of you, little Lumea."

She shrugged, refusing to let him see what she was feeling. "I'm not afraid of you either," she lied.

Gîsal towered above her, and his appearance frightened her. She attacked with all her might, but time and again he deflected her blade. His own sword tore through the cloth of her dress, and with a flick of the wrist he drew blood from her arm. She hardly even felt it as she fought to protect Elion. While Gîsal seemed invulnerable, he wounded her time and again.

"You shouldn't have gotten yourself involved in this, human. This war had nothing to do with you, but now you're going to die for it anyway."

His words touched a nerve within her. In her fight against Gîsal, she recalled her struggle against the demon so long ago. Back then, Wolf had given her the chance to back down, and she had not. The demon had told her she would die in a battle that was not her own, and yet, she had emerged victorious. The same clear calm came over her, and, fully in control of herself, she sprang forward. Not expecting this maneuver from her, Gîsal was too late with his defense. With a lucky jab, she managed to pry her sword underneath his breastplate. Knowing she had won, she remembered everything she had told Elion about her vision, and what he had told her afterward. She wondered what would happen if she gave the choice of the ending back to Gîsal.

"All I have to do to end your life here and now is to push. But I want to give you a chance to end this differently."

Gîsal sneered. "There's only one way for you to stop me, and that's entirely up to you. Your words mean nothing to me, human."

He spat out the last word and raised his sword, but before it had reached its apex, Lumea pushed upward and pierced his heart. She let go of her sword without withdrawing it. The elf dropped down to the floor, opposite of Elion, dead. It was the last straw for the workers and the Hosts, who dropped their weapons as one. The whole reason Hydrhaga had even existed died along with its leader.

29

With Siard, Zephyr and Aeron bringing their prisoners to the cells, Lumea had her hands free to take care of Elion. He was smiling, though his eyes betrayed the pain he suffered.

"We did it, we won!" he said softly.

"Yes, we did. But look at how hurt you are," she answered, the worry for the injured elf clearly evident in her voice, which neared the point of breaking.

"I don't think I will make it, Lumea. But that doesn't matter. The important thing is that we did what we came here to do. Omnesia is safe."

Lumea was powerless to keep her tears from streaming down her cheeks. "It does matter. You can't die, Elion."

The elf seemed resigned to his approaching death. His voice sounded even softer as he said, "Goodbye, my Lady Lumea. It has been an honor..."

His eyes closed as he drifted off into unconsciousness. One of Lumea's tears fell on his face, and she carefully wiped it away. Then her hands felt for his shoulder. With one decisive movement she set his arm back into place. She knew that it must have hurt terribly, but Elion did not react.

In all the rubble and destruction left from the battle, she found the right materials to bind the shoulder, so that it had no chance of moving. Then she moved on to the rest of his body. The worst of the wounds she treated, but her supply of herbs was almost gone, so she had to be careful how much of it she used. At least, so long as she was taking care of his wounds, she could keep her grief and despair at bay.

Siard and Aeron returned with a stretcher they had fashioned, and they put the elf on it when Lumea was finished tending his wounds. What remained of the group of fighters had gathered in the rooms of the Hosts. Even the people who had been too weak to fight had been brought there by Gentil.

Elion, on the other hand, was brought to the most luxurious room of them all, which had of course belonged to Gîsal. Lumea stayed by his side. Siard brought her a glass of water to drink and put his hand on her shoulder for a moment, after which he left her. Through the open doors she could hear the excited murmurings from people who were happy to be alive and to have emerged victorious. The threat was finally over. At times, the murmurings quietened though, as they remembered their losses. Lumea paid no heed, for all her attentions were directed toward Elion.

Later on, Aeron came into the room.

"Lumea, you have to wash and let me take care of your wounds."

She hardly seemed to hear his words. He sat down next to her and put a comforting arm around her shoulders. When he said her name again, she looked at him with intense sadness.

"I don't want to leave him."

Aeron pulled her towards him in a comforting gesture. "I know, honey, but you need to take the time to care for yourself. If you let yourself die, you won't be helping him. Go and wash yourself. I promise I will stay by his side."

She nodded and went away. When she had washed, Aeron tended her wounds and gave her new clothes. Only now did she realize that he had put on something different as well. She looked at the dress he had given her with admiration.

"We got some things from Gîsal's archive. Nobody really wanted to keep walking around with bloodied clothes, so we kind of plundered it. You should come out and look. You've never seen that much color on a bunch of Omnesians!"

It was his attempt at cheering her up a little, but instead of smiling she just sat back down next to Elion.

"I'm so worried about him, Aeron. He really means a lot to me, but I feel like someone is taking him away from me."

"You need to have faith, Lumea. He's obviously still fighting, so you shouldn't give up either. Oh, that reminds me, I have something for you."

Aeron took the bottle he had placed on the table when he had entered the room. It contained some kind of transparent liquid.

"What is it?"

"We found it in the archive as well. The label belonging to it described it as water coming from the Fountain of Life. I have no idea if it's just a name or not, but it couldn't hurt to try, could it?"

Lumea recognized the bottle as one of the things she had seen that time she had been in the archive. She took it gratefully and wet Elion's lips with the water.

Lumea did not sleep at all that night. Instead, she kept vigil next to Elion. Her night was lonely, filled with worry for the man lying next to her. The only thing that could give her some comfort was his regular breathing. It assured her that he was still alive, so she tried to have faith, like Aeron had told her to.

There were times that she drifted off, only to wake up again with a shock. She would not allow herself the luxury of sleep, afraid to miss any change in the elf's condition. She'd blame herself for the rest of her life if he died while she slept. She quickly pushed the thought aside. Maybe Elion would wake up and need her. She had to stay awake.

In the silence of the night, thoughts kept playing through her mind, showing her all kinds of possible scenarios. She tried to push the negative ones away and keep hold on the positive ones.

The next morning, she changed Elion's bandages, but apart from his breathing Elion showed no sign of life. Siard came by to bring Lumea some food, but he hated seeing his friend like that so he quickly disappeared again. Lumea hardly noticed him. She took the food and ate it automatically, without actually tasting it. Slowly, the day dragged on.

Aeron often joined her. Mostly they sat in silence, but sometimes Lumea told him what was going through her head. The woman that had come out of the airship and set foot in Omnesia had been young and uncertain, but determined to lead her life the way she wanted to. She had left Lunadeiron because she did not get that chance there. In the course of her adventures, however, from the moment she walked through the gates of Hydrhaga and up until now, sitting next to Elion's still form, she had evolved into a strong, self-assured woman.

She looked worriedly at the unconscious man and straightened the blankets.

"Elion forced me to become the woman that was hidden inside of me. I really did not have any other choice when he pulled me through that door to escape from the Hosts. I hated him for it, but now that it's all over, I am grateful, in spite all the bad things we have endured."

She looked at Aeron sadly. "What if he dies? There were times when he insulted me, but he learned to accept me for who I am. There are not many who do. I'm afraid that without him, I will just go back to my old life, under the care of my parents."

"I don't think you could do that, Lumea, even if you wanted to. Too much has happened since then. And whatever the outcome, you will always carry part of him within your heart. You will never forget the things that he taught you."

His words made the tension drain from her. "You're right. I know I can take care of myself. And I will never give that up!" she said fiercely. Then she looked over at Elion, adding, "But I'd rather live my life with you by my side..."

The two of them sat together in silence for a while. Darkness was creeping in by the time Aeron got up to go to his own bed. Lumea got up as well and walked over to the window to look at the moon. She hoped that it could tell her something about Elion's recovery, but even though the night was clear, the moon was nowhere to be seen. She turned around with a disappointed sigh.

The lantern spread a soft light, illuminating Elion's face. His skin was pallid, and it was obvious to her that his condition was grave. She walked back to him and knelt by his side. Taking some sage, she lit it in a small bowl. The dried herb flared up briefly, but soon the flame died down, leaving only the smoke to waft up. She cleansed herself and Elion with the smoke, and prayed to the gods for a long time. She begged them to let the elf recover. After the prayer, she lay down and fell asleep next to his bed.

The following days and nights passed without much incident. Lumea stayed with Elion, and every now and then Siard or Aeron would keep her company. She took care of the elf with all the love and devotion she possessed; she kept using the water from the Fountain of Life, she sang to him, she turned him. In the nights she would often get the desperate feeling that he would die, because there were no signs of improvement. She always managed to turn that feeling around, though. After all, at least he did not get worse.

On the sixth night, Lumea awoke with a shock. She knew it had only been a dream, but the uncomfortable feeling that she got from the dream lingered. She looked over at Elion, who was still lying in the same position that she had last put him in. His breathing seemed shallower. She put her hand on his breast to feel the beating of his heart.

In her dream, the two of them had been walking through the Ruin of Achnon, but the place was no longer in ruin. The sun shone through the leaves and onto the courtyard. The moss was soft under their bare feet as they walked hand in hand, talking and laughing happily. Then Elion had let go of her hand, and no matter how hard she tried to keep hold of his, he always seemed to just slip away from her grasp. He disappeared through the gate. Lumea had woken up, sadness oppressing her because she had not been able to follow him.

She got up and walked to the window. The room felt stuffy, so she opened the sash to let in some fresh air. As soon as she did, she felt the comforting caress of the wind, as the coolness of the night touched her cheeks and filled the room. The woman stared up at the stars and the clouds. Suddenly one cloud opened up to reveal a thin sliver of the moon. Lumea smiled as a serene calm came over her.

"A new moon, a new start!" she said.

She thanked Isil, the Goddess of the Moon. For a while, she remained at the window, her mind empty of thought but her heart full of feeling. When she eventually turned back to Elion, she saw that beads of sweat had formed on his forehead. She carefully wiped the drops away, but they returned almost immediately. It was a sign that his body was trying to fight against the illness. She tried to get him to drink something.

From that moment on, she took care of the elf with renewed faith. She made him as comfortable as possible, and, slowly, the fever subsided. He started moving and mumbling something in his own language, which Lumea did not understand. She talked back nevertheless, trying to comfort him, though he was still unconscious. Siard came to join her more often, but she never neglected her task.

Lumea had opened the curtains to let in the light of the early morning sun. She could hear some birds beginning their serenade to the new day. Suddenly she heard a deep sigh behind her, so she quickly went over to the bed and sat down next to Elion, shielding his eyes from the sunlight with her body. She took his hand as he opened his eyes a crack. It was too hard for him to keep them open, so he quickly closed them again.

"Where am I?"

"In Gîsal's room. I hope you don't mind."

He opened his eyes again and looked at her. "Lumea?"

She smiled. "Welcome back to the land of the living, Elion."

Though she forced herself to sound calm, a small catch in her voice betrayed how excited she was. "How are you feeling?"

"Like I got trampled by a herd of horses," he answered dryly.

She had to laugh; she could not help it. He wanted to laugh too, but it hurt too much. She became serious again and she bent over to give him a kiss on his forehead, happy that he was going to be all right.

30

Now that Elion was awake, he quickly recovered from his wounds, and soon he was able to leave the bed, but even so, Lumea stayed faithfully by his side. Now when she bandaged her own arm, he came over and took the bandages from her. He carefully wound them around her arm and fastened them.

"I like how you stay close to me, Lumea."

She laughed. "If you have had enough of me, just tell me!"

"No, I mean it. I know what you did for me when I was unconscious, how you never left my side. I heard your songs. They gave me the courage to fight death."

She touched his cheek and he took her hand and kissed it.

"I'm glad you were the one sitting next to me when I woke up. Your soft hands holding mine, they were a real comfort. I knew I was safe with you."

He suddenly started blushing, and he let her lead him back to the bed, where they both sat down on the edge.

"I'm glad I could do that for you, Elion."

"To be honest, I thought I was back in Arminath at first. Gîsal's furniture reminded me of the old times, and you sitting there in the clothes that my mother used to weave, with the sun shining behind you... For a moment it seemed as though everything had just been a nightmare, and that I was back home."

Lumea's countenance dropped when she heard his words. "Did it bother you when you realized that you were wrong?" she asked.

Elion firmly shook his head. "Not at all. When I heard your voice I remembered everything, but I was truly happy when I recognized you."

He looked at her closely. He said, "If my shoulder would let me, I would lift you up and put you in bed. You look incredibly tired. The gods only know how little sleep you've had lately." He pulled the blankets aside. "Now it's your time to rest, since you don't have to worry about me any more."

Lumea gratefully lowered herself into the bed, and Elion tucked her in. Within moments, she had drifted off into a deep sleep.

Elion slowly regained his independence. His shoulder needed more time to heal, but in spite of that they left Hydrhaga to go back to Omnesia. On the second morning after their departure they saw banners flapping in the wind against the light of the rising sun. It was the Omnesian army riding towards them. The man that had left Hydrhaga alone to find his way through the wilderness had managed to convince the king that war was imminent. They made camp and the survivors explained everything that had happened to them.

The next day, the survivors went on toward Omnesia. The army had given them horses and a few soldiers rode with them as escort. The rest of the army continued on to Hydrhaga, where they destroyed Gîsal's lifework and drowned the land. From that day on, the tower stood in the middle of a gigantic lake as the sole witness to the threat that Omnesia and its inhabitants had only barely escaped.

The Hosts and workers that the fighters had taken prisoner were taken to Omnesia, as well as the bodies of both humans and elves. The elves were buried near the Ruins of Achnon, their living kin brought them there under Elion's guidance. No human was witness to the ceremony giving them their final rest.

During the following days, magnificent parties were held to celebrate their victory. Siard, Lumea and Elion were summoned to the king's palace. In the arena, the fight against the Thurancs was reenacted. It took two whole weeks for the uncharacteristic frivolity in Omnesia to die down.

Some weeks later, Lumea and Elion sat side by side on a bench in the city, very much like the first time they had met. Close by, workmen were repairing one of the last wells of the city. Every once in a while one of them looked up at the two figures sitting in the shadows. Summer was once again in full swing, and the Omnesian sun relentlessly beat down upon the rooftops. Elion looked at Lumea.

"What are you going to do now?" he asked.

She thought for a moment. "I'm going back home. Omnesia has

changed, but even so, I could never live here. I don't belong in this arid land. I need mountains and forests around me. Most of all, though, I want to see my family again."

They sat next to each other in silence for a long time. Lumea made geometrical shapes in the sand with her feet, but she wiped them out again with the sole of her boot.

"What about you?" she asked.

Elion shrugged. Lumea studied his face. After everything they had gone through, his face was even more serious than the first time they had met, but he smiled more often now. At the moment, she detected an unaccustomed sense of insecurity in his features. He did not answer her question.

She asked him, "Do you want to go with me? I remember your saying once that Lunadeiron seemed like a nice place to live. It might not be what you expect..." She looked for the right words, saying, "I'd like for you to come with me."

She felt her cheeks turning red as the smile returned to his face.

Elion answered softly, "I'd like that very much."

She leaned into him and put her head on his shoulder, relieved with his answer. He pressed a kiss on her black hair, and they stayed in that position for a while.

Finally, Lumea got up and walked over to the workmen. After everything that had happened, she was no longer afraid of them. When she was near them the men bowed to her. She talked to them for a while. Judging by their reactions, they agreed with her proposition. Then she came back to the bench where Elion was still sitting. He looked at her questioningly and she explained, "We won't be traveling alone."

He stood up as well and the two of them walked to Siard's house, where Elion and Lumea were staying as his mothers guests.

Not long afterward they said their goodbyes to Siard. He did not wish to leave Omnesia behind, but he did promise to come and visit them in Lunadeiron. By now, the city's streets had been swept clean of the sand and the buildings were decorated with beautiful silken banners, gifts from the elves to the humans of the city. The elves that had spent so long repairing the city's wells rallied around Elion and Lumea.

Together, they all traveled east, with the people of Omnesia waving goodbye to them. The city was part of the elves' past, but now that the wells were all functioning again, there was nothing to keep them there except memory. Although everything that had happened had made the humans look at the elves in a different light, and old grievances had been buried, this place could never again be their home. The elves hoped to build a new future in Lumea's country, free from the guilt of the past.

Near Achnon's Ruin the group halted. Elion went inside, alone. For one irrational moment, Lumea wanted to stop him from going through the gate, but he returned soon enough. He stretched out his hand towards her and she took it with both her own, gripping it tightly. They walked on like that. Lumea felt herself leaving her own past behind with every step that she took. Once more, she looked back at the setting sun as it shone through the leaves and the soft moss underfoot. That was the last time she looked back. Tonight there would be a new moon. Ahead of them was a new beginning.